What the critics are saying:

"With its amazing intrigue and mystery, Forsaken Talisman is a compelling, shocking and often heartbreaking read. Tender concern and compassion are at war with a nearly inexplicable passion that neither Skylar nor Dusty can ignore..."- *Robin Taylor, Romantic Times Bookclub*

"...a strong second book in the fascinating Talisman Bay series...the pace of the story is fast and furious. The loves scenes are very hot...Pick up Forsaken Talisman and become engrossed in the heroic and steamy lives of the Shadow Walkers." *Jenni, A Romance Review*

"Ashleigh Raine delivers a powerful, suspenseful tale with her second book in the Talisman Bay series. In-depth characterization, an intriguing storyline, and of course, the hot sex which rightly deserves its E-rotic rating, make FORSAKEN TALISMAN one for the keeper shelf." - *Sinclair Reid, Romance Reviews Today*

"...a fantastic paranormal story that is rich in plot, characterization and bold imagery...a roller coaster of intrigue, passion and romance..." - *Valerie for Love Romances*

"...wonderfully imaginative...a book that is absolutely not to be missed!" - *RogueStorm for Sizzling Romances*

Forsaken Talisman

Ashleigh Raine

Forsaken Talisman

An Ellora's Cave Publication, October 2004

Ellora's Cave Publishing, Inc.
1337 Commerce Drive Suite #13
Stow, Ohio 44224

ISBN #1419950649

ISBN MS Reader (LIT) ISBN # 1-84360-792-1
Other available formats (no ISBNs are assigned):
Adobe (PDF), Rocketbook (RB), Mobipocket (PRC) & HTML

FORSAKEN TALISMAN Copyright © 2004 ASHLEIGH RAINE

Edited by *Briana St. James*
Cover art by *Jason Stoddard*

Warning:

The following material contains graphic sexual content meant for mature readers. *Forsaken Talisman* has been rated *E-rotic* by a minimum of three independent reviewers.

Ellora's Cave Publishing offers three levels of Romantica™ reading entertainment: S (S-ensuous), E (E-rotic), and X (X-treme).

S-ensuous love scenes are explicit and leave nothing to the imagination.

E-rotic love scenes are explicit, leave nothing to the imagination, and are high in volume per the overall word count. In addition, some E-rated titles might contain fantasy material that some readers find objectionable, such as bondage, submission, same sex encounters, forced seductions, etc. E-rated titles are the most graphic titles we carry; it is common, for instance, for an author to use words such as "fucking", "cock", "pussy", etc., within their work of literature.

X-treme titles differ from E-rated titles only in plot premise and storyline execution. Unlike E-rated titles, stories designated with the letter X tend to contain controversial subject matter not for the faint of heart.

Also by Ashleigh Raine:

Acting On Impulse

Angel In Moonlight

Lover's Talisman

Mesmerized

Forsaken Talisman

Dedication

For Alex and Jason, because they understand — or at least respect — the voices in our heads.

For Bree, because she hasn't killed us yet.

For Kendra, because she let us use her name and physical likeness. She's really not the bitch we made her out to be. Love you, Kendra.

For Tracey. You know why. You'll always have his heart…and ours.

For our guys. Our inspirations. Since you walked into our lives, everything has become real.

Prologue

"I'm not Mariah. I'm not Mariah."

The words had become her mantra, the only grasp on control she had left. The only thing she knew about herself was who she wasn't.

Not even a flicker of who she had been remained.

She knew she was female—large breasts made that obvious—and she guessed she was young by her appearance, but looking in the mirror didn't bring any flashes of insight into who she'd been before. Tangled, limp, light brown hair fell halfway down her back. She had light blue eyes, but captivity had added darker blue circles under them. Pale white skin…she didn't know if she was normally so pale, or if it was the lack of sunlight creating that illusion. Nothing looked familiar…just a stranger's face peering back at her questioningly. She thought she might have been considered pretty once, but imprisonment had drained that spark from her features. Now she just looked tired, confused and scared. At least that was one thing she shared with her mirror's reflection.

The cement floor was cold, her white cotton nightgown too thin to protect her from the chill. She preferred the frigid cement over the neatly made bed because the floor kept her awake and aware, enabling her to fight this thing that was trying to take over, to change her into someone else.

She rocked back and forth, forehead resting on her knees as she continued her mantra. The *clank-clank* of the manacle binding her to the bed reminded her that there was no escape. That her whole world had narrowed down to this tiny room. At times, the fear was overwhelming, but she held on because she wouldn't let this be the end. She had been someone once, and she'd be that person again.

"I'm not Mariah. I'm not Mariah. I'm not Mariah."

A shadow blocked her light, giving her brief warning of his arrival before a cold hand descended on her head, patting her almost lovingly. She flinched. *Damn it! Ignore him! Don't let him win!*

She spoke, this time louder. "I'm not Mariah. I'm not Mariah. I'm not Mariah."

He continued untangling the strands of her hair, murmuring soothing words under his breath. She was so tired and for once his touch felt inviting and calming. As she found herself relaxing into his unexpected gentleness, a spark of the familiar, a memory of someone from her past, slammed into her unconscious. Someone else's hand, caressing her hair, warm gold-specked brown eyes sparkling with laughter, teeth flashing white as he smiled. A friend? A lover? It didn't matter, he was part of who she really was.

Stomach clenching as the memory of what she'd lost quickly faded, she lashed out. The bastard touching her now had taken her away from that life. Whether good or bad it had been hers, and now she didn't even have that.

She threw herself backward, away from his grasp. Glaring up into dark eyes that didn't reflect light or a soul, she screamed her mantra at him. "I AM NOT MARIAH! I AM NOT MARIAH!"

He smiled, the coldness emanating from him so much colder than the floor. He wore his usual black from head to toe, the only color a slash of red across the chest, mimicking the blood of his she'd like to spill. Moving closer, he knelt next to her and smoothed his hand down her face. She cringed.

Gripping her hair, he wound the long strands around his hand and pulled hard, forcing her to look up to him. The pain caused tears to well up in her eyes, which she quickly tried to blink away. She hissed the words at him. "I'm not Mariah."

His grin widened. "No, my little spitfire, you're not. Not yet. But you will be. You will be."

Smashing his mouth to hers, the painful assault began.

She screamed as a bright light invaded her mind, forcing images, memories, thoughts not her own deep inside.

She screamed as her soul went deeper into hiding, retreating to the furthest reaches of her mind.

She screamed as her last hold on everything that she knew to be true slipped away.

And she kept screaming as he left the room, whistling a waltz, a slight dance to his step.

Chapter One

Something wasn't right. As the minutes unraveled, Dusty became certain tonight was not going to be as perfect as he'd previously thought. Too many things could go wrong. Initially, it had looked like everything was going to be just fine, but then one plaguing question came to mind.

Where the hell was his tux?

Dusty wracked his brain, trying to figure out where he had left the tuxedo once he'd picked it up from the cleaners. After spending such a long time in his closet, it had collected so much dust, he knew he couldn't wear it like it was. So when he'd heard he would be working the charity ball with his friends, he had pulled it out of his closet to have it cleaned. But where the hell had it gone after that? Did he get in a demon brawl on the way home from the cleaners? *C'mon Dusty, think! There's no time to get another one.*

Never mind, he remembered he'd put it in Marlin's closet, figuring if it was with Marlin's tux he wouldn't lose it. But where the hell were his shoes?

"Dusty! Yes! Faster! Yes!" Jeneane moaned and writhed as Dusty's cock plunged and retreated. Her pussy was so wet and tight. She was the best fuck he'd had outside of Polgara. The only downside was that while she was always willing, she was always the same. *Harder, faster, yes, Dusty!* He heard the same cries every night, every day and every morning. Whenever they rendezvoused at her third floor apartment. Her neighbors had started recognizing him as the apparent legend they heard fucking through the walls. He'd turned down a few college girls in the building simply because he liked what he had with Jeneane. It was simple. She didn't want a relationship, just a good hard fuck. And that he could certainly serve up at any time.

"Oh, Dusty…" Her voice trailed off as she climaxed. He'd heard that cry so often, he knew what came next. She disengaged from him, pushed him onto his back and slid down his body as she tugged off the condom. She was amazingly agile at applying and removing condoms to the point where he hardly even noticed it anymore—he'd lost count of how many different shaped condoms she'd tried out on him.

But condoms weren't the only things she was agile with. Jeneane had quite a talented tongue. It teased and licked and twisted around his cock as he thrust against her masterful workings. Her reddish blonde hair caressed his thighs and tickled his balls, adding to the sensual torment.

But what the hell did he do with his dress shoes? At the last formal event, he wore a pair of Converse All-Stars and the guys got all upset. What did he know about style? They felt good, and the ladies hadn't seemed to mind. They giggled, but he danced with all of them. He was never the one for fashion. That was Marlin and Ryan. Well hell, even Jake and Stephan were more into clothes than he was. Maybe his shoes were in Marlin's closet, too.

"Dusty…" Her breath was so ragged. She looked like a porn star as she trapped his cock between her large breasts and continued to work on him. "Are you gonna come…by…tonight?"

His hips gyrated to her rhythm. He knew she was getting ready to jump on him again. Everything she did always felt good. But what Dusty wanted was spectacular. He wanted the earth to move. He wanted to be able to lay with a woman without having to fuck her right away. He wanted something deeper. To connect with her. Actually, at this particular moment, he mostly just wanted to come, but Jeneane had asked him a question.

"I have to go to this charity ball thing, and I know you hate them so—"

"Yes! Uh-huh. Oh yeah! I totally hate those things. Oh yes! You're gonna come over after it, though, right? Yes!" It never took much to get her off. Sure his hands and tongue were on whatever he could reach, but he wasn't doing as much as usual to get her off. *Dusty, why do you bother? She's a great lay, but that's not what you really want, is it?*

"I have to…umm…help clean up afterward. Oh, damn you feel so good! Oh yeah. And I don't know when I'll get out." He had to come up with a better excuse than that. But all of the blood from his brain was in his erect cock. He couldn't hold a decent conversation during sex unless it was really important, like who should do the work or what felt better. *Dammit. Where the hell are those dress shoes? There's only about four more hours until I have to get ready.*

"Oh! Dusty!" He knew she was about to polish off another one. She was insatiable. "If you change your mind, come on over. Sandy and Jack are coming over tonight for a little party of our own." Jeneane let out a long, low moan. "I'd love to make it a four way…"

She licked her way up his chest before she straddled him. Somehow, amidst all the unbridled sex, she'd landed another condom in position. Sliding her cunt down him slowly, she leaned over and tongued his ear. He grabbed her ass and helped her on her journey. He knew she would keep going until he came. During their first week of fucking, he'd had to use a bit of restraint to make it last literally all night, but after the first couple months, it got easier. Now, though, he was beginning to wonder if he could come at all. What was this world coming to?

"I don't think I'll be able to make it tonight. Thanks for the invite." Jeneane had tried several times to get him into a group fuck, but once a naked hairy guy entered the room, Dusty lost all interest. He shook off that thought before he lost interest right now.

He flipped Jeneane over and, using thrust after powerful thrust, built her up so high that he figured when she orgasmed, she'd pass out.

She screamed in ecstasy.

It worked.

She lay there with her eyes closed and a grin on her face as she took in deep gulps of air. It had been awhile since he'd gotten her that high. Although last time, they'd both passed out.

"Let's take a shower. You gotta get ready for work," he whispered in her ear in between little kisses.

"What time is it? You rocked my world so hard." She started to roll out of bed as she looked at the clock. "Oh shit! I'm late!" Jumping up, she threw on some clothes then grabbed her hairbrush and a partially used travel size mouthwash as she headed out the door. "Call me later or whatever! Bye!"

"Yeah. See ya." Dusty started to run his fingers through his hair, but it was too bedraggled. He lifted an arm and sniffed. Oh yeah, in definite need of that shower. Between patrolling yesterday evening, and fucking all night long, he'd worked up quite a sweat.

He sat on the edge of her bed, looking down at his still erect cock. Perhaps the cold water would calm it down. *Getting off used to be so easy. Damn it. Maybe I need to find another willing female. Yeah. One who wants more than just my cock.* He smiled as he got into the shower.

"That's right! They're in the box on the shelf in my closet!" Dusty continued to scrub. Perhaps in his penguin suit, he could dance his way into a lady's heart.

* * * * *

"Harder…Stephan…harder!" Mariah panted.

"Are you sure, honey? I don't wanna hurt the baby." Stephan tried to catch his breath.

"You're not going to hurt the baby, I promise. I need this. Give me all you got. C'mon, harder! You know you want to. Pretend I've been a bad girl."

Stephan laughed. "You're always a bad girl, that's what I love about you."

Mariah stuck her tongue out at him and Stephan lunged for her. She ducked his attack and rolled on the floor, jumping to her feet still facing him. She grinned and her eyes sparkled mischievously. "Told you I'm a quick learner."

Stephan looked at Mariah, her cheeks flushed and hair tussled around her. She was amazingly radiant, the magic in his life. And she carried his child. The love he felt for her knew no bounds. He'd almost lost her once, and the fight with the Dread Lords was far from over. He needed to keep her safe and she needed to realize her limits. "It's not that easy on the streets. You're not invincible. Fiero can heal wounds, but he can't raise the dead. Remember that…I'd rather you ran away than tried to fight, okay?" In one quick swipe he grabbed Mariah around the waist, turned and pulled her down on top of him as he landed on the mats covering the floor. "Because it only takes one unexpected move for you to be taken from me forever…and I couldn't live like that."

Mariah pressed her mouth to his, and he drank of her essence. Every kiss, every moment with her was more than he'd ever expected. She began to remove his jeans—one happy side effect of the pregnancy was that she was an insatiable nymphomaniac—and no, that wasn't redundant. He was tired, but so damn happy. Although he couldn't have her right now, not yet.

He reached out and covered her hands with his, stopping her from removing his pants. Mariah broke the kiss and looked at him questioningly, her mouth swollen and irresistible. "What? It's okay. I locked the door. No one's going to barge in on us this time." Mariah grinned. "Although, the look on Dusty's face when he walked in on us last week was priceless. He couldn't figure out if he wanted to stay and join us, or if he should run away before you kicked his ass. I think the running away only happened because you threatened to kill him immediately if he looked any harder at me. You know, he still hasn't been able to look me in the eye since then." Mariah laughed. "No one's going to interrupt us this time. I promise."

She slid down his body, her breasts teasing against him the entire way down. Her hands brushed against his achingly hard cock as she worked on removing his jeans again. His heart raced, but not just because he knew what she planned on doing to him. He had plans of his own. He smiled up at her but spoke commandingly. "Stand up."

"Stand up?" She arched her eyebrow. "Hmmm…what do you have in mind? Do you want me to dance for you?" Rolling back onto her feet, she stood up gracefully.

He shook his head. "Just stand there and let me look at you."

She waited, eyeing him expectantly. "Is this some sort of test to see how long I can last before I jump you? Not fair. You know we both want it."

His hands were sweating…his hands never sweated. He got up off his ass and knelt on one knee in front of Mariah, wiping his hands on his jeans to remove the errant moisture. His right hand slipped into his pants pocket and extracted the small box he'd placed there earlier, keeping it hidden in the palm of his hand. He looked up into her teasing eyes. "Yes, I do want it. But I don't just want it now…I want it forever. Always and forever."

"I know, silly. I do too. But now would be a really nice place to start."

He grinned at her, figuring that she could hear his heart beating its way out of his chest. "I agree. Now would be a nice place to start. So—" With shaking hands he held the ring box out to her, "—Mariah Andrea DeSilva, will you marry me?"

Mariah's eyes widened, her knees slowly gave way and she sank to the ground next to him. "Yes…yes." Tears filled her eyes as she gazed into his. His heart continued its frantic pace as he removed the ring from the box and slowly slid it onto her finger. She looked down at the ring and gasped. "Oh, God. It's beautiful. It's an infinity sign. Oh my God…" As she slowly rolled her hand back and forth catching the light, the alternating emerald and diamond pattern sparkled.

Stephan looked at his woman, his fiancée. "This is forever. We are forever. Always and forever. I will always love you and our children." He placed his hands over her slightly rounded stomach. "I love you."

Tears glistened on her face. Stephan reached up to wipe them all away. He cupped her cheek and she nestled against his hand, closing her eyes. She whispered, "I love you, too. So much."

Moving his right hand to her other cheek, he brought his face to hers. Their lips met, softly this time. Between kisses he whispered, "Always—"

"And forever." Mariah pulled him on top of her as she lay back on the floor. Her eyes gleamed. "Make love to me as your fiancée now, for the first time."

Stephan lowered his mouth to hers, loving her lips, her tongue. God, this woman completed him. His hands busied themselves removing her pants. He couldn't wait any longer.

The door slammed open behind them and Stephan and Mariah turned as one toward the unwelcome visitor. Dusty let out a muffled groan and did a quick about face. "Dammit. In the training room, too? Do you two ever do anything but—"

Stephan growled. "Dusty, you better have a damn good reason—"

"I can't find my bowtie. Hell, it ain't gonna be in here with you two unless you're using it for some kinky bondage game, so if you've got it, I don't want it back. I'll just figure something else out." He continued to grumble as he closed the door.

The room was quiet for 2.3 seconds before Mariah burst into giggles. "Okay, the lock on that door sucks. So much for privacy."

Stephan kissed her laughing mouth. "I'm working on that, sweetheart, but until then…" One hand slid under her shirt, palming her full breast, massaging her nipple between his thumb and forefinger. The other found her clit, teasing it until she arched and moaned beneath him.

"Don't stop," she whispered breathily. "Don't ever stop."

* * * * *

"I see you found your bowtie," Mariah said as she stepped into the main room of the compound.

Dusty smiled in appreciation. She looked like the midnight sky, her dress a deep black lit up with sparkles—knowing Stephan, they were probably diamonds. The dress fastened around her neck, leaving her arms and shoulders bare and dipped low in the front, allowing an enticing glimpse of flawless skin and luscious breasts. Her hair was pulled up in some fancy twist with random strands curling around her face and neck. Those long dancer legs, teasingly visible through the thigh high slit, walked toward where he was sitting on the couch.

He tugged on his bowtie and grimaced. "No, I had to borrow one from Ryan. I couldn't find mine anywhere."

"Do I want to know why you were looking for it in the training room?" she asked, a wry glint of humor in her voice as she sat down next to him.

Dusty laughed. "Probably not, but I'll tell you anyway. Me and Jake were comin' home from a snooty benefit dinner thingie and he ran into a Speint demon, which sprayed vomit all over him. We were getting out of the car, so we were close to home. Anyway, I ran downstairs into the training room to grab the Speint masting bow because I knew Ryan was still working on installing a new shoulder sling after Stephan broke the last one. As I was running upstairs with it, the damn trigger switch broke, so I hooked my bowtie to the free arm and lashed the metal back with my tie. It worked great. I just figured that when Jake brought the masting bow back after the Speint turned on me, he'd have left the bowtie on there, but I guess it completely disappeared. Hell, maybe Ryan tossed it, or the Speint ate it. All I know is I went looking for the bowtie and I found you two instead."

Mariah just laughed. "I think you were right, I probably didn't want to know." She leaned toward him and straightened his bowtie. "How did you guys survive without a woman around all these years to help take care of you?"

He smiled and dropped a kiss on her forehead. "We weren't livin'."

"Dammit, Dusty. She's mine."

Stephan stepped into the living room, his tuxedo jacket slung casually over his shoulder. Mariah turned, allowing Dusty to view the pale skin of her back. "Hello, GQ..." she said, her voice husky, wanting. She approached Stephan, who tossed his jacket onto the couch before placing his hands possessively on her lower back, pulling her to him.

Dusty shifted his gaze and adjusted his pants. The last thing he needed was to add to his discomfort by playing the voyeur...again. After walking in on the two of them going at it last week and again earlier today, he didn't need to watch to know what they were doing. The image of Mariah's head thrown back, Stephan's hand covering one naked breast as he fucked her hard from behind, was one that would stay with him forever. He swore he would never open another door in the compound without knocking first, just to avoid the torture of seeing lust, love and passion that wasn't his to enjoy.

Damn tight pants.

The rustle of clothing, giggles, whispers and quiet moans became impossible to ignore. Dusty avoided shoving his fists deep into his ears and thought about all the alcohol he would have to imbibe in hopes of erasing the need burning deep inside.

He sighed. Alcohol. That was the need, the thirst burning deep inside. But he didn't drink anymore. Would he ever stop thinking of it? Referring to it as though it could ease all his ills?

"Done yet? We gotta get going." Dusty looked at the two of them as they slowly pulled apart. Mariah's left hand slid over Stephan's lips—the heat between the lovers was palpable.

Wait a second. Was that an engagement ring on her finger?

"Something you wanna share with me? As in how much the boulders on that ring on Mariah's pretty finger weigh? And, I don't know, maybe if it's what it looks like it is, 'cause of where it is?"

"Mariah agreed to marry me today." Stephan's proud and possessive grin practically split his face in two.

Dusty scowled at Stephan. "It's about time. If she'd been mine, I would have married her immediately, and not given her three months to come to her senses and leave me." He turned to Mariah with a smile. "See, you should have married me when I asked you."

"My loss," Mariah said with a dramatic sigh, but her hand intertwined with Stephan's and she leaned against him.

Stephan shot both Dusty and Mariah a questioning glance but was interrupted as Ana and Jake entered the room through the open door from the stairway. They both wore black from head to toe.

"Congratulations, you two." Ana smiled softly at them and sat in the recliner. Jake sat next to her on the arm of the chair. Since Ana's surprising return to Talisman Bay, she and Jake had resumed the close friendship they'd had while growing up. But she still hadn't told any of them where she'd been for the last twelve years.

"Did I hear that right?" Jake said with a grin. "You two finally disengaged long enough to get engaged." Everyone groaned as Jake clapped and laughed at his joke.

"Hey, Wonder Twins, why aren't you ready to go?" Marlin joined the crowd, his statement obviously for Jake and Ana, although his eyes focused solely on Ana. Dusty saw her eyes darken before she turned away from Marlin's stare. *Wonder what that's about? Marlin leaving shattered hearts again?*

Jake laughed. "Someone has to patrol while you guys are schmoozing people out of their money. We'll try to show up late if we don't run into any problem critters. Gotta get this girl all prettied up." Jake wrapped his arm around Ana and pulled her against his side. She laughingly attacked him while Marlin watched, his jaw clenched tight. He turned away and frowned when Jake pealed with laughter and gave her a noogie.

"Where's Twyla? Wasn't she gonna meet us here, or are we supposed to pick her up at her place?" Marlin sure seemed interested in seeing Twyla. So, who was he trying to get into bed? Ana or Twyla? Dusty snorted. Probably both of them...at the same time. That was more Marlin's style.

"Twyla's just going to meet us there," Mariah replied. "When we had lunch earlier, she told me she had some stuff to do before the ball and might be running late."

Dusty's gaze took in the room around him. Jake with Ana, Marlin looking on. Stephan and Mariah, still wrapped around each other. Was he the only one flying solo?

He grumbled and stood up, heading for the stairs. "All right, the limo should be out front. Wait a sec...where the hell's Ryan? Dammit, can we just get this ball over with? It's not like I'm getting any prettier sitting around here waiting."

"Well shit, Dusty. Ya sure aren't getting any better flappin' your trap like that." Jake shook his head and grinned. "Someone needs to get laid...in a big hurry."

"If only it were that easy," Dusty mumbled.

"Come on, you guys. Ryan's closing up the shop. He'll be joining us in an hour." Stephan put on his jacket then picked up a fur wrap and settled it around Mariah's shoulders. She smiled up at him as he placed his hand on her back and gently led her to the door. Marlin gave Dusty a raised eyebrow before pushing past him and walking up the stairs.

"Let's go find Dusty a good mood," Stephan said as he guided Mariah after Marlin.

Dusty scuffed up the stairs after them, feeling properly chastised. He really was happy for Stephan and Mariah. But they made him realize how alone he was. Jeneané was great, but there was nothing beyond a fuck on that menu. Although that had been fine for a while, now he was ready for a full course meal. He smirked at his imagery. Jeneane was simply an hors d'oeuvre, and he needed a lot more than a cheese cube to satisfy him.

Mariah stopped at the top of the steps, shooing Stephan forward, before turning to face Dusty.

He sighed and ran his hand over his hair. "I'm sorry—"

She placed her hand on his arm. "Shush, don't apologize. It's all right. Let's just go have a good time tonight, okay? Maybe someone new will surprise you." Humor sparkled in her brilliant blue eyes. "Besides, with those socks, who wouldn't want to dance with you?"

"What's wrong with my socks?" Dusty lifted up his pant leg, showing off black socks with big red hearts.

"Oh, Dusty…" Mariah laughed and linked her arm through his, as they walked together to the limo.

* * * * *

"I wanna sit this one out if you don't mind." Dusty smiled at Jill, the owner of the local flower shop, to soften the rejection.

"Your loss," Jill said with a laugh, winking at him before grabbing Ryan's hand. "Let's dance, sweetie. There's nothing like a man who can move." Ryan twirled Jill around, their bodies already grooving to the beat as they joined the rest of the dancing crowd.

Dusty glanced around the room to make sure no one was watching before he reached below the table and massaged his tender calf. It was really tormenting him tonight. The last thing he needed was for Stephan to find out that his injury still caused him trouble. He'd already taken enough shit over it from Fiero. But Dusty wouldn't have done it any different. He'd never leave a fight. Ever. And that had been a really nasty one. They'd won that battle, Stephan got his girl and they'd sent the big bads to a hell dimension—and had enjoyed a quiet, relatively trouble-free Talisman Bay in the three months since.

As Dusty stretched and flexed his leg underneath the cover of the table, he took in the flash and glitter of Talisman Bay's Fifth Annual Charity Ball. Everyone who considered themselves anyone had shown up tonight, to show off their cars, their money, their jewels and their women — in that order of importance.

This year, the charity of choice was the Family Violence Prevention Fund, which all of the guys supported after their not-so-great childhoods. And that was why all of them were there in force, getting the wealthy citizens to lighten their pocketbooks. Maybe if the fund had been in place sooner, Dusty would've had somewhere to go when things had started to get rough.

Dusty had done his share, smiling and flirting his way through endless dances. So far, he'd secured several hefty donations, and received more than a few interesting sexual propositions, but the women had been far from his type. He had danced with two Jennifer Aniston clones, several sets of fake boobs, and one trust fund princess who spent the whole time talking about the new cars her daddy had just bought her. If these were the only available women left in Talisman Bay, he'd prefer to live his life alone. Even Jeneane had completely lost her appeal. It was time to officially end it with her. Hell, if he was bored, she probably was too.

Dusty stood and headed slowly toward the hors d'oeuvre table. He smiled at a few ladies, but still, there was no one who intrigued him. Nose jobs made him wonder if the woman liked herself both before and after the surgery. The anorexic look made him hungry as though to compensate. Were there any real women in the place? Women who were single and real? Well, other than Twyla.

But Twyla was another story altogether. He watched her swish and sway around the dance floor, taking time to dance with everybody, but at the same time, not really giving anyone the time of day. Her partners only seemed to be moving props — she couldn't care less who or what they were, just as long as they swung around with her. It was impossible to miss her as she bounced from mover to shaker. Her bright blue dress had more shimmer and shine than all the many diamonds in this place.

It reminded him of the first time he'd seen her, probably five years ago now. Milty at the pawnshop had told him about an industrial rave that a group of vamps were throwing. Supposedly it was all innocent fun, but Dusty wasn't going to wait for the blood to start flowing before he investigated.

What he'd found was a pretty good party run by a group of barely legal teen goths who called themselves vamps, but who would probably shit themselves if they ever met a real one. The music was loud, the beer flowed freely and the women outnumbered the men two to one. He had seen Twyla in the crowd, dressed in a next-to-nothing red leather number, her deep brown eyes full of sexual fire. They'd danced their way into a corner of the warehouse and shared a fuck before the night was over. He'd never learned her name.

Dusty continued to watch Twyla as the music slowed and Marlin took her hand. He pulled her against him and whispered in her ear. She nodded and smiled, but the smile didn't reach her eyes. Twyla wasn't the same woman from five years ago. That woman had loved life, lived it to the fullest. This Twyla was more of a lost soul. Her behavior was no longer free spirited, but more…self-destructive. And her eyes were dulled…not lifeless, but as though they were only watching life instead of living it.

Dusty shook his head. Whatever the Dread Lords had done to her three months back had changed her. Something inside of her had died. *Fucking bastards.* He'd like to run into them again. Make them suffer hardcore pain and wretchedness.

"Hey, sexy, can I have this dance?" a voice purred softly behind him.

Dusty turned around with a smile for Ana, which swiftly became a grin of appreciation. "Damn, how could I say no?" He took her in his arms and swept her onto the dance floor.

"You look…stunning. Did you just get here?" He swallowed his surprise at how different she looked all dolled up. She was wearing a Cinderella gown in cream and lace. Her brilliant red hair was left down around her shoulders. The little girl he'd always thought of as a sister had grown up to be an amazing woman.

Ana's face pinked at his compliment. "Thank you. You're looking pretty damn good yourself. And I've been here for awhile, just hanging out in the shadows watching everybody." She grinned up at him. "Can't seem to let that side of me go. Jake and I will be leaving again after this dance. We gotta do another patrol round. It was quiet tonight, but no need to take any chances." She leaned toward him and whispered into his ear. "Besides, I've got to get out of this dress and into some real clothes. This thing itches like the devil!"

Dusty howled with laughter and hugged Ana close. That was his girl, still a tomboy at heart.

He took in the crowd around him. Mariah and Stephan danced a few feet away, their bodies intimately close. Stephan kissed Mariah's eyelids then her lips before she snuggled into the hollow of his throat, a smile of contentment on both their faces.

Ryan still danced with Jill, who looked to be in heaven. Jake was in the middle of a Jennifer Aniston clone sandwich, and looked fully prepared to be eaten up by the both of them.

"So, what's up with you and Jake?"

Ana lifted her head and looked at Dusty questioningly. "What's up? What do you mean?"

"I mean, you guys are always hanging out together. You two hookin' up or something?"

Ana's eyes widened in surprise. "God, no, Dusty. Jake and I…God, he's like an older, really annoying brother." She laughed. "Besides, he and Twyla have been bed buddies lately."

"Really?" Dusty smirked. "Everybody's getting some but me."

Ana grinned and smacked him lightly on the chest. "And me. But I thought you were seeing Jeneane?"

"Yeah, but I think that's over. We're both getting bored." Dusty paused as he tried to decide how much he should say. He brushed a chaste kiss across her forehead before he spoke quietly, "I need something else, ya know?"

"Yeah, I do, Dusty." Ana's eyes met his and she smiled knowingly. "I feel like I've been waiting my whole life for someone." Her eyes seemed to focus inward. "He's out there somewhere, waiting for me…" She shook her head. "I know exactly what you're saying."

Dusty pulled her close and they swayed together for a few more moments in silence.

"Can you turn us around?" Ana whispered against his chest.

"Sure, sweetheart. Someone bothering you?" Dusty turned as he spoke, and saw the reason for Ana's concern. Marlin was still dancing with Twyla, but his gaze was locked on Ana.

"So, you wanna talk about what's going on between the two of you?" Dusty said as he ran one hand soothingly over her hair.

Ana sighed. "Not really. It's something I have to get over. Something from a long time ago."

The song concluded and the band left the stage to take a break. Ana hugged Dusty tightly. "Thanks for the dance, and the conversation. Time to get into some leather and go patrolling."

Dusty lifted her hand and kissed it. "Thank you for making me look good." He winked at her before she walked away.

Marlin approached Ana, but Dusty couldn't hear what he said. She shrugged him off and gestured for Jake, who peeled himself away from the pouting Jennifer twins. Marlin and Jake glared at each other as Jake led Ana out the door.

Marlin turned quickly and stopped when he saw Dusty watching him. He glowered and then shot past him, disappearing into the crowd.

Dusty sighed as he walked toward the hors d'oeuvre table. He checked his watch. Thankfully this thing was almost over. The big dance auction that Stephan was emceeing was the only part left.

A waiter passed in front of Dusty and, without a thought, he grabbed a glass of champagne. Then he stopped. He looked at it there in his hand, willing it to disappear. Memories of stumbling around the compound, drunk off his ass, assailed him. His friends had intervened on his behalf, cleaned him up, got him away from alcohol. What the hell was he thinking picking up a glass again? If the guys saw him with it they'd think he was drinking again—and he'd be back in detox and on their shit list by tomorrow morning.

The only thing to do was to set it down as casually as he'd picked it up. He stepped through the crowd hovering around the hors d'oeuvre table. As he was about to discard the evidence, a hand brushed against his shoulder. He'd been caught. He turned with an apologetic smile, glass still in hand, trying to think up an appropriate excuse.

But it wasn't one of the guys, reprimanding him for his mistake. This was even worse.

Wide green eyes stared up at him in surprise, and pouty lips he still remembered the taste of struggled to smile up at him. Kendra. Dear, sweet, run-away-before-things-could-get-too-serious Kendra.

He waited to feel a stab of heartache, yet looking down at her, he hardly felt any regret that she'd dumped him. When they'd been together, he had thought he loved her, thought he wanted to marry her. But the fact that he'd had to think about it should have been his first clue. His instinct had always guided him without fail. He *knew* when something was right and didn't hesitate to act on it. And as he watched her now, he wondered why he had ever thought she was the woman for him.

A man stepped up next to Kendra, placing an arm possessively around her. Dusty eyed the large ring on her finger where his ring should have been. Between seeing her flustered expression and the guy's confused stare, Dusty made a startling realization. He was actually looking at a cleaned up version of himself.

Kendra's blush deepened at his long appraisal. "Wow! Dusty! It's been…" Her pretty green eyes were alight, but he remembered that look. She didn't really wanna talk to him. She just wanted some more cheese cubes.

"Two years, actually. Nice to see you." He thought about just walking away, dismissing this woman the same way she'd so easily dismissed him. But she interrupted his departure. "This is my husband Donald." Kendra looked between the two of them, her pouty lower lip now being worried between her front teeth.

"Call me Donnie." Her husband extended his hand in greeting.

"Hey, congratulations." Dusty shook Donnie's hand and enjoyed squeezing it a little tighter than necessary. Dusty looked from Kendra's uncomfortable smile to her husband's pale-faced quiet shock. Donnie seemed to realize the same thing Dusty had. "It looks like you're finally happy, huh?" She had wanted him, just not exactly in his faulty packaging.

"Well, yeah…" she stammered. "I am now."

"Now?" Dusty raised an eyebrow.

"All guys are fixer-uppers. Just some—" She bit her tongue and her eyes bugged as she realized what she was saying.

"Need less fixing than I did, right?"

She didn't reply as a dark blush stained her cheeks. Dusty nodded at her husband—who was looking a tad green to match her red—and walked away. He actually felt better about pawning the ring he would have given her. But unfortunately, the truth still hurt.

He cursed Kendra for reminding him of his flaws, then looked at the unfortunate vice he still carried in his hand. The champagne was like a beacon of temptation, calling out for him to indulge. Just one sip…one glass…one bottle.

No!

Summoning a server, Dusty placed his still full glass of champagne on the man's tray and headed for the dance floor. Surely there had to be a way to resurrect this evening. Except his sore calf reminded him that dancing wouldn't be the way to do it. He sat down at a table near the edge of the dance floor. He figured the sour old biddy sitting there couldn't bust a move either. She smiled at him and he couldn't help but return the grin. She looked about as grumpy as he felt. He stole two pieces of chocolate torte from a passing waiter. There was silently understood appreciation as he handed one to the woman.

Tonight was a night best left forgotten in the morning.

* * * * *

Today was a day Mariah would never forget.

She couldn't help the smile that seemed permanently frozen on her face. Her cheeks actually ached, but everything was so right, so perfect with Stephan, she couldn't keep it inside.

Stephan turned toward her and their eyes met. He smiled and winked at her before he turned back to the crowd and continued on with the dance auction.

More than a dozen bachelorettes had offered themselves up, and male wallets had emptied. The Family Violence Prevention Fund would be getting a hefty donation check.

Twyla was up now, the last woman willing to sacrifice a dance for charity. The bidding was going higher and higher, and Mariah couldn't help but clap and laugh as Twyla soaked in all the attention, strutting herself around the stage. She was smiling, enjoying herself and Mariah felt a smidgen of relief. Maybe Twyla was finally healing. She'd never shared details of her final hours of captivity, had only hinted at the way her life had changed. But now it looked like she might be ready to move forward.

"Fifteen thousand dollars," an older, dapper-looking gentleman called out from the back.

Twyla waved and blew him a kiss.

Stephan looked the room over. "Is that all we can get for this beauty up here? Come on, guys. This woman knows how to shake it...just ask my brother, he hasn't left her alone all night."

The crowd laughed as Marlin waved and called out, "Yeah, that's why I'm sitting this one out. She wore me out."

"Twenty-five thousand dollars. I enjoy being worn out by a woman." Dusty stepped to the front of the crowd, a charming, crooked grin across his face.

"Going once, going twice…Harold, I'm giving you one last chance to up the ante…" Stephan glanced at the older gentleman who'd bid earlier.

Harold grinned, his ruddy cheeks a bit redder than they'd been before. "As much as I'd love to dance with that beautiful woman, I'd also like to sleep in the same bed as my wife tonight. I think I'd better back off."

Twyla pouted at Harold, then turned her attention to Dusty who took her hand and helped her step off the stage as Stephan finished up with his duties.

Mariah sat back with a smile. Dusty would be good for Twyla…and Twyla would be good for Dusty. Perhaps…

Leslie Winters, Talisman Bay's mayor, stepped up to the microphone. She was a striking woman in her early forties, her hair prematurely gray, adding to her compelling appearance. She was tall and classy and a powerhouse in Talisman Bay. They'd shared dinner a few times, at a few different events, and Mariah admired her.

Stephan moved to the side, talking to a few others on the charity committee. Things were wrapping up for the evening. A few more dances, a few more thank yous and they'd be able to leave. Mariah was ready to take her fiancé home and show him how much she loved him. She stood up, walking toward the stage and Stephan when Leslie began speaking. Mariah stopped moving, not wanting to be a distraction, and stood quietly in an alcove listening to what Leslie had to say.

"Thank you, everyone, for coming out tonight. We've outdone ourselves this year, and The Family Violence Prevention fund will be receiving a check in excess of one million dollars from all of your contributions." A smattering of applause filled the air. The band began playing softly in the background. "But now I'm going to step back, allow the final dances to begin. I just want to remind everyone that we'll be accepting donations the rest of the night if anyone—"

"One million dollars. One million dollars to dance with the stunning woman in front of me."

The voice washed over her, so close his warm breath caressed the back of her neck. Mariah froze and her entire body went cold. She knew that voice, would never forget that voice, relived it in her nightmares.

Craze was back.

Chapter Two

Stephan faced his nemesis and reached for his weapons before he remembered he didn't have anything with him. Security was too tight at these events; he couldn't have even gotten in a pocketknife.

Craze was here. Standing behind Mariah. And Stephan was unprepared.

He cursed under his breath. He knew better. He was a Shadow Walker and this was the type of mistake that got people killed.

Leslie Winters' voice brought him out of his blind rage. "Mr. Strickland. I'm so happy you were able to join us. I was afraid you weren't going to make it this evening."

Stephan could hear the smile in Leslie's voice, although he didn't remove his stare from Craze and Mariah. She had grown pale, the only outward expression betraying her fear. Only Stephan knew her well enough to recognize the signs.

Craze—the man biology had made Stephan's brother but circumstance and destiny had made an enemy—smiled and the room lit up with women sighing, giggling and whispering. A new, tall, handsome, and obviously wealthy man had entered their midst. He continued smiling at the crowd, before turning his attention first to Leslie, then Stephan. His grin widened as he looked Stephan in the eye and spoke. "One of my recent acquisitions required extra attention. But there was no way I was going to miss out on this..." his calculating gaze swept the room "...magnificent event."

Craze's overconfident stare returned to his half-brother. "I'm a big supporter of the Family Violence Prevention Fund. Family is very important." His attention shifted back to Leslie and he winked. "And you're supposed to call me David."

Leslie giggled. Leslie, the mayor with the backbone of steel, the woman who as a young attorney had scared several gang members straight, had actually giggled. "David Strickland everyone. Most of you have probably heard of Strickland Enterprises. They're involved with just about everything, luxury hotels to real estate development to computer software engineering. David has just moved to Talisman Bay. And, ladies, he's quite the charmer, as Mariah's going to find out."

"No. No way in hell is Mariah dancing with him." Stephan turned his attention to Leslie. Why couldn't she see through David's charming façade? But of course no one here knew him like Stephan did, no one knew what the scheming bastard was capable of.

Leslie tittered, but gave Stephan a quelling look. "Why Stephan, you never struck me as the jealous type. One million dollars to charity for a five-minute dance with Mariah. Then she's yours again." Leslie dismissed him and cued the band. "Thank you again, everyone, for your generous contributions. Enjoy the rest of your evening."

It was done. David laid one hand on Mariah's back , leading her to the center of the dance floor. And Stephan could do nothing but watch.

Twyla and I are set to shadow them. I'll be within grabbing distance if he tries anything. Dusty's voice brought Stephan out of enraged numbness and he open-clicked-in to everyone.

Jake, Ana, Craze is back. I want you outside the reception hall as back up in case he tries anything. Marlin, stay near the back exit. I wouldn't put it past him to try to get Mariah out of here. Dusty, do whatever it takes to stay near them. Ryan, I know you're dancing with Jill, but do your best to stay between Craze and the main exit.

We're on our way, Jake replied. *Take it easy, man. We got your back.*

Dusty spoke next. *Twyla and I are on it. You better believe we're not gonna let anything happen to Mariah.*

Don't worry about me and Jill, I've got my focus on Craze, Ryan said, pure determination in his voice.

And I've got the back exit covered, bro. He ain't getting outta here with Mariah. Marlin paused. *What are you gonna do?*

I'm gonna take care of my family by taking out the enemy. Stephan clicked-out, unwilling to listen to the alarmed responses. He made sure everyone was in place, then stood at the edge of the dance floor and locked his gaze on Craze and Mariah.

Mariah appeared remarkably calm. Craze's hand rested low on her bare back. He leaned in to whisper to her, brushing his lips over her ear. Mariah stiffened and Stephan stepped forward, ready to attack, but they continued dancing.

Stephan felt helpless. His anger and wrath practically boiled over. He wanted to rip David's head from his body, remove the smug grin from his face, end the torture that Craze's presence represented. But nothing could be done. Not here. Not now. Not in front of the citizens of Talisman Bay who Stephan had to protect from his secret.

And that was the kicker. How could he protect them when their biggest danger stood welcome in their midst? This was *his* community and somehow David had managed to make himself a member of it. The rage deepened. Quickly, his gaze swept the room to be sure Craze was acting alone.

A photographer from the *Talisman Bay Report* darted through the crowd, snapping photos. David pulled Mariah into a close embrace, and with one hand, lifted her chin and peered into her eyes. The photographer snapped the picture of the dancing couple as David closed the distance and pressed his lips to Mariah's.

Stephan lunged in primal fury.

The crowd parted around him as he pulled the pretender from Mariah, and slammed his fist into David's smirking face. Stephan heard nothing, saw nothing, knew nothing but that he had to kill Craze and he had to do it now.

But the execution was flawed.

Stephan was wrenched from his prey, who now lay on the ground, wiping blood from his mouth. Several arms held him back, pulling him farther away from Craze. Something cold slammed around one wrist, then the other.

He was handcuffed and surrounded. He frantically searched for Mariah, but in all the chaos, he couldn't see her. He was being led away and he didn't know if she was safe.

Dusty! Mariah, where's Mariah?

She's with Twyla; she's fine. Dusty's disappointment was palpable. *What the fuck were you thinking?*

Stephan ignored Dusty's question as he was shoved into a chair. One of the hired security guards glared down at him. One of the security guards *he* had hired to watch the crowd this evening. Stephan shook his head in disgust. How the hell was he going to get himself out of this one?

Mariah weaved her way through the crowd of people, Twyla at her side. She pushed past the guard, sat on Stephan's lap, kissed him then wrapped her arms around him.

She whispered into his ear, "Oh, Stephan. Why did you do that? Why?" She squeezed him tighter. "I love you. I need you by my side, not in jail. We have to fight this battle away from prying eyes."

Stephan closed his eyes, resting his head on Mariah's shoulder. "I know. I just couldn't handle his hands and mouth on you. Not again."

"Let him go."

Stephan lifted his head and faced David, who stood over him, a handkerchief pressed to his lip. Stephan fought the urge to smile. David was going to have a split lip and a black eye marring his perfect features.

But he should have been dead.

David faced the security guard, but his voice was loud enough for the surrounding crowd to hear. "Uncuff him. I'm not pressing charges. This man is obviously very protective of his woman. And how could anyone blame him? She's beautiful, and I'll admit my interest in her…as I'm sure several other men here would do as well." He grinned at the hovering crowd. "But take it from me, guys. Don't show your interest unless you enjoy a strong right hook."

Several men laughed knowingly and approached him. Hands slapped backs as David was surrounded. Handshakes were given freely while everyone introduced themselves to tonight's surprise guest. In one moment, David was fully accepted into Talisman Bay society. Stephan looked on in amazement. David was smart. Very smart.

David spoke again to the crowd surrounding him. "Someone tell the band to start playing again. The night is young, there's no reason we should stop celebrating. We're donating over two million dollars that will go to help protect families and prevent domestic violence. Talisman Bay should be proud. Let's have a good time." The music resumed and a few couples sauntered back to the dance floor.

The handcuffs were removed and Stephan wrapped his arms protectively around Mariah and stood up, lifting her to her feet in the process. They were leaving now. No way were they going to spend any more time here. He expected he wouldn't be welcome anyway. Leslie was going to have his ass, and he had no idea how he was going to explain his actions.

David approached, his hand outstretched in truce. "No hard feelings. I don't want to start off this relationship on the wrong foot…or fist." He smiled as the watching crowd chuckled. "I concede defeat in this round."

Stephan was stuck. He had to offer his hand or be further damaged in Talisman Bay society. And he wouldn't let Craze win in his town. He tried not to glare at David, but this was far from over. Stephan vowed next time, he'd kill the bastard.

He took the offered hand and shook it. Craze stepped closer, keeping one hand locked in Stephan's and placing his other hand on Stephan's shoulder. "I'm sure we'll be seeing a lot of each other, and working closely together on many projects." His voice lowered so only Mariah and Stephan could hear him. "I hope you're ready, bastard little brother, because round two of this game has already begun."

* * * * *

"All right, David, or whatever you're calling yourself these days. You're dancing with me, now." Twyla elbowed a couple of eager, flirting females out of the way to get to him. David Strickland may have sugarcoated his way into Talisman Bay, but the miscreant would always be Craze to her. And she would be damned if she'd let him go without at least taking her best shot at him on Mariah's behalf.

He charmed the women with a smile. "Sorry, ladies. Perhaps the next one?" He took Twyla's hand and began to sway with her to the music, closing the distance between their bodies.

"Do you always have to be a dickhead?" Twyla rested her free hand on his upper chest near his shoulder. His muscles were firm beneath her fingers. Damn, he had a nice body. Add a black tuxedo and red bowtie and he was almost tempting. Too bad he was such a creep.

"Who me?" He grinned. His lip was still a little swollen, his eye a reddish-purple color. Twyla bet he was going to be hurting in the morning. "I was the one who was attacked for no reason."

"Sure, David. You were groping his fiancée."

With her remark, Craze crept his hand from her upper back, and began gently massaging the base of her spine. Twyla fought the urge to purr. Sure he was an evil, manipulating bastard who relished causing pain with his hands, but damn, he knew how to offer pleasure with them as well.

"Honestly, I'm not that kind of guy. We were merely catching up on lost time."

"Lost time? Yeah…laced with underlying threats of pain and torture, I'm sure."

Craze laughed. "No threats. Only promises."

Twyla shook her head. "Right. Then could you do me a favor?"

"Your wish is my command."

"Quit jabbing me with your cock."

He chuckled. "Funny, you never struck me as the type to shy away from equipment like mine." Okay, so he had her on that one. From what she could feel, it was just as perfect as the rest of his body. Definitely long, hard and hot.

"I'm not shying away, David. I'm just not interested."

"Not interested? Hmmm…I thought you liked bad guys?"

"Don't go there."

"Oh, come on." He tilted his head closer to whisper in her ear. "If it wasn't for me, you never would have met Freeze."

She wanted to step on his toe with her stiletto heel.

"No. Actually, I just like to fuck. Bad guys are always good lays." Her voice was a whisper as she frantically tried to think of a way to divert conversation from the topic of Freeze.

"He was just a fuck, was he?"

Hearing him repeat her lie nearly made her cringe. "I was under the impression that maybe if I fucked him, he'd let me escape. I didn't know what you two had already planned. He was a really great fuck, though." Like she would just tell him that she'd wanted Freeze from the first moment she saw him, that Freeze was the only man who'd ever challenged her in or out of bed.

Damn him.

"I didn't come here tonight to hear you lie to me." His hand slid just a touch lower onto the curve of her ass, his fingers splayed, groping her through her dress. His shaft pulsed hot and hard against her stomach.

Two could play this game. "You had other havoc to wreak, I'm sure." Matching the rhythm of their undulations, she slithered a little lower and cradled his cock between her breasts.

Grabbing her by the shoulders, he pulled her up straight again, a quelling look in his eyes. "An invitation?"

"What do you want from me? What would really turn you on?" She pressed her breasts against his chest and looked up into his midnight black eyes. Ever so slowly, she traced one finger across his closed mouth, along his chiseled jaw and up his cheek. Putting feigned lust in her eyes, she ran her tongue over her lips.

The heat and length of his cock intensified and his eyes flashed red. Twyla swallowed a grin. He looked as though he would start sweating at any moment.

"I don't think I should talk about it here." His fingers bit deeper into her ass, locking her to him. The only way they could get closer was if they were both naked. She could feel every throbbing inch of him. His unwavering stare intensified…she felt as though he were looking deep inside her. Like he sought answers that only she would have. Twyla was impressed. Most men were usually helpless when she pressed herself against them but this man was a surprisingly worthy adversary.

"No one's listening. What do you want from me? I see the look in your eyes. Your cock wants to fuck. Your mind wants something completely different."

"Right you are." His deviously inquisitive gaze still engaged with hers.

She remained pushed up against him, poised to meet whatever he would dish out. "I just appeal to your most base nature."

"I'm sure that's what happened when I left you and Freeze alone together, right?"

Damn him. What did he care about what she and Freeze had done?

"You really wanna know?" The look in his eyes confirmed it, but she'd sooner die than tell him anything that might be important to him. "Well, here's the whole story. I fucked him. He gave me his shirt and left the door open behind him. That's it."

"That can't be it. You were on the pier with the rest of the Shadow Walkers, yet you were supposed to be dead."

"Funny, so were you."

"Funny. I'm not, but Freeze is."

Hearing his words cut her heart like a hatchet. Damn him. And Freeze too for that matter.

"I kinda figured that one out. Something about a fire portal and him falling through it. That usually tends to kill a person. Well, except you." Damn! Damn! Damn! She really wished the song they were dancing to would come to an abrupt end.

Craze's eyebrow twitched but his eyes remained intense. "Yes, poor Freeze…he had no idea." His hand left hers and cradled her neck. Their mouths were so close she could taste the words he spoke. "Why did he scream your name? That was the last word he said." He paused, then grinned. "Twyla."

Her breath caught and she fought the urge to run away. Somehow he'd changed his voice to mimic Freeze perfectly. The melody of her name on his tongue, the sound she'd only heard in her dreams for the last three months, immediately burned an echo in her mind. Craze continued. "You should have seen the anguish on his face, too. It was like he was being ripped apart from the inside out. The flames didn't seem to burn him at all, yet he was full of grief. Something must have happened between the two of you."

"Nothing. There was nothing between us." Her words were vehement. She looked at his chest as she strengthened her composure. She'd built many walls to keep people out, but this one was threatening to fail. She forced herself to look back into his overly pleased eyes. Damn him.

"Hmmm…Why do I think you're lying?"

"I don't know. Why don't you tell me?"

"I'm not daft. I see your pain."

"And you thrive on it, don't you?" She rubbed against him further, hoping that his cock would suck all the blood from his brain so he would stop talking about the one person she couldn't stand talking about. The one person who, with the simple mention of his name, never failed to set her world upside down.

Craze met her grinding with his own and ran his fingers through her short locks of dark hair. She didn't want to fuck him, but there was definitely an air about him that really made her body rise to his challenge. Except instead of bringing him pleasure, she wanted to punish his body with hers.

He closed the remaining distance between them with a searing kiss. She wasn't expecting it, knew she had to fight back somehow. He was trying to blind her mind's eye as he had done months ago, the first time she was kidnapped. He wanted answers again, wanted the truth she'd never share. This time, she knew what to do.

As his tongue plunged into her mouth, she defiantly fought his blinding light with her own. Their minds and tongues both dueled.

Feelings, thoughts, emotions rocketed through her body. She was consumed by the power and heat of magic. So much…too much.

"The song's over. I'm cutting in."

Twyla was abruptly pulled from Craze's embrace and into Marlin's arms. His hands slid where Craze's once were and his warm body nudged against hers. She cast a glance at a rather surprised but clearly unvanquished Craze as he backed away. Her mind still reeled, but Marlin's calming whispers were a lifeline, bringing her back to normalcy.

Her senses returned. Plus a little bit more.

"What the hell were you doing? I know you think you can take care of yourself—"

"Umm…Marlin…I…uh…thank you for cutting in. And also, I think I just…no…I know I just did something to him and—" Words? What were those? Her flabbergasted mind was having trouble stringing them together. When she'd kissed Craze back, she had meant to teach him a lesson not to fuck with her, but instead, she got more than she'd bargained for.

"Are you okay? Did he mess with you? I swear I'll kill that bastard if he hurt you."

"No. You would? Wait. No. That's not it. I was…well…Dammit. Half the stuff I want to say, I can't. And the rest, I'd need about an hour and a half to explain it so it would make enough sense to you."

"Twyla, what are you trying to say?" Marlin's voice was calm, but full of concern.

"I just learned that Craze has kidnapped someone else."

"What? Shit, not again." Marlin's jaw tightened. "Dammit. I wish we could have fuckin' annihilated him before."

Twyla ignored Marlin and rewound what her mind's eye had seen during the kiss with Craze. There was a woman screaming loudly. She was screaming in such agonizing pain. Craze was there with her, but she wasn't screaming at him. She was screaming at something going on in her own body or mind, something he had done to her. And the bastard was clearly enjoying it.

"Talk to me, Twyla. Tell me what you know."

"Yeah, he's got another woman. She's trapped and he's doing some heavy wicked magic stuff to her. I think he has a new compound. He's torturing her. I can't explain all the details. I don't even hardly know how the hell I got this information from him. Well, maybe I do. I dunno. This magic bullshit is really kicking my ass. Freeze didn't exactly tell me how to use what I have…" Her voice trailed off as her body slowly succumbed to exhaustion. She wished she'd learned more from Freeze—or that she hadn't learned anything at all. Talking about him with Craze and then using so much power against him had drained her. Her whole body felt as weak as a day old kitten.

"Twyla? What is it? What did Freeze tell you? What's going on?"

"Marlin…I…I haven't told anyone about Freeze. I don't know what to say. The pictures are swirling in my head." God, she wanted to cleanse her mind of everything connected with Freeze. Damn Craze for talking about him. Damn him straight to hell and then some.

Marlin clasped her hand tightly, seemingly trying to give her some strength. She looked into his eyes, hoping in vain that he could help her sort out her mind and heart. What she needed was her purse and the amethyst tucked inside. She'd taken the crystal point from Freeze's room and it was the only thing that had given her any kind of strength lately. She always kept it with her—except, it seemed, when she needed it most. But her damn gown just didn't have pockets. With the amethyst's help, maybe she could have waged an all out attack on Craze.

"It's gonna be okay. Stephan called a Shadow Walker meeting for after the ball tonight to discuss Craze's return. You gotta come so you can tell Stephan and the rest of us whatever you learned." Marlin cradled her cheek in his callused palm, ready to wipe away a tear she wouldn't let fall. The feel of his touch was so refreshing after Craze's closeness. He brushed his lips across her forehead, then leaned his head against hers. "I'm always available if you need something…anything. Are you sure you're okay?"

"Dammit, I'll be fine." The words quietly fell from her lips as she allowed herself to sink into Marlin's caring embrace. Somewhere, there was a defenseless woman whom Craze was torturing. Everything else going on in Twyla's heart and mind would have to wait until the girl was rescued.

Chapter Three

Stephan placed his hands firmly against the tabletop as his eyes sparked. "No way we're going in to rescue the woman tonight. Not until we know Craze's movements and can get in and out of there safely." Stephan turned his glare on Twyla. "What else did you get from him when he kissed you? I need more to go on."

Twyla returned Stephan's glare. "I don't normally read minds like that, okay? That's all I got from him. I don't wanna talk about Craze anymore. This is about the woman he's holding." Twyla fought the urge to get in Stephan's face, to forcefully make him understand the necessity of rescuing the woman now. Why couldn't he see how much this woman needed help? And what else could she tell Stephan about Craze? That his hot and powerful magical kiss was the first thing she'd actually *felt* for months? No, she wasn't going to talk about that—she didn't even want to think those thoughts. She turned from Stephan and looked at everyone else in the room, wondering if maybe she had an ally among any of them. Her eyes met Dusty's and she recognized understanding there. Perhaps he at least saw things her way.

Stephan leaned over the table toward Twyla. "Don't fuck around. We don't know exactly what's up with Craze so we're not going in until we have more info. You gotta tell us everything you know if we're going to take down this asshole. Holding stuff back will only put Mariah in jeopardy again and I won't let you do that."

Put Mariah in jeopardy? That had to be the most asinine thing the man could have said to her. Did he really think she would let Mariah be endangered again? What a dickhead.

Marlin leaned forward as well, facing off with his brother, looking prepared to strike if Stephan tried anything. "Lay off, man. Twyla's been through enough, don't you think? She already told you everything she knows."

Twyla kept her voice just barely above a whisper. "Don't you think you're putting Mariah in jeopardy by keeping her away from this meeting? I look around this table and every other Shadow Walker is here. How soon you forget Mariah's one as well." Twyla's voice rose as she released some of her pent up anger. "She's a lot stronger than you think she is. Don't you get it? Everything that affects you will eventually affect her. Keeping her in the dark was what almost got her killed before." Twyla carefully refrained from going further. She'd made her point. Mariah was not the issue here. Maybe he'd get his head out of his ass long enough to realize that.

Stephan's gaze darkened further. "I *won't* take any chances with her and my family. After what happened at the ball, she needs to lay low until we know what else Craze has up his sleeve. The last thing she needs to worry about is this." His voice slowed as if he were talking to an indignant child. "So, what else do you know about Craze?" Stephan began drumming his fingers on the table. Twyla considered slamming her fist down onto them.

Regrouping her thoughts, Twyla attacked in the only way she could. Her words were slow and taunting. "I already told you what I know. And I would never put Mariah in danger. Did you forget that I've loved her a lot longer than you have?"

"I don't fucking believe this." Stephan blasted out of his chair, his face red with fury. Before Stephan could move even a foot toward her, Marlin rushed to his feet and stood between the two of them.

Twyla watched with pleasant awe at the sight of the two brothers facing off. She'd obviously hit a button. Good. Maybe Stephan would finally see things her way.

Marlin's voice was low as he spoke to his agitated older brother. "If you gotta let it out and punch someone else tonight, go for it, but I ain't gonna go down like Craze."

Dusty stood up and situated himself between the two brothers. "Dammit, Stephan. Calm the fuck down. Mariah is safe here. We can't say the same about the woman that Craze has. How can you willingly leave a helpless woman in his grasp? She may not have the time you want to wait. What the hell is wrong with you? It's our job to help, not sit around with our thumbs up our asses, waiting for a convenient time."

Stephan shot Dusty a hard look, ran his hand over his hair and took a deep breath, visibly calming himself. "You're right. Craze is a brutal killer. But we are not just gonna go into his house. Getting ourselves killed won't help anyone. We gotta plan this out first."

Damn, the man was dense. "The woman has no time. She's in utter agony. I really believe he'd kill her in an instant just for sport."

Twyla paused for emphasis and her tone became indicative of past events. "You already know what it's like to be held captive by Craze. Even the great leader of the Talisman Bay Shadow Walkers nearly died at his hand. How can you honestly think this woman stands a chance?"

A hush fell over the room as the Shadow Walkers all looked at one another. The outcome was usually grim for anyone who taunted Stephan.

He paused and eyed her fiercely as though he was going to reply, but he turned his attention to Jake instead. "So you did follow him home, right?"

"Yeah, of course." Jake glared at Stephan, then softened his expression as he turned to Twyla. "Any idea what room the woman's in? The house ain't that small."

"Not exactly. It didn't seem like she was being kept in a regular room. I think it's another dimensional portal, like the room down here. But I also don't think he's gonna keep her there much longer."

"All right." Jake got up and strode to the map of Talisman Bay on the wall next to the head of the table. He grabbed a pushpin and pressed it into place. "29322 Flowing Water Drive. It's not quite a mansion. Maybe 4,000 square feet. It's in that new section around the corner from Twyla's place." He put another pin where Twyla's house was located.

Under his breath, Stephan cursed. "Fucking bastard must have somehow known..." He sighed hard and looked at each of the Shadow Walkers. "Dusty, you're watchin' his place tonight while Jake gets some shut-eye. I gotta do some quick thinking about how we're gonna get that woman out of there. You tell me immediately if anything at all looks suspicious or if he makes like he's even thinking about leaving."

"It'll be my pleasure. Craze won't even breathe without me knowing how deep." Dusty grabbed his jacket and checked the pockets for weapons. Twyla's eyes followed his movements. He shot her a quick glance and nodded. Relief washed through her body. They were both on the same team.

Twyla turned back to Stephan as he looked intently at Fiero.

Fiero nodded. "No worries, man. Themonius said your Watcher is ready and will be here tomorrow for certain."

"Good." Stephan glanced around the room. "I'll have the rest of this figured out in the morning. We all need some rest." Stephan nodded at Twyla. "Especially you. I don't know what possessed you to dance with Craze tonight, but I'm glad you got a glimpse inside his head. You should cool off a little. We'll get the woman. I promise. But I gotta make sure it happens the right way or we could be setting ourselves up for some real bad shit."

"All right. We'll just wait and see, then." Twyla stopped herself from fighting with Stephan any further. Arguing with him all night wasn't going to get the woman rescued any sooner.

"Besides, there's nothing else you can do if you already told us everything you got from Craze. But you might wanna stay here as well in case Craze wants more than just a dance with you." Stephan sat back down in his chair. He'd gotten his way and was obviously just waiting for everyone to do as he said.

Twyla stood up. Enough was enough. She didn't even try to hide her anger. "No, Stephan. I don't need to stay here under metaphysical lock and key. I'm going home. Don't underestimate me anymore, okay? I can take care of myself."

The room was silent enough to hear a pin drop. Twyla gathered her purse, slung it over her shoulder and walked toward the exit, wondering if anyone would try to stop her. She took a few steps then paused. Freeze's amethyst rattled against something in her purse and all the emotions she'd kept locked inside for the past few months finally got the best of her. She slowly turned back around, her hands clenched in tight fists at her sides. "By the way, Stephan, in case you care…because I think you probably do. If it wasn't for me, Freeze might not have interfered with Craze's plan to kill both you and Mariah. So don't tell me I'm endangering her again. You barely know shit about what I've done on her behalf and would do again in a heartbeat if I had to. Even with every godforsaken thing that has happened to me because of it."

A flicker of movement from the hallway to the living quarters stopped Twyla from going further, from spilling her guts about Freeze and the hell she lived in because of him. Mariah stepped into the room, a soft robe wrapped haphazardly around her lavender nightgown, a look of quiet betrayal on her face.

"Why didn't you tell me?" Mariah walked toward her, one hand reaching out to offer comfort. But Twyla didn't want comfort, not now. She just wanted to get the hell out of there.

Twyla backed away from Mariah and cringed at the look of hurt crossing her friend's face. "Now that I pointed you toward heaven, I'm in hell and I would never drag you down here with me."

Mariah let out a quiet gasp and tears welled in her eyes. Twyla's heart shattered. Maybe she'd gone too far with what she had said, but she couldn't take it back now. And maybe now Mariah would understand…or maybe she had just lost her as a friend forever.

The room echoed silence as Twyla turned and exited the compound.

* * * * *

Dusty wasn't surprised to see Twyla waiting about a block away from Craze's house. Placing something in her purse, she smiled sheepishly as he approached. Dusty noticed silver trails along her cheeks where she hadn't completely wiped away the evidence of her tears.

"You ready to go in?" She walked next to him as they turned the corner onto Craze's street.

"Hell, yeah. I was actually surprised you waited for me. I figured I'd catch up with you as you were climbing in through a window or something." He knew better than to ask if she was all right, but it was still on the tip of his tongue.

"I'm not that stupid." Twyla's smile widened and a bit of life came back into her eyes. "Besides, I knew from the look you gave me that you also thought Stephan was full of shit. And neither one of us could do this by ourselves and you know it."

"Yeah, but I still would've tried." Dusty laughed as Twyla rolled her eyes.

"And you would've died. Real smart." Her demeanor changed as she got down to business. "Okay, so I'll distract Craze and you get the woman out of there."

"Yeah, just be careful. Are you sure you're up to this after what happened back there?" Dusty couldn't help it. He knew Twyla didn't want to be coddled, but he wouldn't just let her walk in there without making sure she really was okay.

"I don't need coaching. And you don't need to worry. I'll stall him no matter what. You just get your ass in there and find her. I'll do whatever it takes to give you the time to get her out of there." Twyla placed her hand on his arm. "We're doing the right thing. Stephan's not thinking clearly. No matter what happens, you just get the woman away from Craze."

"Go for it." Dusty nodded. "I'm with ya all the way."

Twyla gave him a peck on the cheek. When she stepped away, her eyes were slightly glazed over. "This woman needs you Dusty."

"What—?" But before Dusty could finish asking her exactly what she meant, Twyla darted up the walkway to Craze's house and knocked on his door. Dusty slipped behind some bushes and positioned himself near the house where he had a clear view of the front room.

Through the window, Dusty watched Craze get up from his couch and head to the door. Dusty smirked. For once, David didn't look perfect. His wrinkled white T-shirt was untucked from his tuxedo pants and his hair looked like he'd been running his hands through it. An empty bottle of some expensive looking wine lay on the floor near where he'd been sitting.

Dusty felt a perverse pleasure on seeing that the wounds Stephan had dealt Craze would be visible—and painful—for at least a day or two.

"Twyla. I didn't expect you to take so long to hunt me down." He looked her up and down with a sneer. "Oh, that's right. You surround yourself with people who skulk in shadows. This is their time of night."

Twyla crossed her arms over her chest and met Craze stare for stare. "What the hell was that kiss about earlier? Were you trying to mindfuck me or what?"

"No hello? Just straight to the point now, aren't you?" He leaned against the doorframe.

"Dammit, Craze. Can I come in?"

Craze slowly shook his head. "I don't think so."

Twyla inched closer and lowered her voice to a seductive whisper. Dusty strained to hear what she was saying. "I'll tell you whatever you wanna know about Freeze."

It appeared she'd spoken the magic words. Craze moved away from the door and motioned for her to enter. She stepped inside and he closed the door behind her. Dusty listened carefully, but there was no extra click of a lock.

Once they were inside, Dusty could no longer hear what Twyla and Craze were talking about. After a few minutes of wondering if he should try to find another way in, Twyla opened a set of French doors and Craze followed her into the backyard. Bingo! Dusty took his cue.

He breezed through the front door and silently whizzed through the lower rooms in what felt like seconds. There was no sign of a secret door and no sign of a prisoner. He listened carefully to make sure it was still clear to get up the stairs. Just as he put his foot on the first step, the doors came back open and he heard Twyla.

"Yeah, when I said the view was nice, I was talking about the view of the pier, not your view of my ass. Where's the bathroom in this place?"

Dusty threw himself into a room then realized it was the bathroom. He ducked behind the shower curtain before she got all the way into the room and closed the door.

"How are you holding out?" Dusty whispered as he peered around the shower curtain.

Twyla gasped then spoke in a furious whisper. "Dammit, Dusty! Don't startle me like that. I almost blew your cover." She took a deep breath. "Sorry. He was being a dick. The world has no shortage of them these days. Don't worry about me. I've handled much worse. Did you find the woman yet?"

"No. You came in when I was gonna go upstairs. Can you get him somewhere out of the way?" He reached out and touched her shoulder. She looked distraught. "Am I interrupting your piss break?"

She bit her lip and grinned. "No. I just needed a break from the bastard. Sometimes guys like him are tough to read and steer the way I want to."

Dusty reached over and flushed the toilet. "Well, if he starts fucking with you, scream and I'll kick his ass. Make some noise like you're washing your hands."

"Yeah." She turned on the faucet and played with the water. "Thanks, Dusty. I'll stall him as long as you need. I know he just wants to talk about Freeze anyway, so I'll just fight my way through his grilling."

"Okay, but you better get back out there before he suspects something."

Twyla dried her hands and took one more deep breath. "Here I go." She walked out of the bathroom and turned off the light. Dusty waited anxiously. He just hoped that Craze didn't have to take a piss.

"Everything okay?" Craze actually sounded a bit concerned.

"Fine. Back to my question. So you weren't messing with my head when you kissed me? You were just caught up in the moment?"

"Yes." He paused. "Now it's my turn. Why did Freeze turn against me?"

"Because I fucked him."

Dusty couldn't believe what he'd just heard. Suddenly so much about Twyla's recent behavior made sense. He finally understood the pain in her eyes. The bastard had fucked her, hurt her, and she still hadn't recovered.

Twyla continued, her words syrupy slow, oozing with sarcasm. "I don't know why he turned on you. I mean, you're such a nice person. It's not like you were killing people all the time or anything."

"So was Freeze," Craze said with finality.

"Hey, I do know how to pick 'em, don't I? Can we go back outside? I think I need some more air." Twyla's voice retreated.

Dusty waited until he heard the French doors close before jumping out of the shower and heading for the stairs. His foot was on the bottom step when the doors slammed back open.

He looked around frantically before dodging into a sparsely furnished bedroom. Dusty braced himself behind the door, listening for any hints that he'd been had. He practically jumped out of his skin when Marlin clicked-in.

Are you already in? I hear Twyla in the backyard.

Yeah, I'm already in. What the fuck are you doing here?

Come on, man. You know we're on the same team on this one. Marlin paused. *And I knew you weren't gonna listen to Stephan…I mean, I didn't either. Look, I'm out here in my car if you need me. I ain't leavin' until you do.*

I'll be out soon. Dusty clicked-out.

He heard the sound of someone moving around inside. Then Twyla's voice, muffled as though she were still outside. "No, Craze. I know it's not like that. Come back out here with me. Just tell me the truth."

"Okay. Yeah, I did fuck with your mind. But you blocked. How the hell did you do that?" Craze accused.

"What are you talking about?" She paused. "Craze?"

Dusty heard the sound of glass clinking and perhaps liquid being poured.

"So, you have no idea what you did?" His voice changed from questioning to seductive. "My finest Syrah. Drink with me Twyla. Share what you've learned." Craze's voice trailed off as the French doors closed once more.

Dusty blasted up the stairs and rushed through the first room. It didn't seem like Twyla would be able to hold off Craze much longer. If the creep started going for her throat, Dusty couldn't live with himself for letting her help him with this rescue.

He checked every wall for hidden portals, but continually came up empty-handed. His frustration mounted. He knew the woman had to be here; Twyla wouldn't have led them false. There were only two doors left. He listened once more for Twyla and Craze. All was still silent.

Dusty placed his hand on the next doorknob, not realizing until too late that the door was already opening. There was no time to run. He looked up in dumbfounded surprise at the familiar face staring back at him. Either he'd really had too much to drink tonight...

But he hadn't had anything to drink tonight. Although what else could explain the impossibility in front of him? Wide silver-blue eyes, long brown hair and lots of luscious curves teased him through the pale translucent lavender nightgown she wore. She looked exactly the same as the last time he'd seen her, except for a purple bruise shadowing one cheek.

Was this who he was supposed to rescue? It had to be. But where were the chains, the locked doors? How come she wasn't restrained? This made no sense. What the hell was Craze doing?

Snapping out of his daze, he pushed her into the room and shut the door behind him.

"Dusty, what the hell are you doing here?"

"I'm takin' you home."

She stepped away from him, backing closer to the bed. "I won't go back to Stephan."

"Dammit, I don't know what to say. Sorry 'bout this." Dusty grabbed a scarf from a coat hanging on the back of the door and, giving her no time to protest or fight, gagged her with it as quickly as possible. He secured her hands with a purse strap.

She flailed and fought him, managing to kick him in his injured calf. Pain shot up and down his leg and he bit back a growl. There was no time for weakness. Ignoring the pain, he kept one hand on her as he undid his belt and pulled it off. Her eyes widened in fright and she thrashed harder. He bound her ankles with the belt, turning away from the betrayal he saw in her eyes.

"I am so sorry." He had never felt so bad about a rescue in his entire life. For the first time ever, it appeared the victim didn't want to be saved.

Running out the door with her over his shoulder, he clicked-in to Marlin.

I'm runnin' out. And you ain't gonna believe this, but I think I just rescued Mariah.

Chapter Four

Marlin stayed silent for several long moments, digesting Dusty's declaration. Struggling with the woman, Dusty tried to keep her quiet and still in order to get them out of there unscathed. Marlin finally replied, sounding shocked. *What the hell are you saying, Dusty? Did I hear you right?*

Yeah, man. Pull around next door. I'm bringin' her out and she's pissed. Dusty ran down the stairs, the woman still fighting against him. The aching burn in his leg caused him to stumble down a step. He swallowed a curse then paused on the landing to listen for Craze and Twyla…nothing.

She just looks like Mariah, right? There's no way Stephan would let her out of his sight after what happened tonight. We would have known…

Dusty left the house as quietly as he'd arrived, which wasn't easy with the woman wiggling like crazy. "I'm sorry, sweetheart. I really am. I'll make it up to you. I promise." He barely got the door shut behind him before tearing over to Marlin's black Jaguar XKR. *Well, whoever she is, I'm taking her to the compound.*

Marlin already had the door open for Dusty to get her into the car. His eyes widened when he got a good look at the woman in Dusty's arms. *Damn, she does look just like Mariah. Don't take her to the compound. Let's not get Stephan involved yet. He's gonna kill us when he sees her and realizes we went against everything he said.*

Dusty put the seatbelt around the defiant woman. She continued to glare at him and squirm as much as she could. *Yeah, I'm not lookin' forward to that at all. But she's the victim here. I wasn't going to leave her there any longer. Where the hell else can I take her where she's still gonna be safe?*

Marlin scrutinized Craze's house. *Take her to the cave. I'll stay here and make sure Twyla gets out okay.*

Good idea. On both counts. Dusty hopped into the car and closed the door. *Twyla says she can take care of herself, but if Craze finds out the woman is missing while Twyla's still in there…it's good you're here for her. I'll get the woman to the cave where she'll at least be protected, and if anything goes wrong, I can chain her to the wall or something.*

Yeah, just don't fuck up my car unless you really have to. Marlin laughed nervously as Dusty sped away. *I'll talk to Stephan come morning. It'll give you some time to see what answers you can get. Let me know if you need anything else.* Marlin clicked-out.

With Marlin tracking Twyla's every move, Dusty felt less guilty about letting her participate in the rescue. It didn't seem like Craze really wanted to hurt Twyla, but Marlin's presence guaranteed there'd be no chance to even try.

Dusty looked at the tiny woman in the seat next to him. She stared insolently back at him. Craze had already hurt her, and Dusty vowed that he'd never let it happen again. He just wished he could remove the bruise on her cheek and her memory of how she got it.

Dusty wondered how many wounds she had that he couldn't see.

He forced those thoughts away. This woman had probably faced more tortures in her time with Craze than he'd faced in years of Shadow Walker fighting. Dusty had to figure out how to make things better for her.

She was growing tired, but she still tried to get out of the car a few times. He'd fastened the seatbelt through her bound wrists to make sure she couldn't actually get away. He wished he could make her understand that he wouldn't let anything happen to her. At a stoplight, he gently brushed a stray lock of hair off her forehead and she flinched. He swallowed hard.

"You're in luck, sweetheart. I'm not takin' you back to Stephan. I promise I'll keep you safe."

She glared at him, but Dusty saw a faint spark of hope in her eyes. No matter what abuse she'd suffered, he would find a way to bring her out of its torment.

The beach was dark and empty as Dusty parked on a neighborhood street close to the cave. He wasn't surprised. It was still several hours before sunrise when the early morning surfers would ride the Talisman Bay waves. Right now he'd be able to slip her into the cave unnoticed.

Dusty shuffled the mystery woman out of the Jag, receiving a few well-placed kicks in the process. As he lifted her into his arms, one hand accidentally slid under her nightgown, landing on her bare ass. Her skin was so soft to his touch, he wanted to stay and explore it for hours, to learn every dip and curve of her body's shape. He quickly removed his hand and cursed himself for not being careful enough. If he was going to gain her trust, feeling her up was not a good idea. No matter how damn sexy she looked...and felt.

After smoothing out the nearly transparent fabric, he held her tightly against his chest. She did lean into him, but he figured she was just gathering her strength before trying to beat him up again. His words of comfort had apparently been dismissed, but considering he'd been an ass and accidentally groped her, he didn't blame her.

Holding her close, he couldn't help but notice the sweet scent of apples and honey. Her hair, her skin, the smell of her surrounded him. Dusty's mouth watered. This woman was intoxicating every one of his senses until he couldn't think of anything but her. His calf burned with every step and he tried to use the sting to clear his mind. He'd surely pay in pain for what he'd gained in knowledge of her flesh. Dusty gritted his teeth and traversed the short distance to the cave, making sure he didn't trip and land on the woman. Then again he'd much rather land *in* her and he had to stop thinking about how delicious that would be.

In an effort to help his situation as well as hers, he kept whispering words of promise and protection as he clicked-in to Fiero. *I need you at the cave if you can make it. A little bit of healing to do. Hopefully nothing worse than a bruise or two.*

Sure. Be there in a few. I'm lookin' in on some stuff for Stephan but I'll get over there as soon as I can. A demon get the best of you, or somethin'? Fiero chuckled, then the tone of his voice changed. *Wait, you were supposed to be watchin' Craze's house. What happened?*

It isn't me. Look, don't tell Stephan yet, but I went in and rescued the woman. She's got some bruising, but I don't think there's anything worse. She's fighting me and she's scared and really pissed off. And she looks...well, I'll leave that for you to see when you get here.

You do realize Stephan's gonna lose it when he finds out you went against orders?

So what else is new? I saved her, he can deal with it. Just get here soon, okay? I'm gonna need your help. Dusty clicked-out.

Dusty stepped through the rock wall and into the cave. At his entrance, sconces along the wall burst into flame, lighting the interior. As he passed by the manacles on the walls they used for subduing unruly demons, her fighting resumed with ferocious intent. Her eyes widened and she made screaming sounds through her gag.

Dusty ached for her. He wanted to comfort her, remove the fear and anger from her eyes. "Look, I swear I'm not gonna hurt you. Here." He gently laid her down on the soft white sheets covering the mattress that was set in a natural indentation in the rock.

He was suddenly thankful that Mariah had taken it upon herself to keep the living area of the cave clean and well-stocked with all sorts of necessities. He would've hated to put this woman down on dirty sheets. And tomorrow he'd be able to offer her a fresh change of clothes when they woke up. They could even take a bath together in the hot springs...

Where the hell had that thought come from? He would be watching this woman all night, *not* fucking her. There would be no baths, no sex, and no stroking those long, long legs teasing him from beneath her nightgown. He swallowed hard as he took off the scarf that had served as her gag and did his best not to notice the inviting curve of her calf and the smooth flesh of her thighs and the perfect—

"Dammit Dusty!" Her voice came out on a harsh whisper and she coughed. As he leaned forward to tug the skirt of her nightgown down over those bewitching legs, she backed away and glared up at him. "What the hell are you doing? Where's Stephan? He's not coming over here, is he? He's gonna kill me." She pressed herself against the stone wall, as far away from him as she could get.

Dusty froze. She spoke as if she were Mariah. She knew him, knew Stephan... Who was this woman and what was she talking about? He had to think of the right questions to ask, the right way to approach her without scaring her further. And, he reminded himself, he had to stop looking at her nipples showing through the nightgown.

"Okay, slow down. You think Stephan wants to kill you?" He desperately tried to get his mind back on track.

Her eyes flashed angrily at him as she spat her reply. "Who do you think punched me and left this bruise on my face? And promised to kill me if I ever left him? You saw how angry he was with me tonight."

Dusty's mind raced. Hearing those words coming out of this woman's mouth was disquieting. Stephan was overprotective, but he'd never hit Mariah, would he?

Dammit, of course he wouldn't. Stephan would *never* hurt Mariah. And this wasn't Mariah...couldn't be her. He spoke slowly. "When was Stephan angry with you? Was it after the meeting?" Something had to start making sense. Nearly everything about her was shrouded in mystery. Well, except for all those graceful curves underneath that nightgown.

He forced his gaze up to Mariah's eyes—no, not Mariah's eyes, he couldn't think that way—and they looked at him confusingly as she spoke. "What meeting? What are you talking about? It was after the ball. Stephan was mad at me after I kissed David. I didn't mean to kiss David but he was so...*nice*." Her lower lip trembled and her eyes beseeched him to understand.

"Nice? The guy kissed you—Mariah—not the other way around. I'm thinking the man who held you captive in his house roughed you up."

"Held me captive? He took me in, gave me a safe haven away from Stephan. David was never anything but a perfect gentleman to me. Why did you take me from him? I thought you were my friend. I thought I could trust you. I guess I should have known. You protect Stephan's interests, even if that means getting me killed in the process." She closed her eyes in resignation and rested her head on her bent knees.

Dusty sighed. It was hard for him to balance his instinct. His gut was telling him that she was in serious need of help and his Shadow Walker brain was telling him that she could be a deadly trap if he fell into her. And unfortunately, his cock was telling him that it wanted to slide into her slick pussy and never leave. But all of those feelings just seemed to be an amplification of his need to keep her close to him, to take care of her, to make her realize that he would never do anything to hurt her. He shook his head to straighten himself out. "I am your friend. I always will be. Nothing can ever change that. Look, I promise to keep Stephan away from you if you don't try to fight me anymore. I want to untie you, but I don't know if I can trust you to stay here with me. Can I, Mariah? Your name is Mariah, right?"

She raised her head from her knees and looked at him like he'd gone crazy. "Yes, you stupid ass. Did Stephan hit you, too? Just let me go!"

"Take it easy. I can't let you go just yet." With insults flying at his back, Dusty walked over to where the miscellaneous demon restraining and torture devices were kept. Some were rusted from lack of use and others were in complete disrepair. It'd been a long time since they'd used the cave for its original purposes.

There had to be something small that she couldn't escape from. Some old manacles would do the trick. The length of chain between them was long enough that she'd be able to get off the bed, but not get out of the cave. And there was no way she could chew through metal.

Dusty turned around in time to see the woman undoing the belt binding her feet together. He couldn't help but grin. She was a firecracker. And pretty damn flexible if she'd been able to get her still tied hands from her back to her front. In spite of himself, he couldn't keep his mind from wondering what she'd look like with those arms wrapped around him as he brought her to orgasm.

She looked up and met his eyes as she slipped the last loop of belt free from her ankles. Jumping to her feet, the belt still held in her bound hands, she glared at him. "I won't let you chain me up."

Dusty sighed. Shit. He was stuck. He couldn't *not* chain her up. Yet more than anything, he wanted her to trust him, to understand that he wasn't the enemy.

She advanced toward him, holding the belt in front of her like a weapon. Dusty swallowed hard. How was he supposed to deal with this? A beautiful woman facing off with him made it hard enough to focus, but add in the fact that her nightgown was nearly transparent from the light shining behind her, and he was useless.

Raising his hands in the air, he approached her slowly. "Look, you know me. I'll go up against Stephan for you. But until I know what happened to you—"

She darted around him, wielding the belt like a whip, but her escape attempt was over before it had begun. He grabbed the belt, yanked her to him and caught her around the waist while she kicked and screamed at him. He inhaled her sweet scent, nearly able to taste her on his tongue. Gritting his teeth, he laid her back on the bed, using the full weight of his body to hold her down. During the struggle, her nightgown had twisted up, allowing him a glimpse of the pussy he'd been fantasizing about. He quickly pulled the fabric back down to avoid doing something he might regret. She bucked against him and he fought the unheroic urge to kiss her into submission. His body could only take so much and just looking at her almost had him over the edge.

With most of his weight still on her, he pulled off his shirt. Her eyes flared and she stopped fighting. "J—Just what are you planning on doing to me?"

Dusty gave her a sardonic stare. "Not what I'd like to." He caught her feet and clipped one manacle around her ankle after using his shirt to protect her delicate skin from the rusty metal.

"What's that supposed to mean?" She looked up at him, the fight still visible in her eyes.

With increasing difficulty, he climbed off her body, trying to hide the evidence of what their tussle in the bed had done to him. Could she be more enticing?

Her eyes widened. "Oh."

He obviously hadn't hidden it well enough. He clipped the other end of the manacle to a steel bench that was bolted into the bedrock and then returned to the bed, sitting on the edge. She watched him closely but remained silent as he untied her wrists. When they were free, he massaged away the marks left by the purse strap. "Sorry about that. I don't like having to keep you restrained, but I need you to talk to me. You're not the real Mariah."

"What?" She jerked her hands free from his grasp. She appeared briefly stunned and then laughed like he was some kind of idiot. "Real funny, Dusty. I'd forgotten about your odd sense of humor."

As she'd laughed, her breasts had bounced, teasing him with their fullness. He forced himself to stare not at her, but at the wall behind her. She was too damn tempting. There had to be a way of cooling himself off, but then again, she would just reignite his fire as fast as he could extinguish it.

Fiero appeared in a quick flash of light, in effect saving Dusty from further torment.

The woman looked up with a wry smile. "Hi Fiero. You didn't happen to come rescue me from my kidnapper, did you? The oaf here doesn't trust me." She sighed and gave Dusty a sideways glance. "I don't blame him." Her eyes returned to Fiero. "You're not gonna take me to Stephan either, are you? Please don't."

Fiero clicked-in as he approached the woman. *Damn, Dusty. Craze must have done a pretty hardcore mindfuck on this woman. I can tell without even touching her that she absolutely believes what she's saying. I'm gonna go in and see what I can do other than just healing the bruises.* Out loud he spoke to the mystery woman. "I won't take you to him. Especially if he was the one who hurt you like this."

She vigorously nodded. Dusty could see the fear in her eyes.

Do what you need to do. Just see if you can get her to understand I'm not gonna hurt her. Hopefully she'll figure it out on her own that we're the good guys.

I'll do what I can. Fiero sat next to the woman and placed his hand over her bruised cheek.

"I'm not in any pain, Fiero. You don't have to heal me. I'm fine."

Dusty climbed off the bed to give Fiero more room to work and to help cool himself off. The woman shifted into a fetal position, pulling away from Fiero's healing touch, tucking herself as far away from the two of them as she possibly could. Her voice was a small whisper. "Would you both just leave me alone? I've had a long night and would like to sleep."

Fiero leaned over her, placing both hands on the top of her head. "I just need to check—"

"I said leave me alone!" She kicked out with both feet and would probably have shot Fiero straight off the bed if he hadn't quickly changed to his intangible form. Although Dusty was worried about the woman, something within himself cheered at the sight of her tenacity. In her own way, she was a fighter, too.

Fiero shifted back to corporeal form and placed both hands on her forehead. "I'm sorry," he said quietly as her eyes closed and she slipped into unconsciousness.

"Is she okay?" Dusty rushed back to her side. She looked so innocent and helpless and worst of all, trapped. He smoothed out her nightgown once more. He noticed his hands were shaking as they slid the fabric over her body and he instantly felt guilt for the pleasure touching her allowed.

Fiero's hands remained on her forehead. "Physically, she's fine. It's her mind I'm worried about." He closed his eyes and green light sparked from his fingertips. "She's had severe memory rearranging, if you will. She has some of Mariah's memories, but not all. In her mind she absolutely believes she is Mariah. I dunno how Craze did this and I don't think I can completely undo it, but let me at least see if I can get her to understand that she isn't Mariah."

Dusty watched in silence for several minutes as Fiero remained locked on to the mystery woman. Drops of sweat glistened on Fiero's face and his jaw clenched in concentration. Finally, Fiero lifted his hands from her forehead and let out a sigh of relief. "It's done. I untangled the weave of Mariah's memories…removed the hex on them that made her believe they were hers. I tried to break through to her real memories, but it's like a huge barrier is in place. I can't get through it. Funny thing is, I think she threw the wall up herself, to protect her mind from Craze. I don't feel like it's dark magic in place. She's gonna have to lower her defenses. Until then, I have no idea who she is."

"Thanks Fiero. I don't wanna keep her all locked up, but I don't want to chance that she's gonna freak out and run, either. Poor thing is terrified."

Fiero climbed off the bed and stood next to Dusty. "Well, all I can say is watch your back when you're around her. I don't know what she's gonna be like when she wakes up. She might be even more terrified or she might be just fine and be able to tell you who she is. Or maybe none of the above. All we can do is wait and see."

"Thanks, man. And don't let Stephan know about her yet, okay? I don't want him to be pissed about her because I went against him. Give me some time with her, see what I can find out." Dusty smoothed the hair back from her face. In the short time he had been in this woman's presence, she'd really brought out the protector in him. He placed a blanket over her and tucked her in, thanking his lucky stars that she had fallen into his life.

"You've got until morning. You know that Stephan will figure it out by then when he starts planning her rescue. If she's still pretty messed up when she wakes, let me know and I'll see what I can do." Fiero disappeared.

Dusty watched the woman sleep. She'd turned on her side, curling one hand underneath her cheek. She let out a quiet sigh and snuggled deeper into the bed, a small contented smile covering her face.

He gave in to his urge to touch her, tracing his fingers down her cheek and along her jaw. Her skin was so soft, so delicate, belying the strength and determination she'd shown earlier. Now that Fiero had removed the bruise, she looked even more like Mariah, although at the same time he could see subtle differences. Her face was slightly rounder, her hair had a bit of red tint. And her body wasn't as tightly molded as Mariah's. This woman didn't have a dancer's body; she was more naturally shaped with feminine curves in all the right places.

What was it about this woman that made him want to hold her tight against him, soothe away her fears, and promise her things he'd never promised anyone else?

Instead of climbing onto the bed and wrapping himself around her, Dusty sighed and ran his hand through his hair, settling himself in a chair next to where she lay. This woman was a mystery, her presence creating so many questions for him. Who was she? Where had she come from? What did Craze have planned for her? What part did she play in Craze's game of revenge and death? How could he protect her?

And how the hell was he gonna keep his hands off of her in the process?

Chapter Five

Twyla managed to hold back her grin when she glimpsed Dusty run out of Craze's house with a woman in his arms. They'd done it! Now it was her turn to get out of there.

She followed Craze back inside the house, celebrating her multiple successes tonight. He had yet to learn that she'd picked up images when she had blocked his invasion of her mind. She wanted to be far away when he made that discovery.

But then an hour crawled by and she was still there with Craze, purse strap *still* over her shoulder ready to leave, *still* talking about the latest Talisman Bay gossip, fun places to hang out on Saturday nights and how nice the weather had been. Every time he asked an inane question, she tried to steer him back to something of substance but it never quite worked.

Her role as the welcome wagon in his charade of being a new neighbor had to end before she lost all of her patience. He was acting like a different person—almost devoid of bitter hatred. But Twyla wouldn't let herself be fooled. She drank her wine and let him talk even though she couldn't get much out of him other than that he wished the local wine store had a larger selection of French Bordeaux. And that didn't tell her anything about him that she didn't already know—that he was a snobby rich boy who wouldn't know anything truly worth having if it bit him in the armpit.

Craze set his wineglass down on the coffee table and turned to face her. "It's nice to see that out of his many faults, Freeze's taste in women was not one of them. I am starting to see how you mesmerized him into betraying me."

So the small talk was finally over. She didn't know whether to be relieved or worried. Twyla lifted an eyebrow and returned his stare, pretending nonchalance. She didn't want to talk about Freeze anymore…she didn't want to talk about anything with Craze anymore. She just wanted out of there. "I didn't do a damn thing to him other than fuck him. Then again, men really are that easy, aren't they?"

The corners of Craze's mouth tipped up slightly as though he were holding back a full grin. "Now, Twyla, how could he resist a woman with the kind of power you have? Blocking my attack on your mind as well as launching your own attack? Hmmm…you can't play dumb on that one now."

She swallowed hard. Had he discovered what she'd done? "And just what do you mean by that?"

He took the wineglass from her hand and abruptly changed the subject. "You know, you still owe me the rest of tonight's dance." He walked over to the incredibly high-end stereo system and put on some slow jazz. Then he dimmed the lights and held his hands out to her.

Dammit. Switching gears again. There had to be a trick up, his sleeve, but she knew she'd look too suspicious if she made a lame excuse to get out the door. And with the darkness back in his eyes, running out of there would likely mean certain death. Then again, when they were outside, he'd practically gotten off on their conversations about her power so maybe he simply wanted to explore some of that a little further. He was clearly seeking more than just small talk from her now and wouldn't kill her until he got it.

And that was her best card to play. She would tolerate his games, talk to him about Freeze. And maybe this time, learn something from him in the process.

With renewed confidence, she stepped into his embrace.

He remained quite the gentleman, moving her slowly to the seductive jazz rhythm. Using the natural flow of the dance, she snaked closer, pressing herself tightly against him. She couldn't mistake his body's interest, whether in her power or in her actions she didn't know. Not that it mattered. She was leaving him cold and alone once this song was through.

Unexpectedly, he whirled her around a corner, pinning her against the wall with his body. There was no room to struggle, no way to escape.

Lifting her up, he brought his face to hers, his words whispered into her parted mouth. "Let's not make this into a scene. I know you got the woman out of here. Come on, Twyla. I think you know me better than that, don't you? It's okay, though. I'm not in the least bit concerned. In fact, I'm more concerned about who's gonna break into *my house* to pull me away from you. Because this time, there won't be anyone to stop me from killing him, whoever *he* might be."

His calmly spoken words tasted sweet like the wine they'd shared. "You really didn't think I'd be taken by surprise with your little rescue, now did you?" He smirked. "I'm disappointed in you, Twyla, underestimating me like that." He tilted his head as though he were listening for something and applied more pressure against her body with his own. He slid his thigh up between her legs, grinding against her pussy, holding her to the wall. "Where's your cavalry, Twyla? There has to be another Shadow Walker ready to break down my door to steal you back from me. Maybe if I just hold you a little longer…or make you scream…"

She gulped and forced herself to match his intensity while trying to ignore the heat of his body so intimately close to hers. She would not let him scare her. "There is no one, Craze. I am alone. Go ahead. Finish what you started." She rode his thigh, letting go of her fear, and mustered all of her power. With Freeze, she'd evoked a weapon tornado. Perhaps against Craze, she could do something similar and force enough power to annihilate him—or at least give her enough time to get away.

His tongue found the base of her neck and licked upward, leaving a trail of erotic fire in its place. She knew what that one lick meant. Months ago when he'd captured her, she'd licked him to show that he couldn't control her. Now he returned the favor.

Her thoughts spun angrily as his teeth deliberately sank into her earlobe and another wash of red heat shot through her. His hands found her ass, guiding her back and forth along his leg, creating a burning, throbbing need in her pussy until she had to fight her body to keep from coming. Damn her attraction to bad boys. Too bad Craze was beyond even her preference. There had to be a way to punish him for manhandling her, but her mind wasn't clear enough.

With the same slow movements, Craze released her from his body's trap. Through his removal, she regained her breath, but full recovery of her senses was another matter altogether.

He grinned wickedly. "Go home, Twyla." He shoved her through the house and out the front door.

* * * * *

Marlin moved from window to window. It had been two minutes since Craze had danced Twyla out of his view, two minutes of wondering if she was being hurt or tortured. He couldn't hear anything above the jazz music. If something bad was happening to Twyla while he stood there waiting…

That was it. He was going in. He reached into his jacket and curled his fingers around his .38. At such close range, he wouldn't need to use one of his larger guns.

Marlin stepped toward the front door when an inside light flicked back on and Twyla came into view, being pushed by Craze. Marlin ducked out of sight as the door opened and Twyla was shoved out.

"We'll be in touch." Craze's voice sounded normal, but there was an edge of malice to his words.

There was no verbal reply from Twyla as she abruptly turned her back on Craze and walked down the front path. Her eyes were somewhat dazed, though anger showed in the death grip on her purse.

Craze lingered in the doorway, watching her walk all the way to the street before closing the door.

Marlin waited to make sure the coast was clear before creeping through the shadows, following Twyla. She sighed and shivered as she passed the next house, folding her arms around her purse in front of her, closing herself off from the world around her.

After edging along a low fence to a bush, Marlin emerged, directly blocking Twyla's path. Her eyes were downcast and she didn't even notice she was about ready to collide with him. "Twyla. You all right? If he fucked with you, I swear I'll kick his ass right this time."

She stopped in her tracks and quickly looked up, her eyes registering surprise. Then, just as rapidly, there was a visible shift in the way she carried herself. She looked Marlin up and down with a smirk. "And you're here why? I can take care of myself, Prettyboy." She briefly glanced back toward Craze's house before continuing on her way. Marlin fell into step next to her.

"Sure you can, but I'd feel better knowing I at least tried to help. Dusty already took my car. I'm walking you home." He put his jacket over her shoulders and she sighed. *What the hell had happened to her in there?*

"Thanks, Marlin, but I'm fine. He was remarkably…um…well-behaved." Twyla turned the corner onto her street.

"Right. You know I'm not buying that."

Twyla came to a halt and turned to face him. She lifted her chin and met his eyes. Pain blossomed in his chest at the raw emotion visible there. She took a deep ragged breath before speaking. "He knows we got the woman out of there. But he doesn't care. I don't know why he doesn't care, but he doesn't. And that's what scares me the most." She lowered her eyes and continued up the pathway to her house.

"And I hate to tell ya, but the woman looks just like Mariah."

Twyla paused for a moment. "And I hate to tell ya, but I don't think I wanted to know that, Marlin. That just makes everything worse."

"Yeah, I know. Sorry." Marlin blindly followed Twyla as she sat down on her front porch swing. His mind was awhirl, trying to make right what she'd said. Craze had known about their rescue of the woman and he didn't care. So what did he have planned? Fuck! Had they walked right into another trap? He clicked-in to give Dusty the news and was met with an eerie silence.

Dusty? Dusty? Are you there? Adrenaline raced through his veins and his heart began pounding painfully. Why wasn't Dusty responding? Had something already happened and he didn't have enough time to click-in?

Dusty! Answer me dammit!

A low rumble of sound, then, *What the fuck do you want? I'm trying to sleep here.* There was a brief pause and Marlin could almost hear Dusty's mind waking up. *Shit! Is Twyla okay?*

Fine time for you to decide you wanna sleep. Twyla's all right considering she just spent the last hour with a killer. How's the woman? Marlin took a deep breath and waited, trying to decide the best way to break the news. To hell with it, there was no easy way to say this. *Shit, Dusty. Craze knows we got her out of there.*

What? Is he comin' after her? How'd he find out?

Twyla just told me he knows we got her and for some reason he doesn't care about it. I dunno about you, but that tells me he planned this whole thing out. You have to be careful. Watch your back. Don't let her out of your sight. I'll talk with Stephan about it come morning. Until then, stay away from her. Don't fuck around.

Dusty's voice quieted. *Yeah. Whatever. I'll make sure she stays here. Let me know if you learn anything else. I'm goin' back to sleep.* He clicked-out before Marlin could object.

He turned his attention to Twyla, sitting silently next to him, staring up into the night sky. She'd been holding an awful lot in lately, he knew. He recognized that sad look in her eyes as a mirror of his own in the months after Judy had been taken from him. At that point in his life he'd been almost suicidal, stepping into fights with a foolhardy attitude, truly not caring if he won or lost. And that seemed to be exactly what Twyla was doing.

She broke the silence. "You sure got quiet. You all right? I was expecting a scolding for what me and Dusty did tonight."

"Oh, you'll hear about tonight from Stephan, not me." They lapsed into silence again as he tried to think of what he could say to get her to talk to him. His mind latched on the one thing he could ask Twyla about without her accusing him of digging into her life. And maybe if he offered up his own problems, she'd be willing to share as well.

"Hey, can I ask you something? I think I need a woman's point of view because I have no idea what's up."

Twyla finally shifted her gaze from the distant stars and focused on him. Her lips curled into a half smile. "You're asking me for advice on women? You? Mr. Prettyboy, ladies' man? What the hell is wrong with the world when you're needing advice?"

"It's not funny. This is somethin' I can't figure out." He grinned as her smile widened. "C'mon, I'm serious here. I'm wondering what's up with Ana. She avoids me like the plague."

Twyla settled deeper into the swing. "I haven't talked to her much, but there's definitely weirdness between you two." Her grin widened and she winked, her words turning saucy. The old, cocky Twyla that he hadn't seen in months was back, if just for the moment. "I can't imagine *why* any woman would avoid you, Marlin. I'll bet you and Ana had something going on. Something she maybe hasn't gotten over?"

"Well, nothing happened. I mean, we were close. We slept together once, on the night we became Shadow Walkers. But her mom moved her out of Talisman Bay right after that and I never heard from her again, until she showed up three months ago to help us fight Craze."

"Any idea where she went?"

"None. Well, I think Jake heard from her a few times. They were always close. Like brother and sister, ya know? But I never heard a thing about her. She just disappeared out of our lives. I mean it's not like we made any promises to each other. We slept together that night to celebrate life and our survival. And I do care about her. But why is she staying so distant from me? She's fine with everyone else, but when I walk into a room, she pulls away. What am I'm missing?"

"Marlin, you care about every woman you sleep with. I can see it in your eyes. But I also know you won't give your heart to any of them. Did Ana want your heart or something?"

Marlin shook his head. "No. We were just friends. That was it. We'd talked about it a lot. Both of us knew our lives were taking us other places."

"Maybe she did want more and you just didn't give it to her."

"No."

Twyla shifted positions, tucking her legs underneath her. She wrapped his jacket tighter around her shoulders like a blanket. "Look, before you dismiss my advice so quickly, at least think about cornering her and asking her what's going on. Neither one of us can read her mind, you know."

Marlin ran his hands over his face in sheer frustration. "I tried talking to her tonight but she pushed me away." He laughed at himself. "First time that's happened to me in a long time."

Twyla choked out a sarcastic laugh. "It's funny. I watched you tonight and saw how every woman tried to throw themselves at you, yet you just weren't interested. You wanted to be, but it's like you just couldn't go there. Maybe that's what's up with Ana. Think about it. I mean, I know that one night with you would make me want more. Maybe she still wants you but doesn't know how to get past the memories." Twyla grinned. "I know I'd fuck your brains out, too, if given the right opportunity. It's those damn chocolate brown eyes of yours. They scream sex whenever you look at a woman and you don't even realize it." She shrugged. "But we both want more than that. I can tell."

Marlin stared at her in astonishment. She'd just gone from talking about talking to talking about fucking in one breath. "What, exactly, are you saying?"

"Both of us are wishing for the one who was taken away from us. Jake told me a little about Judy and how you lost her. I think your Judy is my Freeze. We both lost the half of us that made our worlds make sense. But you know what, Marlin? Tonight, while talking to Craze, I actually had a revelation about that."

This was getting interesting. "A revelation?"

"Yeah." She opened her purse and pulled out an amethyst crystal, pondering it as she spoke. "If I continue to let Freeze live in my life even though he's dead, I'm gonna end up dead right alongside him." Her voice trailed into a shaky whisper as she closed her hand around the amethyst.

Marlin placed a hand on her shoulder as she continued. "That's not something I was put here for. I have to take what I learned from him and put it to good use. Sure I miss him and what could have been, but who knows? In any case, I'll bet my memories of what happened plus my fantasies about what will never happen are better than whatever our reality would have been. He's a memory I'll cherish forever, but if I let him take over my life, I might as well not live. Have you gotten to that point yet? Or do you still hate waking up in the morning alone?"

"Yeah, I still roll over sometimes looking for Judy. But it does get easier."

"Maybe you'll find the woman who makes you want to get up in the morning—or should I say will make you want to stay in bed all day with her." She smiled up at him, but this time the smile didn't reach her eyes. "Maybe that girl is Ana."

He shook his head. "No, not Ana. I do love her, but not in the way you mean. Even growing up, she always seemed distracted. Like she'd be on my arm, but always looking for someone else. That's one of the reasons nothin' ever really became of us. We both had our hearts in separate places. But I do want to be her friend again. It seems that lately, we need all the friends we can get."

Twyla nodded in understanding as she put the amethyst back into her purse. She slipped her legs out from underneath her, placing them back on the porch. "It's cold out here and there isn't much night left. Come inside with me. I don't want to sleep alone tonight."

Marlin stood up, his feet already moving him away from Twyla. "I dunno. Seems like it could be a bad idea. We've both got too many open wounds."

Twyla laughed lightly. "Come on Marlin. Like you've never slept with a woman without having sex. And there won't be sex tonight. I'm too damn tired." She sighed and the weariness seemed to surround them both.

He turned back around to face her. "I haven't. Not since Judy."

"Well, let me show you how nice it can be." She held out her hand to him.

Marlin hastily considered the options but it was an easy decision. He didn't want to be alone tonight either. He took her hand, letting her lead him into the house and up to the bedroom. She quickly shed her dress and slipped under the covers, closing her eyes on another weary sigh. He removed his clothes and slid in next to her, letting their bodies fit comfortably together. Their shared warmth lulled him into a much-needed rest.

He smiled as he fell asleep. Twyla had been right. This was nice. There was nothing between them.

* * * * *

I'm not Mariah…

She drifted almost casually into wakefulness, sure of only two things: one, although she still had Mariah's memories, she wasn't her and two, because of those stolen memories, the man sleeping in a chair with his feet propped on the bed was someone she could trust with her very existence.

Careful to remain quiet, she turned her head. Before her rescuer knew she was awake and aware, she wanted time to look at him. It was very strange for her. Part of her knew this man, had conversed with him, shared laughter and dreams…but that part of her wasn't really her. It was like she was looking at him through two very different sets of eyes.

The side of her that didn't know him indulged her curiosity. His dirty blond hair was longer than was fashionable and unkempt as though he never did more than run his hands through it. His hair had brushed against her face during their earlier struggles and it had been soft, like the caress of a feather.

His eyes were closed, but she could remember their light brown color. He had small wrinkles at the corners of his eyes and mouth. Laugh lines. Under better circumstances he probably was a lot of fun to be around…but she already knew that, had seen his playful side through Mariah's eyes. She tried to clear her mind of the foreign memories, wanting to focus on what she knew and not what had been forced inside.

He wasn't relaxed in sleep. His body remained taut, ready to spring to life at the slightest noise or movement. His hands were crossed in front of his naked chest…he'd never put another shirt on. She swallowed hard as she took in the full view. He had large hands, strong arms, and a torso of pure, rock-hard muscle. A fighter's body. She didn't know how she knew that, but she knew without a doubt that this man could take someone down with one punch. He had a light smattering of blond hair on his chest, and a darker patch of hair that started around his belly button and disappeared into his jeans.

She followed the path of the hair, lowering her gaze to his jeans. She was looking almost straight up the long stretch of his legs. His bare feet were crossed at the ankle merely a foot from where she lay. The denim showed more than it hid, a bulge obvious beneath the tight fabric. Her nipples beaded beneath her soft nightgown. She remembered the way he'd looked at her earlier, the effect she'd had on him. She swallowed again and licked her lips.

A low, deep moan startled her and she looked up into Dusty's passion-slitted eyes. A slow grin full of erotic promise covered his face. "I know I told you earlier I'd keep my hands and body to myself, but if you keep looking at me that way with those big, gorgeous eyes, I just might change my mind."

The red heat of a blush, mixed with the heat of his stare, warmed her body. She rolled onto her back but not before she saw his grin widen even further. The bed shifted as he moved his legs to the floor, and then dipped again as he sat down on the edge.

"Sorry about that, sweetheart. I promise, hands to myself. I swear it. You just caught me by surprise. How are you feeling?"

She rolled back onto her side facing him but didn't meet his gaze. "Okay, I guess." She paused. "I'm sorry for fighting with you earlier, Dusty. I wasn't in my right mind, although I still don't know what my right mind is."

"Look at me, sweetheart. You know my name?" She lifted her head and met his confused stare. "Mariah?"

She reached out her hand and touched his arm, then pulled it away as his heat sparked a fire inside her. *Why did I touch him?* But she knew the answer. It was a familiar touch, one that Mariah had done to Dusty often.

"No, not Mariah…not anyone." She sighed then gave him a small smile to cover her body's confusing reaction to his closeness. "I know you because I still have Mariah's memories. I think. I mean, I think they're Mariah's memories because they're not my own. I don't have any of my own..." She struggled to find the right words but didn't know how to explain her strange situation. "I'm not explaining this very well. I *remember* you, but I don't *know* you or me for that matter, and what I remember may not be altogether correct. Does that make sense?"

Dusty smiled at her. "Yeah, I guess it makes about as much sense as everything else that's happened tonight." He stretched his legs out on the bed, reclining upright against some pillows. His body was only about six very short inches away from hers and impossible to ignore. She tried to minutely distance herself by pulling the blankets up tight around her neck.

At her actions, he threw her a concerned glance. "This all right with you? I promise I'll be on my best behavior."

She gulped. What kind of behavior would be the best? Hell, doing a strip tease in front of him would probably produce a desired response in both of them. The man was certainly built to physically please a woman.

His concerned look slowly morphed into a seductive grin and he winked. "Do you trust me?"

Oh, so he was teasing her now, was he? She was tempted to call his bluff, say a few things to shake that cocky grin off his face. *Yes, I trust you and no, don't be on your best behavior? Help me create some memories of my own?* But what would she do if he took her up on her offer?

She sighed and rolled over in bed, giving him her back and dismissing her mischievous thoughts. "Sure. Whatever. Doesn't matter to me. Just don't hog the blankets and do stay on your side of the bed. I'm going to sleep."

He chuckled and then she felt something soft and fluffy being pressed against her back. She sat up. "What are you doing?"

"Pillow barrier." He raised an eyebrow. "It'll keep me on my side."

"Oh. Good idea." She lay back down, this time focused on the rock ceiling above her head. Dusty finished setting up the pillows then lay down next to her. She couldn't think about his nearness, about how Mariah's memory of Dusty's sweet and funny side was wearing down her defenses. But she could add that to the things she knew about herself. She had defenses against hopping into bed with an unknown man. Good for her! Although Dusty wasn't completely unknown. She mentally smacked herself, trying to take her mind off her inner struggle. "So, we're in a cave?"

"Yep."

"Cool."

Silence followed and she started to relax, eyes closing, preparing to go back to sleep. Maybe she could do this, sleep with a strange man and actually sl—

"So, you don't remember who you are?"

Or not… She closed her eyes and tried to focus on memories, her memories, something below the now obvious layer of implanted ones. She came up empty-minded. "Not at all. When I try, there's nothing there."

She'd spoken too soon. A spark of who she used to be shone through the darkness of her mind. She focused on that spark of life, tried to pull it closer. She was in there! Her heart raced as she battled with her mind. A single fragment of light split from the spark, shooting at her fast, furious, painfully. She screamed as it slammed into her consciousness.

And then it winked out and was gone.

"Whoa, sweetheart. You okay? C'mon, baby, talk to me."

She blinked her eyes open. Dusty's face, tense with worry, was right above hers. His body partially covered hers, almost as though he'd been holding her down. One hand was on her face, wiping away tears she didn't remember shedding. "What's going on? Are you okay, sweetheart? Tell me what happened. Is something trying to hurt you?"

Slowly, she shook her head. Even that slight movement caused residual pain to flare up inside her mind. She knew there would be no more memories uncovered tonight. But now she had a place to start.

She took a deep breath, trying to bring herself back to full awareness. How long had she been out? Moments? Hours? It was too hard to tell. Her body felt tense and tight as though all of her muscles had gone rigid during her internal struggle. She shifted under Dusty's weight and realized something else. Her left hand was locked around his forearm, his blood wet beneath her fingers where her nails had pierced his skin.

With a gasp, she unclenched her hand, sliding it uselessly down his arm. A smear of blood followed her hand's path. "Dusty, I'm sorry. I didn't know…didn't mean to hurt you."

"Shhh...it's okay. What happened?" He cupped her face in the palm of his hand, showing such tender concern for her it almost made her cry again. How did he know exactly what she needed him to do? With his other hand he brushed several strands of hair away from her face.

"I remembered something, Dusty." She met his caring eyes and gave him a small smile. "Skylar. My name is Skylar."

Chapter Six

"That's a beautiful name, Skylar. It fits you." Dusty smiled down at the woman still trembling beneath him. He ran his hands over her hair, trying to comfort her. "Don't try to remember anything else, okay? You scared the shit out of me."

That was an understatement. One minute they'd been talking, and then the next she'd been convulsing on the bed next to him, the expression on her face one of sheer terror, her eyes darting back and forth under her closed eyelids. Whatever Craze had done to her, Dusty swore he'd make the bastard pay. She'd latched her hand onto his arm so tightly she'd drawn blood, but that was nothing compared to the blood of Craze's that Dusty wanted to spill.

Skylar's tongue darted out to nervously lick her lips. "I think I'm okay now…just tired."

"All the same, don't do that again." Dusty forced a grin. He couldn't take his eyes off those lips or the moisture she'd left behind. His gaze returned to her scared blue eyes and he warned his growing cock not to get too excited. But being this close to her was incredible. She could consume him in a split second with just a glance.

"Dusty…I…"

"What, sweetheart? You okay?" He gently smoothed her hair, then cradled her cheek. If she were to freak out again, he would try to be her anchor even if he couldn't eliminate her pain.

She gave him a small smile. "Yeah, I'm fine. It's just…you're…ummm…" She shifted beneath him and he realized what she was trying to say. What had gotten into him? Overstaying his welcome wasn't going to get him in her good graces no matter how fucking fantastic it felt to be pressed up against her body. Too bad his cock didn't understand that. He just hoped she hadn't noticed.

"Sorry." Silently cursing himself, he retreated to his side of the bed and readjusted the pillow wall. "I wasn't trying to feel you up. You were shaking like you were gonna come off the bed or something. I didn't want you to hurt yourself."

Even though he hadn't tried to feel her up, he couldn't forget how right it had felt with her lying beneath him. Every part of his body had come to life when pressed against her. Hell, his fingers wanted her, his cock wanted her, even his damn knees and elbows wanted a piece of her! But he would have to wait until a cold day in hell before acting on it. He'd never take advantage of a woman who had no memory. *But maybe if she jumped on me…*

"It's okay, Dusty. I'm sorry I hurt your arm. I—"

"What?" He couldn't help but smile. "Don't even worry about it. I'm fine." Dusty glanced down at the superficial wounds. "They're not even worth a band-aid."

"Good." She let out a quiet sigh. "I wouldn't want to hurt you."

"Believe me, you'd have to try a lot harder than that." He chuckled in a desperate attempt to lighten the mood. She didn't know it, but she *was* hurting him. His cock was so hard it could be mistaken for the sizzle probe on an Iznoyian torture device and there was just no cooling it off. Being this close to her while knowing what he'd rescued her from made his heart ache…and everything else about her made his cock ache.

He flopped about on the bed, searching for a position that would allow enough room in his pants. Lust clouded his thoughts. There had to be a way to get comfortable, think more clearly…and somehow stay on his side of the bed. *Dammit, Dusty. You should be thinking about protecting her, not fucking her. Find out what she remembers.*

"Do you remember at all what Craze did to you?" His conscience was right, he did at least need to see just how much she remembered. Maybe there were hidden memories that would explain why Craze didn't care that she was no longer in his cage. Maybe she would magically remember who she was, discover that she was hot for him, and then they could fuck like there was no tomorrow. *Stop it, Dusty!*

It must have been the plan all along to let her go. Otherwise, how could he have so easily stolen Skylar from that evil bastard? Then again, stealing women from jerks was easy, but stealing hearts was more Marlin's style, something that Dusty had never even come close to mastering. And with this woman, oh how he wanted to try. *Just find the willpower to stay on your side of the bed. Imagine the pillows to be as impenetrable as a fortress wall. Okay, so feathers and cotton don't exactly equate to stone, but imagine that they do, dammit. Don't screw this up.*

"Who's Craze?"

What? "Didn't he ever tell you his name? You know...the guy who had you trapped in his house. The one who put that bruise on your face. The cruel degenerate who stole your memories and put Mariah's in their place."

Skylar's voice registered her confusion. "But...wait... It was Stephan that hit me. And I was at David's house. He was taking care of me, keeping me safe. He loved me." Her voice quieted.

"No, Skylar, he didn't." Dusty spoke with more conviction than he thought he had. "If he loved you so much, why can't you remember meeting him? Why can't you remember making passionate love to him so hard all night that you woke up blissfully sore? He didn't love you. You don't really believe that, do you?"

"I don't know. Everything's all screwed up. Too many things don't make sense." Dusty heard the underlying frustration in her voice.

"Come on. Think through your collection of memories from Mariah. Do you honestly believe that a man as loving as Stephan could have it in him to hit you? Hell no." The idea of Stephan hitting a woman was more absurd than the idea of pigs flying. "Hell, if I had a woman like you, I'd make love to her as often as possible just to show her that she is all I have ever wanted with my entire being. She wouldn't have to wonder if I loved her. And no one could ever question my love for her. It would be so obvious in everything that I do and say. Craze was never like that with you, was he?"

Whoa. Take it down a few there, buddy. Don't give yourself away. Chill out. But would she figure it out for herself? Would she think he was just some creep trying to get under her nightgown? Hell, either way, he wasn't ashamed of what he'd said. She could either go on thinking Craze was some kind of saint or think the creep next to her was some kind of hard up fool.

"Oh God..." She took a loud, shaky breath. "It wasn't Stephan who hit me. The David that invited me into his home, who promised to protect me from Stephan and told me he loved me, is the same person who forced these memories on me. I can see it so clearly now." Her voice hitched and Dusty could tell she was trying not to cry.

Was she going to be okay? Sure, it was great that she was getting her memories straightened out, but he cursed the pillow wall he'd erected, wishing he had x-ray vision to see her sweet face through them. His heart went out to her, but he forced the rest of himself to stay put.

Finally, the silence was broken as she softly spoke, her words barely more than a whisper. "It's so weird, Dusty. I've got these memories of David holding me, telling me that he'll keep me safe, that he loves me and won't let Stephan hurt me. I can feel the tenderness of his kisses. But why would the same man who told me he loved me keep me chained to a bed and try to turn me into someone I'm not? I feel like an idiot. How come I didn't make this connection before?"

Shit! "Same reason I didn't realize how much of an ass I am. Hell, I'm no better than Craze. Let me take that thing off of you." *Dammit. Of all the things I could've done to keep her here, I had to choose that one! I am such a fucking dimwit!*

Without further delay, he climbed off the bed and retrieved the key to the manacle. Returning to the captivating woman he hoped wouldn't completely hate him forever, he leaned over the pillows and unlocked the manacle, tossing it to the floor with a loud clang. Then he gingerly unwrapped his shirt from where it had been protecting her skin from the rusted metal. Gently, he massaged her ankle.

He glanced up and met her eyes. They were full of so much damn fear and worry and confusion, but there was a sparkle of wonder and interest as well. Did she feel an inkling of what he was feeling? He knew he should pull his hands away, but she wasn't retreating even in the slightest. Stroking her skin felt too damn good in more ways than merely tangible.

"All I know is that if I was the one taking care of you and keeping you safe, as you said Craze was, I'd have done things a whole lot different." *Get your ass on the other side of the pillows now before you accidentally massage all the way up that gorgeous leg of hers!*

With trembling hands, he gently laid her ankle back down onto the sheet and dragged himself back over to his side of the bed, completely against the wishes of his cock.

This was not the time to let a woman get to him. Maybe that was the reason Marlin stressed staying away from her. He of all the Shadow Walkers would know when to stay distant from a woman. If Dusty got too close and bad stuff happened… Shit, it could mean even worse trouble for the Shadow Walkers…Twyla…everyone David had set his sights on destroying. Hell, maybe even the whole of Talisman Bay and beyond.

Skylar was like a gift from the enemy. A gift he shouldn't unwrap. But he couldn't deny that he was drawn to her in more ways than he could logically explain. "Actually, what I mean is that I would never do anything to hurt you or that you wouldn't want me to do." And much to his surprise, that came straight from the bottom of his heart. *Back it off a little, Dusty. Don't scare her away.*

Something tapped against his thigh. Shit! Was his cock trying to climb out of his pants and go dive into her? Then the something moved, and he realized just what that something was. Skylar's hand. And it had landed on his cock.

He gritted his teeth as his cock twitched against her touch. Like she'd been bitten, she quickly pulled back, but didn't return to the other side of the pillow barrier. Instead, she placed her hand in his, curling her fingers around his palm.

Rip-roaring excitement shot through him hard enough to make him wonder if he was dreaming. He slowly wrapped his fingers around her hand. Maybe he could work his way closer to her. Take in her sweet feminine scent. Maybe she was warming up to him and he did have a chance tonight.

And maybe hell would freeze over and monkeys would fly right out of his butt.

* * * * *

Skylar shook her head. She was a slut. She had to be. How else was it possible that after such a short time in Dusty's presence, she wanted to climb over the pillow wall and mount an attack on him? Or just mount him. She liked that idea even better.

Not that she would act on her attraction. Dusty had made it fairly clear that he wasn't interested by jumping away whenever he got too close. Although sometimes his signals were a bit confusing. When he'd massaged her ankle, she could have sworn he was interested in her. But then he'd retreated like he'd smelled a foul odor…

Oh God, did her feet stink? Great. She'd turned Dusty off because she had offensive foot odor. Wonderful. And she wasn't into rejection sex. Or pity sex. At least she wasn't now—who knew what she'd been like before.

So maybe she wasn't a slut. It had taken a huge amount of internal coaxing to convince herself to reach for his hand. But touching him, or being touched by him made her feel safe and…well…loved, and took her focus off the fact that she had no idea what the past held or what the future would bring. There were so many things about Dusty that drew her to him. His teasing banter, the way his smile lit up his entire face, his strength of presence and the way his eyes seemed to look deeply into her soul. Not to mention the way he looked in that pair of jeans. Yowzers and yum!

And maybe self-consciously she had wanted to touch his coc—okay, scratch that, she definitely wasn't a slut. She couldn't even say cock-a-doodle-doo in her own mind! But she had noticed his very nice, very large, very hot, very scrumptious penis in the half second she'd touched it before she'd turned into a coward and pulled away.

But was it possible to climax just because a guy was holding your hand? Liquid heat trailed a fire of sensation from the hand he cradled, up her arm and throughout her entire body. Even her smelly toes were curling at the base of the bed. What would happen if he held her in his arms or threw himself over her again? Her whole body quivered at that thought.

She was pathetic. Nothing was going to happen. She just had to get over him.

Dusty's thumb rubbed circles into her palm and Skylar began quivering all over again. If she wasn't careful she was going to cause an earthquake.

She was supremely pathetic.

Dusty cleared his throat and shifted in the bed. Was she making him uncomfortable? Before she could ask, he spoke. "So, ummm…you don't have any of your own memories of before you got to Talisman Bay except that your name is Skylar?"

She frowned, concentrating. Her headache was mostly gone, but she still couldn't remember anything beyond her name. "Not a one."

"Not even your favorite color?"

"No, not even that."

"Well, if you had to choose a favorite color right now, what would you choose?"

"What would I choose? I don't know. Ummm…puce, maybe?" She laughed.

Dusty squeezed her hand. "Hey! I'm being serious now. C'mon. What color?"

"I don't know. Maybe blue?"

"Yeah, I kinda thought that about you. It fits."

"What, I look blue?" she teased.

She could hear the smile in his voice. "No, blue is just a calm kind of color…like a river, or the ocean. And your eyes are blue…"

Her heart fluttered. She was so damn pathetic. Dusty wasn't even poeticizing her eyes. He'd only made a statement of fact. She had to stop making more out of everything he said and did. "Okay, so what about you? What's your favorite color?"

"Me?"

"Yes, if we're asking questions…" *Can I see you naked?* Stop! Stop! Stop!

"I like plaid."

His answer caught her off-guard and Skylar snorted out a laugh before slapping a hand down over her mouth in embarrassment. Great. What a way to turn him on, sounding like a rutting pig. Plus she had the smell to go with it. Just wonderful. Trying to detract from her barnyard animal sounds and odor before he noticed, she asked, "So, what's with all the questions? Did you start a game of twenty questions without me realizing it?"

"I'm just trying to jog your memory." He paused. "How do you feel about Talisman Bay? It's got some of the nicest beaches in California."

"I love the beach."

Dusty enthusiastically squeezed her hand. "You do?! That's great! I mean, that's good you know you love the beach. See, you're in there somewhere…you just don't remember where."

"Wow…I do know that. It's strange, I think of the beach and I feel warm and happy inside…a good memory. I don't know why I like it. But I do."

Dusty's enthusiasm was contagious. It was only a simple memory—well, not even really a memory, more just unexplained knowledge—but it meant so much more than that. It was part of who she was. Unable to stop her increasing joy from bubbling over, she laughed.

"What's so funny?"

"Nothing, really. I'm just…" *enjoying this time with you more than I should.*

Like a little kid demanding an answer, he tugged on her hand. "Oh, come on. What?"

A warm blush crept over her face. What could she say to him? "Just…oh God…I'm going to sound stupid."

"No. What is it? You won't sound stupid." There was both honesty and laughter in his voice.

She took a deep breath and squeezed her eyes tightly shut as if she could hide herself from the impending embarrassment. "I like the way you talk. The things you say. They're sweet and cute and…" Her voice lowered to a whisper. "You make me feel okay inside."

"Really? I do that to you?" Was he genuinely surprised? He paused for a deafening moment. "Well, the feeling's mutual, y'know."

In for a penny, in for a pound. "You're the only person I know I can trust and I know you'd never hurt me. You know as much about me as I do. Heck, I know you better than I know myself."

"Wow, yeah. Hell, that's probably a good thing right about now. See, you know what I can do. And I can do just about anything if you need me to. You can trust me completely. Even with—" He interrupted himself as though searching for better words. "Well, you're definitely safe with me. I promise." Dusty chuckled, but it sounded nervous. "Hey, are you cold at all? Do you need another blanket or something?"

I need you… "No. I'm fine for now."

"See, you know all sorts of stuff about yourself. You've been holding out on me," he teased.

"I know stuff about me in a vague, nonsensical way."

"Yeah, but that's what makes you who you are, whether or not stuff makes sense, it's still you."

Skylar laughed. "Are you saying I'm vague and nonsensical?"

"Isn't everyone?"

"Good point. If I knew who I was, I think I'd tell you. So I guess add honest to the list of stuff we know about me."

"Oh, believe me, I've been taking good mental notes on everything about you. Stuff you figure out. Stuff I figure out. Y'know, you can tell me absolutely anything." As if to reassure her, he stroked the inside of her wrist. That simple touch seeped into her bloodstream, traveled throughout her body, until it became a warm throb beating in her breasts and…nether regions. She squirmed in the bed, trying to relieve the aching need that was building inside.

"You okay?"

"Uh...yeah...just fine. Trying to get comfortable." She wracked her brain to think of something to say, something lighthearted, funny, something to take her mind off of how much she liked being around Dusty. "So, I can tell you anything about me I remember?"

"Of course."

"Well, what if I'm a mass murderer, or a lawyer, or a nymphomaniac..." Darn it! Why'd she have to go and mention something sexual? "I might not want to tell you that."

He chuckled. "Hmmm...so you wouldn't want to tell me you're a nymphomaniac? Somehow, I doubt you are. Mass murderer...nope you don't seem psychotic. Lawyer...you're not devious enough."

"Wait a second..." Not giving herself a chance to think better of it, she sat up and peered over the pillow barrier. Giving her a surprised and questioning look, he quickly bent his knees. But not before Skylar saw what he was trying to hide. His penis strained the front of his jeans. She wished she had the courage to reach out and cup it again, but instead she returned his look with a not-so-innocent grin. "So you're telling me that I don't look like a sexual deviant?"

A mischievous smile grew wide across his face, and those gorgeous eyes of his sparkled. "Well, definitely not a deviant..." He swallowed. "Hey, you're trying to get me in trouble now, aren't you?"

She tried to keep up the not-so-innocent act, but a telltale burn lit up her cheeks. "Who? Me?"

"You're trying to bait me into saying stuff that would get me slapped."

"I'm the passive, non-deviant, non-sexual person. How could I get you in trouble?"

His eyes still sparked with laughter, but there was something more there...something deeper. "I didn't say anything at all about you being non-sexual. Hell, no. You are very far from non-sexual."

"Oh."

"Well, yeah. Okay..." He swallowed hard. "Ummm...I'd be lying if I said I wasn't attracted to you. And I don't wanna lie so I just won't say anything."

Had he just said he was attracted to her? She rewound the statement in her head. Yes, he had. She nervously licked her lips and then realized what she was doing when his attention shifted to her mouth. Oh wow...was that longing in his gaze? Or was that just a reflection of her feelings? Unconsciously, she lifted her hand from his and wiped it over her mouth, transferring the heat of his touch to her lips, wondering what it would feel like if he kissed her.

Dusty frowned and redirected his stare to the ceiling, crossing his arms over his chest with a sigh. "Sorry. I didn't mean to make you feel uncomfortable."

"What? You didn't make me feel uncomfortable."

One corner of his mouth tilted up in a half grin. "Well, here we are laying in bed for goodness sake. The last thing I'd want to do is make you feel uncomfortable in bed with me." He grimaced. "I'm sorry. That came out wrong. I just don't want you to ever feel uncomfortable with me…even though we happen to be in a bed. Shit." He wiped his hands over his face, then crossed his arms over his chest again.

"I don't. I didn't. You're really bothered by this bed thing."

A big sigh of relief escaped his lips then his eyes widened and he turned to look at her. "No…are you!? I'm not bothered by being in a bed with you at all."

"Then why did you think I was uncomfortable with you?"

"Well, because of the way I said it. I didn't mean to imply that anything would happen between us if we were in a bed. But if it did…I mean…oh hell, I'm just gonna shut up now." He looked up again and sighed, one hand tangling in his hair.

"But something is happening between us in bed."

He cleared his throat. "Ummm…yeah, we're…uh…t-talking and stuff." His jaw clenched.

"Well, what else could we do in a bed?" she bantered. He was cute when he was nervous, unable to look at her for more than a moment without getting flustered and turning away again. She knew she should stop teasing him, but for some reason, she just couldn't stop herself.

"Well, shit, I know I can think of all sorts of things. Can't you?" First his eyes found hers, then his head followed. A sexy grin slowly crept over his face and his eyes sparkled.

Skylar couldn't help but return his grin. "Sleeping. Definitely sleeping. But I'm not tired."

He cleared his throat, but his words still came out hoarse. "Me neither."

"Okay. Good."

His fingers drummed the sheet next to him as he looked back up toward the rock ceiling. "Yeah. In a bed...yeah...here with you in a bed...yeah..."

"Yes, Dusty. Bed." She began bouncing up and down on said bed, hoping to bring back his grin. "Bed. Bed. Bed. Bed. Bed. Me and Dusty in bed. Together." And at that exact moment, as she bounced up and down on the bed anxious for Dusty's reaction, Skylar recognized the signs. She was totally falling in love with this man. Irrationally, inexplicably, and so unbelievably right. Dusty made her otherwise insane and scary world an okay place to be. Four hours ago, she'd been held hostage by a madman and her own mind. Now she was happily bouncing up and down on a bed alongside a sweet, cute and loving man who completely dissolved every ounce of her helplessness.

Dusty chuckled. "Yeah...I like the sound of that. T-together...uh-huh." He nodded and swallowed hard. "This is...this is really..."

"What?"

"I don't think I've ever talked this much with a woman while in bed...in a bed with her." His breath was quick and he tightened his jaw as though to keep from saying anything more.

"You don't usually talk when you're in bed with a girl?"

Dusty shook his head and locked his gaze with hers. "They don't usually want to talk when they're in bed with me, they just want me to get down to business. Wham-bam. They never wanted me to use my mouth for anything other than fucking."

"Well, you must not have cared either if you were there."

"I guess not. Wow! I'm learning as much about myself as I am about you. Here in bed."

They were both quiet for several moments, but it wasn't an uncomfortable silence. Skylar pulled her legs up against her chest and rested her chin on her knees. "Have you ever been in love?" she asked.

He didn't answer right away. Skylar watched him, enjoying the play of firelight across his skin. She hoped she hadn't opened up a bad memory for him. Then a smile crept across his face and he began to speak. "Just once. A long time ago. A cute little firecracker of a redhead named Tracey. But then my love affair ended when she decided she'd rather play hopscotch with Phillip Stedman." Dusty snorted. "Damn. I guess I really have had girl trouble ever since that brush off in first grade."

Skylar couldn't help but laugh. "Sorry she broke your heart. Silly girl. If only she could see you now, she'd be smacking herself for her hopscotch betrayal."

He shook his head and smiled but didn't say anything.

"Do you think I'll ever get my memory back?"

"I hope so. I know I don't ever want to forget this."

"Me either." They shared a smile and she wished she could reach out and take his hand again. "It's strange, I don't even know what it's liked to be kissed…except by David."

"I've always hoped that when I kissed a girl, her knees got weak. I don't think that ever really happens though."

Skylar closed her eyes and imagined being kissed by Dusty, and oh how her knees got weak. Her breasts ached and her whole body throbbed in want of that kiss. She opened her eyes, trying to move past her desires as she spoke. "It would be nice to be that caught up in a kiss. To be so intent on a person that nothing else matters."

Dusty nodded. "Yeah, and you find yourself in a world where only you and the girl exists and that's it. Everything belongs only to the two of you. God, what I want is a woman I can kiss and just *connect* to on every level. A woman I can have and hold and kiss and caress for hours so that by the time we're ready for me to slide in, we're so hot for each other I can be a one-stroke wonder and it doesn't even matter because we're in our own world and everything in it is beautiful. Damn…I can't believe you got me talking about all this stuff so easily."

"Dusty…"

"Yeah?"

Could she tell him that she was burning up inside for want of him? That her skin felt too tight for her body and she ached for his soothing touch? She wanted to, but the words stayed locked inside.

"Aw shit, Skylar, did I say something wrong? You got me going and I just started telling you my deep dark secrets and stuff you probably don't even care about. I'm sorry."

Like a volcano, blistering heat bubbled up inside of her, and the words erupted from her soul. "You didn't say anything wrong. Dusty…what you said you want. It's beautiful. God, I want that too." The words froze in her throat, but she forced herself to keep going. "But I know almost nothing about myself. If I were to walk out of here, I have nowhere to go. Nowhere. Nothing exists outside of this bed for me. You are all I have and I can't put that on you."

"Y'know, right now, nothing exists for me outside of this bed, either. And I want to be here with you. I like the way you think. The way your mind works is fascinating. The way your body works is fascinating. Skylar, I find you incredibly fascinating in every sense of the word. But I can't put that on *you*…or can I? Can I tell you that you are my world right now? Is that gonna scare the shit out of you?"

"It doesn't scare me. Except that you have a tomorrow and a next day."

"So do you."

Skylar shook her head, the words all tangled up inside. "I'm sorry. This isn't coming out right." Taking a deep breath, she opened her heart completely. "Tomorrow doesn't exist without you."

"But I will be here tomorrow…and the next day…whenever you need me." He reached over the pillows and laid his hand on hers. Their gazes met and held. By the look in his eyes, she knew that he spoke the utter truth and that even if the world were crumbling around her, he'd be there when the sun came up.

"Will you?" She placed her free hand over his, wanting to keep him with her forever.

"Yes. I promise you I will be here. No matter what. I couldn't leave now even if I wanted to." He smiled, shook his head, and let out a quiet chuckle. "You're driving me crazy."

"Crazy, good? Or crazy, bad?" Her heart seemed to pause in her chest as she waited for his answer. Little did he know, he was driving her crazy, too.

"I'm laying here next to you and all I can think about is loving you." He took a shaky breath as his fingers stroked hers. "I mean, I wanna caress your entire body with my hands and then follow that up with my tongue. And I want to take my time. I want to know every inch of you inside and out. I want to press your body against mine and share your heat. I wanna kiss you and show you without all these damn words, how I feel about you…take you into my arms and hold you so tight you…you…you…"

His words had mesmerized her, pulling her closer to him until she was leaning over the pillows. Her question was whispered into the few inches of air separating their faces. "So tight I what?"

As though continuing her same breath, Dusty huskily replied, "So tight you don't want me to let you go."

Skylar closed the remaining distance between them, breathing her words into his mouth as she placed her lips over his. "I don't want you to let me go."

Dusty began to drink of her with a vehement thirst, one arm encircling her, pulling her completely over the pillow barrier until she rested solidly against his naked chest. His other hand gently cradled her cheek, drawing her mouth closer as his lips parted and begged hers to follow, as his tongue licked the seam of her lips until she opened wide enough to receive him.

His kiss overwhelmed her senses, stealing her breath, making her body buzz with indescribable pleasure. He alternately suckled her lips, then her tongue, sweeping through her mouth with masterful strokes. He tasted of passion, fire and barely restrained desire. A desperate need to know more of his body rippled through her. Tentatively, she stole into his mouth, wrapping her tongue around his. His response was a low, drawn-out growl of need, and an infinitesimal tightening of his arm around her waist. But that slight reaction urged her on and she pulled him closer, tangling her fingers into his silky soft hair.

Under her nightgown, her nipples beaded painfully, aching to rub against his naked flesh, to be suckled into the warm wetness of his mouth. But his sole focus was still on her mouth, as though he was afraid to do more.

Lightly tugging on his hair, she separated their mouths. His eyes followed the path of her tongue as she licked her swollen lips. Her mouth felt bruised, but she relished that feeling. "More, Dusty. I want more. All of you. Please."

"You've been through so much. Believe me, you've got all of me, but I don't wanna scare you, sweetheart."

"You don't scare me." Her hands slid from his neck, down to his chest, playing with the short curly hair there. "You make me feel alive and free. All I know is that I don't want tonight to end. I don't want you to ever stop touching me."

Skylar's eyes fluttered shut as Dusty leaned in to kiss her again. His lips brushed lightly over hers, then continued up her cheek to her ear where he whispered, "I'm gonna taste you now. Run my mouth all over your body. Is that okay?" He nibbled her earlobe, lightly tugging on the tender flesh there.

Her eyes shot open and an involuntary shiver rocked her. "Yes, Dusty…God, yes." She didn't even sound like herself, her words husky and wanting. She curled her fingers into his shoulders, clinging desperately to the man who concurrently made her feel safe, yet desperate to lose control.

"Good," was his only reply, then he arranged their bodies until she lay flat on the bed and he was above her. He lowered his mouth to her neck and began to feast.

Her body came alive under his touch. The warmth of his tongue as he tasted her flesh. The rough burn of his whiskers against her sensitive skin. The gentle nip of his teeth as he suckled at the rapidly beating pulse in her throat. She arched her neck back, silently begging for more.

Slowly, torturously, he moved from her neck to her shoulders, stopping to explore every dip and curve with both his hands and mouth. His fingers teased along the top of her nightgown, running back and forth over the lacy edge. "God, you take my breath away, Skylar."

His mouth lowered until she could feel the heat of his breath against her breast, through the material of her nightgown. "You nearly killed me laying here all this time, watching your nipples swell and darken through your transparent nightgown, figuring I'd die without a taste."

He swiped his tongue over her right nipple and she nearly came off the bed. Her breath came in rapid pants and she surprised herself by groaning, "Again."

"Oh, hell, yes." He latched onto her areola through the nightgown, pulling it into the warm recesses of his mouth. His hand explored her other breast, plumping the soft flesh there, his thumb and forefinger gently pinching her already erect nub. The fabric separating their bodies frustrated her. She wanted to rip it away and bare herself completely to his touch. Instead she looked down her body and watched their bodies react to each other.

His dark blond head nuzzled at one breast, his large hand covered the other. His need was her need. She ran one hand through his hair, pressing him even closer to her and she trembled as he reacted to her unspoken request and suckled harder and deeper, his hand switching from gentle to harsher tugs of her pebbled flesh.

A warm rush of liquid flooded her core, leaking from her body, dampening the flesh between her legs. Desperately, she arched upward, seeking more…knowing only Dusty could provide it.

He moved back up and owned her mouth again with long, slow sweeps of his tongue. As though her body had a wanton mind of its own, it arched and rubbed against him, needing to feel his chest against her breasts, desperate to feel his hardness enveloped in her heat. She could barely breathe, her arousal was so strong, yet at the same time, she wanted to prolong everything he did to her, make every moment last forever.

Dusty's breathing was staggered when he finally pulled away. Light brown eyes sought hers and she saw his deep level of desire, but an even deeper level of caring and concern resided there as well. She knew that he'd back away in a heartbeat if he thought she wasn't ready. He smoothed her hair. "If it's okay, I'm gonna take your nightgown off now. I wanna see all of you."

She nodded, almost too choked up to speak. What had she done to deserve this man? She'd do it all again, her time with Craze, the fear of not knowing what would happen next, if it meant she could stay in Dusty's arms.

He wiped those thoughts away as he slid down her body, stopping to kiss each nipple before moving down to where her nightgown rested just above her knees. His hands slipped beneath, resting on her outer thighs, and he paused, looking up to meet her eyes. "You're trembling."

"Only because I want you so badly."

Their gazes stayed locked as he brought his hands to her hips, bunching up the nightgown. Cool air hit her inner thighs and she struggled not to moan, afraid he would take it the wrong way and stop. She sat up to give him the freedom to pull the nightgown over her head.

When it was gone, puddled on the floor next to the bed, neither of them moved. Skylar remained sitting up, her hands pressed into the bed at her sides. Dusty straddled her legs, his hands fisted on his denim-clad thighs, caressing her body with his worshipful gaze. She returned the favor, looking her fill of his body, coming to rest on the front of his jeans and the very large distraction hidden there. With the removal of her nightgown, it was as though she'd shed all her inhibitions and she lifted her hand and placed it over Dusty's straining cock.

Even through the denim she could feel his heat and strength. Not to mention his extra large size. He had to be uncomfortable trapped in those jeans. Wanting to explore every delicious inch of him, she stroked her hand down lower between his legs. He shuddered and let out a garbled moan. Eyes wide, her gaze shot to his face and she pulled her hand back, afraid she'd hurt him.

He grabbed her rapidly retreating hand. "Don't stop." He exhaled shakily. "I—I mean, don't stop unless you want to."

A mixture of awe and utter feminine power came over her, that she could make this man moan. She slipped her legs out from between his, and rose to her knees in front of him. One hand rested on his magnificent chest, the other lowered to the chiseled six-pack of his stomach. His muscles tightened beneath her exploring fingers. With one finger she teased the dark trail of hair, following it to where it led under his waistband. She lifted her face to meet his eyes, then gave him a wicked grin. "I want to see where this trail—" she ran her fingernails over the coarse hair, "ends."

His eyes smoldered and he crashed his mouth over hers. The kiss was primitive, primal, and she reciprocated, growling and pulling his tongue deeper into her mouth, giving back tenfold everything he gave to her. She got lost in the rhythm of the kiss, the frantic lovemaking of tongues and teeth and lips.

Dusty pulled back, taking in a ragged breath. "Goddamn, Skylar. I'm trying to go slow, but—"

"You don't have to go slow."

"Oh, but I want to. I wanna take my time." Wrapping his arm around her, he gently lifted her until she was reclined on the bed again. "I can see the dampness coating your pussy and I'm dying to taste it. Is that okay?"

"You don't need to ask."

"Yes I do."

"My answer will always be yes," she replied throatily. "I need you, Dusty." Spreading her legs, she invited him in. Warm hands roamed between her thighs, gently nudging them open even further. He let out a low groan at her obvious willingness and settled between her legs.

Starting at her hip, he traced a finger along the top of her leg, moving slowly toward the heat of her. Skylar kept her eyes on his bent head, as he studied her open body before him. His finger moved to her folds, delving carefully between them, spreading her ever-seeping moisture over every stretch of skin. His slow, simple touches had her ready to scream out her need, and she arched her hips into his touch, silently demanding that he give her more. He chuckled. "I know sweetheart. I want this too. But first..." And then his mouth lowered and his tongue tasted the very flesh he'd just been pleasuring with his touch.

Sublime torture. His tongue explored every crevice, dipping inside, pulling moans and need and desperation she couldn't explain from her very core. She thrashed beneath him, wanting more, wanting him to fill her until she would never be empty, to slip inside her, wrap himself around her, connect them in every way so they would never be apart.

She sobbed, on the edge of something unexplainable. And then he added a finger to his torment, pumping into her sheath and she wanted to beg, plead with him, to make it stop, to make it last forever.

He added a second finger, pressing deeper. He lifted his mouth from her and moaned, "Shit, Skylar, you're so hot and wet and tight. I want to feel you ride me. Your pussy clenching my cock the way you're grabbing onto my fingers, trying to pull me inside, deeper and deeper into you."

Skylar didn't recognize her voice as she choked out her response, nearly sobbing. "Yes, Dusty. God, yes. Just...please...I'm burning...so hot..."

His fingers continued their thrusting and he lowered his mouth. Matching the rhythm of his fingers, his tongue lightly danced against the bundle of nerves he'd previously ignored. He worked the movement deeper, circling her clit and taking it into the heat of his mouth.

Skylar screamed, "Dusty!" as every bit of tension released at once, exploding from her core, taking her on a wave of pleasure so extreme the world lost focus around her.

But she knew there was still so much more where that came from. The eyes she didn't remember shutting fluttered open to meet Dusty's lust-filled and very pleased grin.

She met his stare with one of her own and simply said, "More." His eyes widened and he chuckled as she sat up and reached for his jeans. "These are coming off now, mister."

"Yes, ma'am."

So quick she could barely see it, Dusty swung off the bed and ripped his jeans from his body.

Skylar blinked.

Then she gulped.

He was magnificent. And huge. So huge she began to have doubts on just exactly how it was going to fit inside her. But she'd never heard of anyone being split asunder during sex…well, at least she didn't remember anything like that.

And if the height of her demand for him came into play at all, he'd fit like he was made to be there.

Dusty was watching her watch him. On trembling legs that still hadn't recovered from her first orgasm, she stood up and closed the distance between them. "Can I touch you now? Is that okay?"

His only reply was a quick nod and then a rapid exhale as she grasped the base of his cock. With her other hand, she traced the large veins bulging along his angry red shaft, tracing them up to the thick purple head standing away from his body. *I did this to him.*

She continued to study every inch of him, lowering one hand to the heavy sac between his legs, stroking the soft fur that covered him. A low growl filled the air and Skylar shifted her attention to Dusty's face. His eyes were closed, head thrown back, jaw clenched tightly.

Smiling at what she did to him, she stood on tiptoe and kissed his cheek. Then she whispered, "Can I love you now, Dusty?"

"Hell, yes." In one swift maneuver, he lowered his hands to her ass, picked her up and carried her to the bed. She wrapped her legs around his waist forcing his cock toward the entrance to her body. They both groaned.

Dusty settled back onto the bed, keeping Skylar straddling him. His cock pulsed hot and hard against her opening and she knew that he wouldn't take it any further than that. His hands guided, but didn't coax her. She was in control of the situation, and only she could decide when she was ready.

She was ready.

Skylar stroked her hands over the light layer of sweat covering his chest while she circled her open pussy over his length, coating him with her moisture. It felt so good to feel him throbbing there, hot and ready for her. Wanting her. Needing her.

Carefully, she shifted positions, centering the tip of his cock at her open portal. Lowering herself just a fraction, she moaned as the full, thick head breached the opening and slipped inside. She froze as her body adjusted to the welcome invasion.

Dusty's hands roamed over her back. "It's okay, baby, go slow. You're so damn tight, I don't want you to hurt yourself."

But she didn't want to go slow. It felt so good with him there. So right. Like this man completed her.

Biting her lip, knowing it would probably hurt but not caring, she thrust down, taking his full length inside of her.

Then she stopped.

She had something else to add to the list of things she knew about herself.

She was a virgin…or had been until five seconds ago.

Dusty tensed beneath her. "Skylar…?"

Quietly, she replied, "Ouch."

Chapter Seven

Dusty was afraid to breathe. For the very first time in his life, he wished he had a small cock. And not just shorter, thinner, too. He wrapped his arms around her but tried not to jostle where they were still connected. "Oh shit, don't move, sweetheart. It'll stop hurting, just give it a minute. I'm so sorry. Are you okay? God, Skylar, please tell me you're okay." He should've known why she was so exquisitely tight. It just hadn't dawned on him that this was possibly her first sexual encounter.

"Well, that was a surprise," Skylar stated rather matter-of-factly considering the circumstances.

And that was an understatement. Dusty brought his hands to her hips in order to pull out of her a little bit. His fervent wishes hadn't produced a miniature cock so maybe having her take less of him would help. Hell, she probably felt like she'd been split in two.

"No, Dusty, wait." She shifted her hips and her already tight pussy contracted further around him. Dusty couldn't hold back his moan. God she felt so good. But dammit, this wasn't about what felt good. He had to make this right for her somehow. He countered her movement with a roll of his hips. This time she moaned and arched her back, forcing him even deeper. "Oh, God, Dusty, don't stop. I need more of that. More of you."

"Okay, but you gotta tell me if I hurt you again." He began slow small circles with his hips, grinding against her without adding the potentially complicating friction of pumping in and out.

"Dusty, you didn't hurt me. I needed you…needed this." Skylar kissed away his protest. Hell, she was practically making him forget his own name. He massaged her perfectly round ass in unison with their rhythm. Hopefully, if she felt up to it, he could make the movements bigger, gradually building her up. This had to be a night she would remember for the rest of her life because Dusty was positive he could never forget it.

Once more, the woman had completely astounded him. Throughout their conversation, he'd found himself desperately wanting to sink himself within her. Not just within her cunt, but her entire being. When she'd taken control and straddled him, sliding down his length, it was the most erotic moment of his life. Her pussy so tight, her eyes clouded with need for him. But when she'd taken him inside herself completely, instead of it continuing to be one of the most amazing moments of his life, it had nearly torn him apart. The last thing he'd wanted to do was hurt her. Nothing in his life mattered except for Skylar.

Her hands skimmed along the sides of his rib cage as she laid her full weight on him. She felt about as heavy as a feather. Then, she began a slow retreat off of his cock. He was about to ask if she was okay when she crashed her hips back down, taking every inch of him in her tight passage. It felt so good, he practically saw stars. And then he realized something.

She'd never been anyone else's before him. And that knowledge brought forth a responsibility. It was up to him to make this moment perfect. But not just this moment. Every moment they shared.

On her next thrust, he took the lead, adding further gyration while caressing her body with his hands and kissing her. She was small enough that he could reach one of his arms nearly all the way around her. His fingertips grazed the side of her breast where it pressed hard against his chest.

The magic between their legs continued with each stroke until he felt her trembling on the edge, her exquisite pussy clamping down on him. As her sheath contracted around him, he locked his lips with hers, sinking his tongue into the sweet recesses of her mouth. Consuming her as she'd consumed him until she cried out in ecstasy. He swallowed her cries as she came, the furious clenching of her spasming pussy taking him over the edge with her. His seed exploded from his body with a violent need he'd never before experienced. A wild mixture of sensation and emotion flowed from within him as well, his heart awash with devotion to this woman.

Her body quivered over his and her breath came out in soft warm pants against his neck. She spoke against his throat, her voice an understandably exhausted whisper. "I...I love you, Dusty."

Heavenly warmth surrounded him, taking away that gnawing ache of emptiness inside. It even brought tears to his eyes. He'd never heard those words said with such feeling behind them. Every other time, the words had been used as empty promises, tools for manipulating him, or simply what he'd strived for as a child, but never got. But when Skylar said those words, his whole life took on new meaning.

He was in love with her, too.

Dusty smoothed a tendril of sweat-soaked hair from her brow, then proceeded to place kisses all over her face while he ran his hands up and down her skin, memorizing the feel of her body joined with his. His world simply did not exist without her in it. And he never wanted to be without her again.

"Marry me?" he asked between kisses.

She sat up quickly, her blue eyes wide circles in her face. "Dusty? What?"

He grimaced. Although every word he spoke was true, he cursed himself for blurting out his raw feelings and screwing everything up. But he *knew* this was right, that she was the woman he'd been waiting for. "Shit. I—I… Lemme try this again. Skylar, I just can't imagine a life without you in every minute of it. I love you. Marry me, please, and I will take care of you forever."

She was quiet. Too quiet as she stared down at him, gnawing on her lower lip. Shit. He should have waited. She was going to say no. He should have done it right with a ring and flowers and a candlelight dinner and all that shit that he knew he was supposed to do. All the things Skylar deserved. But he just couldn't have waited. His heart wouldn't let him. It didn't matter that she didn't know who she was, he knew they belonged together. He'd never felt this way about anyone before.

"Dusty—"

"Skylar—"

They spoke at the same time and then grew quiet as they looked at each other. He silently willed her to make his life complete by just uttering a simple "yes", but instead of speaking, she lowered herself back over him and kissed him sweet and passionately. Not quite the exact answer he was looking for, but at least she didn't say "no" and throw him out of bed. Even if his ears wanted something else, the rest of his body responded to her kiss all the same. His cock, still tucked inside her warmth, began to thicken and harden again.

Skylar sighed into his mouth and tilted her hips, then her whole body tightened and she let out a quiet whimper. Her cunt rippled around him, pulling him in as she began to slide up and down on his length. But he knew it was hurting her, could feel it in the tension of her body.

Lacing his fingers into her hair, he pulled her lips from his. "Whoa, sweetheart. As much as I'm always game for another round, I definitely don't want you in any pain. I want you to enjoy this as much as I do. Lemme take care of you."

Without giving her a chance to protest he sat up, biting back a groan as her sheath pulsated around his cock. Ever so slowly he lifted her off him, cringing at the ruby red blood smeared on her thighs and on his cock.

Dusty gathered her into his arms. Even if she never agreed to marry him, he knew she loved him and that was more important than anything. He already knew he would love her for the rest of his life whether she married him or not. She wrapped her arms around his neck and leaned her head on his shoulder as he walked deep within the cave where the air was warmer and heated water flowed into a pool. He slowly stepped into the warm spring and sat down with her on his lap, content to just hold her close if only to memorize how it felt to truly love and be loved.

Her eyes filled with awe as she looked around the dimly lit paradise. "Wow…this place is amazing. It's so beautiful. An oasis of serenity…I don't ever want to leave."

"Well, you never have to leave if you don't want to." He kissed her temple. "Now, I promised to take care of you. So just sit back and enjoy the water."

He slid out from underneath her and she reclined back in the water and closed her eyes. He'd never felt so much love as at that moment with her and he wanted to keep her with him so he'd never feel anything but her love. She offered herself so freely; he knew she was meant for only him. As he washed his hands over her body under the water, he moved so that he was kneeling below her, reaching all the way down to her dainty little toes.

As his gaze trailed back up her body, he began to smile, but as he saw her face, his smile faded. She was looking at him, her eyes full of love and mystery and a gnawing uncertainty he wished he could wipe away as easily as he had washed away the signs of their earlier lovemaking.

"Dusty, I'm scared." She swallowed. "But no matter what happens, know that I do love you. Tonight...I'll never forget it. I'll never forget you. No matter what the future has in store for me."

"Are you still worried that you're gonna wake up and I'll be gone or something?"

"Yes...no...I don't know. This is crazy. Too good to be true. I—"

"What is your heart saying?" Dusty interrupted, because while he was feeling the same way, he knew they were both where they should be. "I know mine is saying that I've finally met the woman I will cherish for the rest of my life. Maybe it's crazy, but I trust it because I know it's right. This is right. And yeah, my brain kinda agrees with you that we should be a little scared. But if there was no fear of the unknown, would this even be real? Look, nothing's ever sunshine and roses all the time, but we'll get through it together. All of it. For our entire lives. Because with each other's help, we will make the unknown become known. And facing it together is ten times easier than having to face it all alone. I'm up for the challenge and my heart is telling me you are too."

Her gaze never wavered from his. "Yes."

"Yes, what?"

She stood up and water sluiced down her heavenly body. Either he'd said something incredibly wrong and she was standing up to leave, or he had said something incredibly right and she actually wanted to be closer to him. His fears were allayed when she reached him and knelt down, knee-to-knee, thigh-to-thigh, sex-to-sex.

Her lips brushed his jaw as she spoke. "Yes to everything, Dusty. Because the moment you stole into my life, I knew I'd never be alone again. Does that make any sense? My life changed when you stepped into it. You keep the fear at bay with the strength of your words." She lifted her head and met his eyes. "I don't know what tomorrow will bring, but I do know I want to discover it with you...I love you and just want to be with you."

Dusty choked past the tightness in his throat. "You will be." He knew there was plenty more he should say, but for some reason, the words completely escaped him. And hell, hadn't she said everything he was feeling in his heart?

Their lips met hungrily, feasting on the promises they'd just made to one another. His hands swept down her body, grabbing her by the ass and lifting her. He'd thought to take her back to the bed where she'd be more comfortable, but she surprised him by locking her ankles behind his back and taking his cock all the way inside her. Pure bliss. He was surrounded by so much heat—the water, his Skylar—he relinquished himself to the burn.

When they came, they came together, falling into each other over and over again, a seemingly unending cycle of pleasure and love.

Sometime later, Dusty lifted the sleeping woman into his arms and returned to the bed where they'd fallen in love. He pushed the pillow barrier against the wall as he laid her down. Such beauty and passion within her small frame. As long as she was right there beside him when he woke up, everything would be okay. He lay down, kissed her hair and fell asleep with her tucked against his chest, right next to his heart.

* * * * *

The sound of air whizzing just in front of his nose awakened Dusty in time to see and feel the full force of a fist landing squarely in his eye. How the hell had he slept through the man's approach? He managed to block the next punch while blitzing out of bed, then tried to deliver a bash of equal vigor as his mind fully awakened.

"God damn it, Dusty! You could have gotten all of us killed! When did your Shadow Walker training *ever* include disobeying the orders of your leader?" Stephan shouted as the two men pummeled each other like the worst of enemies.

"Fuck you, Stephan!" Dusty took a hard punch to the gut after delivering a perfect left hook to Stephan's eye. Hopefully, it would match the black eye Dusty felt developing on his own face.

Launching himself at Stephan, they began to wrestle on the ground. With such matching strengths, neither got in more than a few punches. Although Dusty's landed harder than what he received from Stephan.

"Stop hurting him or I'll kill you, Stephan!"

Both men abruptly stopped wrestling and looked up at the naked woman before them. Skylar must have grabbed the iron poker from a pile of old demon torture instruments near the opening of the cave. She scowled at Stephan, ready to slam the poker down on his head.

Stephan expertly rolled away as Dusty jumped up and wrapped himself around Skylar, snatching the poker from her hands and tossing it to the side. "No, sweetheart. It's okay. It's okay."

Stephan replied before Skylar could even open her mouth. "No, it's not okay, Dusty. Now you've really got a helluva lot of talking to do."

"Dusty, don't let him near me. I swear I'll kill him," Skylar snarled vengefully.

Dusty held her even tighter. This was not the morning after he had envisioned. "Shhh…Skylar. You're safe with me. You know that. I won't let him anywhere near you. It's okay. I promise." He pulled a blanket from the bed to wrap her in it. Surrounding her with his protective embrace, he defiantly returned his attention to Stephan. "Damn you. Get your ass over there and sit the fuck down before I really let you have it." He pointed toward the bench. "You have *no idea* what this woman has been through. Before you go berserk, listen to the whole story first."

Stephan didn't show any signs of calming. Shaking his head, his eyes shone of fury, but he sat down on the bench as though he didn't quite know what else to do. His eye was already starting to turn red from Dusty's punch. This spar had escalated into an all-out brawl…something that had never happened between them before. And Dusty hoped would never happen again.

He managed to unclench his fists, although he had trouble unclenching his jaw, but at least Stephan was willing to listen. "She doesn't know who she is. Craze erased her memories and gave her some of Mariah's. Fiero was kind enough to straighten her out enough to realize that she is not Mariah. But Craze set her up to believe that you—yes, you, Mr. Wonderful—were abusing her. So shut the fuck up before you even tell me what it means to disobey you. Dammit, Stephan. Where is your brain?" Dusty kissed Skylar's hair and whispered into her ear. "I'll kick his ass again if he comes over here. Don't worry. I might even let you help if you want to."

Stephan glared. "So, who else knows about this other than me? You think you can just take the lead? There's a reason The Order put me in charge here. What the fuck are you doing, man? We're supposed to be on the same team." His knuckles went from red to white as he gripped the edge of the bench. Dusty had never seen Stephan this pissed off before. Then again, no one had ever dared disobey him quite like this.

"I did what I knew in my heart to be the right thing to do. You can't fault me for that. The operation was flawless. Marlin stayed behind to make sure Twyla made it out of Craze's house okay. He clicked-in to let me know everything was fine."

"Great. You, Marlin, Fiero and Twyla?" Stephan shook his head. He looked like he wanted to launch off the bench, even though he still gripped it tightly. Holding onto it was probably the only thing keeping him still. "Dammit. I should have known. And now you've really gone and screwed things up even more. Here, no less. You know the rules regarding safe havens but apparently, you can't keep your head out of your ass long enough to see just how vulnerable this makes us."

"Oh, don't you even start in on vulnerability, Mr. Double Standard. You can't sit there and tell me that bringing Mariah into the compound wasn't the same as bringing Skylar here. You're full of shit, Stephan. I don't care what you say. This woman is not my weakness. If anything, she brings out my strength and I would sooner quit being a Shadow Walker than let her go. I need her more than I need you."

Dusty ran his hand over Skylar's blanket-covered back as he nudged her toward the bed. This was the first time he'd ever threatened dissension and while it should have surprised him, it didn't. He meant every word. He grabbed his jeans from the floor and slid them on while he waited for the St. Stephan volcano to erupt.

But the illustrious leader remained silent.

The calm before the storm, Dusty supposed. He stood there, watching Stephan stew. The gears were grinding. Dusty knew that if he didn't pay now, he'd surely pay later. But which would it be?

"You need her more than me, huh? I wouldn't go there if I were you, Dusty." Stephan stood up, facing Dusty down with each approaching step. Then Stephan clicked-in. *You think about what you're saying. I need Shadow Walkers who don't shirk their duties when a piece of ass walks by. Maybe after the lust clears we'll both see where your loyalties lie. I need your help against Craze, but if you choose to cavort with his leftovers, I'll find my way without you.*

It was an involuntary action. Dusty could not have stopped even if he'd been cognizant of it. His left arm wound up, and as he unleashed his fist toward Stephan's jaw, Skylar hollered, "Stop it! Both of you!"

But it was too late, Stephan had already gone into Shadow Walker defensive mode and jerked to the side away from the punch, while countering with another left hook aimed at Dusty's jaw.

Evenly matched, they both missed. Skylar darted from the bed and Dusty backed away toward her. *Get the fuck away from us, man. Before this gets even further out of hand.*

Shit, I'm sorry. You just keep her away from Mariah. Stephan let out a pained breath as he stormed out of the cave.

Dusty's mind was a jumble of emotions. And it somehow tore its way down into his heart as well. He almost wanted to cry. He knew he'd done what was best, but in the process, he had also betrayed his best friend…a man who had pulled the alcohol out of Dusty's hand when all he'd wanted to do was waste himself into oblivion…a man who had taken many a knife, bullet and numerous other demon-inflicted wounds in order to save Dusty from being killed or maimed. But through all of those betraying thoughts, the woman Dusty had risked everything for was right here with him and his heart kept assuring him he'd done the right thing. Now, if he could just numb his heart and mind for a moment, give himself time to clear his head and figure out what his next move should be.

He wrapped his arms around Skylar. "Everything's gonna be okay. I promise."

She reached up and put a gentle hand on his cheek just below his eye. He forced back a wince so she wouldn't see his pain. "It's no big deal." Hell, who was he kidding? Everything hurt. He kissed her fingertips.

"Oh no you don't. You sit right here. I need to make sure you're okay." Skylar pushed him down onto the bench.

"I'm fine, Skylar. I mean, yeah, it hurts, but it's nothing that won't go away by tomorrow." He hoped she wouldn't realize just how much Stephan had wounded him.

She inspected a scratch on his chest. "I think Stephan hurt you more than you realize." Skylar skimmed her hands lightly over his body, examining every wound. She was incredible. Did she know how to read minds or was his pain so obvious? His training included hiding emotions. The woman must truly be his soulmate if she could figure him out that easily.

She stood back up and brushed a kiss over his lips. "Let's go to the hot springs. This time I'll take care of you." Shrugging her shoulders, she let the blanket fall to the floor.

Behind them, at the entrance to the cave, Dusty heard two footsteps. Shit. Hadn't Stephan said more than enough? "Fuck you. I'd sooner brawl some more over her than let you tell me what to do."

Skylar looked up and her face went pale. Dusty turned, ready to fight Stephan some more, but instead, there was a different man standing there. One with brown eyes locked on Skylar and a look of distressed surprise on his face.

"I didn't come to brawl. But if Skylar's the prize, I might have to give it a go."

"Who the fuck are you?" Dusty turned to completely face the man who had somehow found the hidden entrance to the cave. Sizing him up, Dusty knew he could take the fellow if it did come to blows. The man was much smaller in mass. Maybe he was some kind of thief or prowler. Except the man knew Skylar's name. What else did he know? Had Craze sent him to take her back?

The man's gaze never left her. "I'm Skylar's fiancé."

* * * * *

"Adrian?"

Skylar stood frozen, locked in Adrian's somber gaze, unable to move, unable to breathe as the memories of her life slammed back into her consciousness with the rapidity of machine gun fire. Summers at the Cape. Getting her tonsils out when she was eight. Learning to drive a stick shift. Her parents' funeral.

She wasn't even aware that she had fallen to her knees as the second wave of memories hit her with more extreme force. Following Adrian around like a puppy dog when she was ten. Their first kiss when she was home on break from college. Late night phone calls when she should have been studying.

The night he'd asked her to marry him.

Oh Jesus, what had she done? How could she have forgotten him? Adrian was her best friend, had always been there for her. Almost every good memory tied back to him.

As if from a great distance, she heard Dusty's voice. "Skylar, come on, don't do this to me again. Come on baby, are you okay? You gotta come out of this." He cradled her against his chest, then stood up, carrying her. Try as she might, she couldn't speak or move, as though with the return of her memories, she'd lost control of everything else.

He lowered her to the soft comfort of the bed, sitting himself next to her before taking her hand, lovingly stroking her fingers like he'd done last night in this very spot.

"What the hell did you do to her?" Adrian this time, animosity and worry evident in his sharply spoken words. If only she could open her eyes, let them know she was okay…except she was far from being okay. The vicious pounding in her head, the stabbing pain in her heart…

"Get the fuck outta here, man. I don't know who you think you are to her, but just get away from us." Skylar could barely recognize Dusty's voice. The anger, the pain. The fear for her.

Adrian spoke quietly…forcefully. "I've been trying to track her down for two months and now that I've found her, I'm not going to leave her in any danger."

"Yeah, well, she's not in any danger with me." A blanket settled over her, Dusty's warm hands soothing as they swept down her body. "This woman is my life."

"This woman is my fiancé."

Dammit, Skylar! Open your eyes! Wake up before Dusty punches someone else this morning! This is your fault. Her whole body felt weak but she needed to stand up and figure out how to make everything right. She choked out, "Dusty, Adrian…I'm okay."

She tried to say more but before she could, Dusty pulled her into a tight embrace. For one moment, Skylar let herself pretend everything really was okay. She rubbed her face against his chest, inhaling his sweaty, masculine scent. She loved him, loved his fierce protectiveness, the way he touched her so deeply with his complete honesty and heartfelt words. She knew he'd never do anything to hurt her, just as she knew there was no way she could avoid hurting him.

Why the hell had she let herself fall into him last night? If she could have kept her wits about herself…

No, no, no. She'd been in love with Dusty before she'd made love with him. Having her memory back didn't change the way she felt for him. It just made things a hell of a lot more complicated. How could she be in love with two men at the same time?

But she was, and she had no idea what to do about it.

Then Adrian's voice broke the silence. "Skylar, what the hell happened to you?"

She lifted her head from Dusty's chest and met the bitter fear and betrayal lurking deep in Adrian's gaze. Dusty kept his arms around her, covering her nudity, for which she was grateful. It was hard enough to be staring into the eyes of the fiancé she'd never had intercourse with while she was in the arms of her lover and second fiancé.

Oh what a tangled web we weave, when first we practice to deceive... But what recourse did she have if the deceiving was unintentional on her part?

She couldn't hide in the shelter of Dusty's arms forever. With a sigh, she pressed her hands against the hard planes of his chest. His muscles tightened beneath her fingers and then he stood up just out of reach. The chill he left behind froze a part of her soul. Skylar held the blanket tighter, as though it alone could warm her again.

"I—I don't know what to say. I don't know where to start." She looked at Adrian, needing an answer herself. "How did you find me?"

He slipped his hand into his pocket and removed a small gold object. "I used this."

Although she'd only worn it a short time, it was instantly recognizable. "My ring...but how?"

"I became a Shadow Tracker so I could find you."

"Un-fucking-believable." Dusty ran his hand over his hair, then stopped mid-stroke. "Wait, The Order sent a Tracker for her?" His gaze bore into Adrian's with much distrust and chagrin.

"How do you know about The Order?" Adrian asked sharply.

A twisted chuckle escaped Dusty's lips and he faced Adrian squarely. "I'm a Shadow Walker."

Adrian was silently taken aback. The cave grew quiet, the only sounds the harsh breathing of its inhabitants.

Skylar broke the silence. "A Shadow Tracker? But Adrian...how?"

A tick throbbed in Adrian's jaw as he slid her engagement ring back in his pocket. "You know, it might be easier to hold a conversation if you put some clothes on."

Skylar blushed as she looked down at herself, then at the nightgown she'd worn last night, still crumpled on the floor where Dusty had thrown it in his haste to get her unclothed. The chill inside settled deeper as she remembered David giving her that nightgown, a gesture of love and respect for Mariah—another act in his little game.

There was no way in hell she was going to put that on again. "I—I don't have anything to wear."

"He kept you here naked?" Adrian growled as he angrily advanced toward Dusty. "What the hell kind of cruel—"

Dusty launched toward Adrian and Skylar threw herself between them. Barely restrained fury resonated from where Dusty was pressed against her back. She clutched the blanket in one hand over her breasts and placed her other hand on Adrian's arm to keep him still. "Stop. Please. Both of you. I'm trying to get my head on straight, and I can't do that with you two facing off every thirty seconds. Please." She licked her parched lips. "Adrian, Dusty hasn't hurt me. And Dusty," she turned toward him, "Adrian would never hurt me. So just…I need you two to stand down."

"Stand down? You want me to stand down?" Adrian's words panted from his throat. "I didn't come here to stand down. I came to take you home." He took her hand in his, a simple gesture that said so much. It didn't go unnoticed.

"Well, then maybe you should go. Alone." Dusty was still ready to strike, but when he glanced toward Skylar, she begged him with her eyes to just stop fighting. He looked back to Adrian and continued. "Look…Adrian…we're both here because of Skylar. She's been through hell already. Let's not compound the issue 'cause you know as well as I that if it comes to blows, you're gonna go down so hard you—"

"Dusty!" Skylar warned and he immediately shut his mouth although every muscle in his body was tight and ready for release.

"Hawke," Adrian said through clenched teeth. "Only Skylar calls me Adrian. Everyone else calls me Hawke…whether I like them or not. And if we do go to blows, do you really want another black eye? I can easily arrange that."

A stony silence simmered, nearly drowning out any breathable air. The two men kept their gazes locked, as though the battle would end when the first one blinked. Neither of them would ever willingly walk away from her—that was clearly obvious. She had to separate them before this got even further out of control.

"Dusty…" Skylar faced him, placing her hand on his chest. "Is there anything here I can wear?"

He looked down at where her hand rested on him. "I'll find something," he said as he backed away.

"What happened to you, Skylar?"

Tightening her hold on the blanket, she turned back around. Adrian had stepped closer, within arms reach, and she wanted to go to him, hug him, tell him she was sorry. But even though he stood so close and she knew he'd take her in his arms if she went to him, there was something shuttered and closed off about him that she'd never seen before. He was changed. Still her Adrian, but different all the same.

She laughed shakily, a nervous reaction, but still hoping to bring a smile to his face or some light to his eyes. It didn't work. "I'm trying to piece it all together myself. My memory—seeing you brought it back. I hadn't known anything but my name, and I'd only remembered that last night when Dusty rescued me."

"What? Dusty rescued you?" Adrian closed the distance between them but still didn't touch her. "From—How the—Who?" He shook his head, aggravation clear in every movement. "Shit, I can't even—I just don't know where to start."

She gave him a half smile. "Me either."

He tucked a lock of hair behind her ear, then caressed his hand down her face. "God, Skye, I missed you." His eyes registered all the love she remembered from before. It seemed everything in her life would now be categorized as either before or after she'd been taken.

An ache blossomed in her chest, closing off her throat, tears blurring her vision. Adrian ran a thumb over her cheekbone, his skin callused and rougher than she remembered. He leaned closer and whispered, "We'll make this all right."

"Put these on." Dusty thrust an armful of clothing between her and Adrian. Forcibly separated by cotton and denim, Skylar stepped away from Adrian and swiped a hand over her eyes. Breaking down into useless tears wouldn't make this situation any better. She took the offered clothing from Dusty's trembling hands. He'd brought her a complete outfit. Jeans, sweater, bra, underwear, socks and tennis shoes. A foreign memory surfaced—the clothing was Mariah's. At least she knew it would fit.

At some point Dusty had put on a clean white T-shirt, the soft cotton clinging to every tight muscle she'd kissed and loved last night. A pang of loneliness hit her. Why did him getting dressed make her feel like he was pulling away?

"Tomorrow doesn't exist without you," echoed in her head. The words she'd spoken to him last night. The words she still meant with every fiber in her being. How could she walk away from Dusty? She

couldn't imagine a life without him in it. But how could she walk away from Adrian and the life they'd planned out together?

As though Dusty was reading her mind, he swallowed hard. Ragged pain and raw emotion shone from his eyes suggesting the same betrayal she'd felt from Adrian.

She looked away, unable to handle all the blistering pain festering around her. There were no simple words that could make everything right. But at least she could get dressed, the clothes providing a simple, flimsy barrier between her and them. Naked, she felt like she was exposing her soul even more than her flesh.

Unless she walked deeper into the cave, there was no place she could get changed without being in full view. And she couldn't leave Dusty and Adrian alone together. Although it appeared they had settled into an uneasy truce, if she stepped away, she couldn't trust things not to change.

To hell with it. Putting her back to them, she dropped the blanket and, aiming for a dressing speed record, quickly donned the clothing.

She turned around and sat on the edge of the bed to put on the socks and shoes, sighing as she looked at Dusty and Adrian. She needn't have worried about them watching. They were sizing each other up. Again.

This had to stop. Determinedly, she got to her feet. "I can't do this. I can't stand here and watch the two men I—" *Shut up, Skylar! Now is not the best time to mention you love both of them.* "I need time to think. Time to put together the mess my life has become."

Dusty faced her, his gaze locking on hers. He opened his mouth to speak, then seemed to think better of it. His hands unfurled and he lifted his arms like he'd given up the fight or just wanted her to run into his embrace, but then they fell back to his sides, defeated. Casting one more glance at Adrian, Dusty stepped back toward the entrance to the cave. Looking down, he shook his head, his jaw tightened and his hands balled into fists like he was going to punch someone.

But she knew he wouldn't. He was going to leave instead. Skylar's heart screamed that she couldn't let him walk out. That if he did, she'd never see him again. She bolted to Dusty and wrapped her arms around him.

His arms circled her, but it felt reluctant, like he'd already completely withdrawn from her. "I'll be at *Rare and Unusual Imports* if you need me."

"I'm sorry. I'm so sorry," she whispered against his chest.

"I know." Then he pulled away from her, turned around and walked out of the cave, never looking back.

Time stood still and Skylar waited for something to make sense.

"You love him, don't you?"

She continued staring at the entrance to the cave, ignoring Adrian's question. She didn't know how long she'd been standing that way, waiting for Dusty to come back. Waiting for the hurt to dissipate just a little bit so she could take a breath without choking on the sharp, burning pain.

Almost viciously she rubbed her hands up and down her arms, trying to bring some life back into her body. A coldness had seeped so deep inside of her, she figured she'd never be warm again.

"Well, I can see this won't be as easy as you coming home with me, will it?"

Shakily, she turned around, facing the first man she'd ever loved. The tears flowed uncontrollably. She knew it wouldn't help, but everything hurt too damn much to keep it all inside anymore.

"Shit, Skye. I'm sorry. God, don't cry. You know I can't stand to see you cry." He closed the distance between them and pulled her into his arms. He stroked her hair, and whispered softly into her ear, "It'll be okay, baby. I promise. Somehow we'll make this okay."

"How? Adrian, I'm in love with two men. How can that possibly be okay?"

His whole body tensed at her admission, but when she tried to pull away, he held her tighter. "I don't know, Skylar. I don't know."

They stayed that way for several minutes. Finally, Adrian broke the silence. "Where do you want to go? What do you want to do?"

Skylar stepped away from him, looking around the cave and at the memories of a short-lived love.

As she looked at the rumpled sheets on the bed, fierce anger surged through her body. Anger at David for ripping her away from her life. Anger at the impossible situation she'd found herself in.

But the majority of her anger was focused on Dusty. How could he have so easily walked away? Had what they shared last night meant so little to him? She didn't want to believe it, but he'd left her behind. He had given up on them...on her.

"I don't want to stay here anymore," she whispered harshly.

"Before we leave, do you need anything?"

She shook her head. "There's nothing left for me here." Without another word, she walked out of the cave, Adrian at her side.

Chapter Eight

Stephan allowed himself a war cry as he charged the bedroom window with a wooden post. The post splintered, but the window held fast. He walked out of the room, then pulled out his silenced .38 and fired a round at the glass. Peering back in the room, he was pleased to see that the glass was still intact. He wanted to test every window in his and Mariah's new house with equal vigor to release his anger, but there wasn't enough time. One bullet to each window would have to do.

This whole morning had been a string of wickedness. One upsetting thing right after another without enough time for Stephan to get anything in enough order to act on it. It all started when Marlin clicked-in to tell Stephan that Dusty had rescued the woman. Marlin had mentioned that she looked similar to Mariah, but that had been an incredible understatement. Her resemblance to Mariah was uncanny. Either her looks had been altered or there had to be some long-lost relatives Mariah didn't know about. So where had the mystery woman come from? Why had Craze made her believe she was Mariah? Too many damn questions. Stephan fired another shot at a pane of glass, wishing there was a way to really unleash serious furor just to get it out of his system.

Right after Marlin's click-in, Stephan had grabbed the newspaper. Big and bold on the front page had been two photos of last night's debacle complete with an article. "A kiss is not always just a kiss, at least not when it leads to two prominent businessmen coming to blows over a woman. And how ironic that the charity of the evening was preventing domestic violence..." The photo of David kissing Mariah had made Stephan's blood boil and the photo of him punching David put everything in a red haze. David had probably paid a good sum to get all that on the front when it should have been buried much deeper within.

By that point, Stephan had been so incensed, he'd gone to the cave in hopes of getting answers, but instead he'd found his best friend in bed with the woman. What the hell was Dusty thinking? Not only had his best friend disobeyed his direct orders, but now he was irreparably involved with a woman who looked just like Mariah and was stolen from Craze. Nothing about that was going to be okay any time in the near future. All Stephan could do was keep the two women apart until he knew more about what was really going on. There could be no effective countermove until then.

Walking down the hall to the bathroom, Stephan fired a round at each windowpane in the hall. The puzzle pieces were starting to fit together and it was so huge, he wasn't sure he had even close to enough pieces to see the real picture. So far, he wasn't liking any part of the image because everything seemed to be closing in on him. Craze's game was far too random this time and with too many key players.

Stephan reloaded his gun and went downstairs. Knowing Dusty was a wildcard and not to be trusted hurt very deeply. Not only did Stephan need Dusty's firepower against Craze, but he needed the friendship. They'd never sparred that hard before. And now their friendship was in tatters.

Dusty was just too easily addicted. This time, to a woman. The last serious time, it was to the bottle in his hand. Thankfully, Stephan and the guys had successfully forced Dusty out of his daily drunken delirium, and once he'd fired himself back up, he always got Stephan's back no questions asked. But now there were too many complications. The fool was tangled in Craze's web for sure. And Stephan couldn't blame Dusty. It was a mighty beautiful web this time. Dammit. Why'd it have to be Dusty? Any of the other guys could've gotten out of Craze's game without getting insidiously involved. Stephan fired three rounds into a guest bedroom toward the window. This was not supposed to be happening.

After testing all of the glass satisfactorily, he started to feel like this house could withstand a full-scale nuclear attack. He just wanted Mariah to have a place that resembled the normal life he'd never be able to offer her. The house was his gift to her. He'd been making it ready for the past month and she had no idea of its existence. The idea was to sweep her off her feet and carry her over the threshold. But he wasn't going to do any of that until the place was absolutely ready.

Stephan tested the outer walls all the way around the house. No worries just yet. Everything remained solid. Everything except his resolve.

He walked the perimeter of his yard while staring in the direction of Craze's house. Stephan couldn't see the bastard's house, but he could feel the evil presence all the same. It ate at him that Craze had moved in just around the corner. The cur had clearly done the research before buying that house, thereby crawling under his "bastard little brother's" skin. But Stephan would give his life to protect his family before he'd let Craze chase him away. No matter how hard he tried, he could never come between Stephan, Mariah and his family. Their love was eternal.

So what was Craze expecting to achieve by making a mystery woman believe she was Mariah, being abused by Stephan? It didn't make sense. Between the newspaper and Skylar, it was obvious Craze was trying to make Stephan look bad, but there had to be more to it. The pieces just weren't adding up.

He walked back into the house and began testing dimensional portals. Nearly every room had a portal into the bunker below. Just like the compound at *Rare and Unusual Imports*, the bunker lay in another dimension. Stephan had been thorough in his instructions to The Order, and they had obliged him on every request. He had a house more secure than the White House, and would soon have a Shadow Watcher well-trained in every manner of attack and defense. That was the only way he could be sure that if he brought his family here, they would have a chance of surviving an attack if for some reason he was not around to protect them.

He trusted Mariah's strength and had complete confidence in her. God, he loved that woman. Everyday she showed him just how much they belonged together. She'd adapted to the Shadow Walker life with ease, surrendering her everyday freedom for a life of necessary precautions.

Stephan smiled in spite of himself as he walked into the nursery. He and Mariah had decided to keep the sex of the baby a surprise until birth. One of the few surprises in their lives they were able to look forward to.

Like the rest of the house, the nursery was unfurnished, except for a hand-carved wooden cradle. When it had arrived at *Rare and Unusual Imports*, Stephan couldn't pass it up. The symbols etched into the wood were ones of health and protection. His chest tightened as he looked into the empty cradle. His baby would sleep there. So tiny. So helpless. Fear strengthened his resolve. He would keep his family safe. Nothing else mattered.

Hey, Stephan. Fiero clicked-in. *The Watcher is here. He goes by Slade.*

Okay, good. I'll be right there. I want to talk to him and make sure he knows what he's doing before he's introduced to Mariah.

The Order readied him for an apocalypse, but I knew you'd still wanna double check. That's cool. And Ryan's training Mariah with his blades right now. I'll make sure they keep working until you're ready to have them meet.

Thanks, Fiero. Check ya later. Stephan clicked-out and walked into the hallway. Down the hall was the master bedroom suite. To the left of the nursery was the room where the Shadow Watcher—Slade—would sleep. He hated the idea of another man, a relative stranger, sleeping in his house. At least they would be able to keep his presence quiet. Slade could slip in and out of the house through the portals and no one in the neighborhood would be the wiser. The last thing he wanted was for the residents of Talisman Bay to think that Mariah and he had a third party in their relationship—no matter what David wanted the town to believe.

Stephan did a final sweep of the master bedroom. The fort was secure. He ran through the portal in the back of their closet and landed in a truncated hallway. It was capped on both ends by brick walls, the one behind him disguising the return portal to his house. There were four doors to his left and another four to his right. Was this some kind of new defensive feature? Which one led to the bunker?

He started opening them to double check The Order's logic. All of the doors revealed small closet-sized spaces. Stephan tested all of the rooms for secret exits, but there weren't any. He stepped back into the hallway and threw himself at the pink door. Sure enough, he fell right through into the main bunker. To test his theory, he went back into the hallway. All of the doors were like that. If you touched the handle, they opened on closets. But running through them caused a fissure, which allowed a quick escape into the bunker.

Once in the bunker, Stephan scrutinized The Order's design. The walls were made from cement and the room was furnished in such a manner that Stephan knew he and his family could sustain long periods down there. A full kitchen area, preserved food, beds, a small bathroom area and other necessities likened the room to a bomb shelter. But if The Order had done it right, this room would also connect him to the compound below *Rare and Unusual Imports*.

All of the six different-colored doors in the room opened on closets. Stephan crashed into empty closet after empty closet until he blasted through the blue door and found himself in a rather full closet...the back of Dusty's closet at the compound. Goddammit. Everything was fine up to that point. Why'd The Order fuck it up at the last second? Stephan fought his way through clothes piled knee deep and stepped out into Dusty's room. Was that The Order's idea of a joke? From one closet to another? He shouldn't have to wade through Dusty's shit every time he had to make a quick trip from his house to the compound.

He exited Dusty's room and headed straight for the meeting area where the Watcher waited. The man had strikingly dark features. He almost reminded Stephan of a stereotypical Hollywood villain. Stephan extended his hand as the man stepped forward. "Stephan Rashleigh."

"Slade." Deep voice. Very firm handshake. Probably decent with blades, guns and potentially pugilism. Reflexes seemed quick as well.

"You are aware of what's at stake here? You are aware that you would sacrifice your own life for the child?" Stephan continued to size the man up. He actually had to look up slightly to meet Slade's eyes, so the Watcher had to be a few inches taller than Stephan's own six-foot frame. Slade's clothes were neat enough for Stephan to believe the man did pay attention to detail without losing track of what was truly important.

"Yes, Stephan. Have no fear. The Order sent me through refreshers on all of my watching capabilities plus hand-to-hand, weaponry, thievery and survival. I'm beginning to think that I am the most trained Shadow Watcher in the history of the organization. I will not let you or your woman and child down. You have my word."

"Good to know. You will be using all those skills, I'm sure." There was one more question. "Do you have any attachments? Any family?" If the man had a family of his own, Stephan would have to send him back to The Order. Slade would have to focus on Mariah and the baby completely or there was too much risk of failure and loss of life.

Slade's jaw tightened and his eyes darkened further. "There is no one."

Stephan nodded. "Good." Clearly there was more behind Slade's words than he was saying, but Stephan believed the loneliness in the man's eyes. The Order had given Slade their approval in his training. Stephan trusted his gut that this man would absorb himself in his duty as a Watcher. There was something about Slade that Stephan related to in regard to duty.

Stephan motioned for Slade to follow him. "We've been training her on as many weapon and combat techniques as we can. When she gets further along in her pregnancy, she might not be able to fight as much, but at least she'll know how and be prepared in case something happens that neither you or me can get her out of."

They crossed the meeting room and headed for the door nearly hidden by the weapon's cabinet. Opening the door, Stephan beckoned Slade inside. The training room was more of a dojo instead of a gym like the back room of the import store. Mats protected the trainees from hard landings on most of the wood flooring. Training weapons were kept against one wall. A mirror made the space deceivingly larger. Ryan and Mariah were embrangled in a tricky spiral stance. Her teacher clearly showing her evasive maneuvering.

Watching Mariah spar with Ryan was an unbelievable turn-on. Her hair pulled back crookedly, clad in gray stretch pants and a sports bra, she looked even more gorgeous 'than she'd looked dressed up at the Charity Ball. Her skin was coated with a thin sheen of sweat and he wanted nothing more than to strip her naked and fuck her there on the mats. Her back was to them and she hadn't noticed their arrival yet. Ryan looked up with a grin, releasing her.

Stephan stepped onto the mat with Slade following behind him. Mariah spun at their approach, blades in both hands, ready to attack. Her eyes focused on Stephan's and she smiled, dropping her guard.

"So, did you come to watch me kick Ryan's ass?" Mariah laughed, her cheeks bright pink with exertion. Then a frown dampened her expression and she gestured toward his face. "Baby, what happened?"

Stephan lifted his hand to the bruises Dusty had left on his face and grimaced. "Just the usual hazards of the job, sweetheart. I'm fine." He changed topics before she could question him further and end up worried. "I have someone to introduce you to. The Watcher's here. Mariah, this is Slade."

Mariah's focus shifted to the man standing slightly behind and to Stephan's right. Her smile froze and her face grew instantly pale.

"You fucking son of a bitch!" Enraged, Mariah charged past Stephan, raising her daggers as she attacked Slade.

The moment was over before it had begun. The blades were knocked out of her hands and she was spun around and immobilized within Slade's embrace. Mariah struggled but was effectively pinned to the man. Stephan and Ryan charged Slade, but he let Mariah go, pushing her toward Stephan. Ryan remained ready as Stephan pulled her safely behind him.

Blood dripped from Slade's left hand, but it was his face that captured Stephan's attention. Shock and pure wonder. And relief? "Mariah? I—I thought you were...."

Mariah growled. "Surprised, Michael? It's not often someone you leave for dead comes back to haunt you."

"You better get the fuck out of here before you end up dead," Stephan snarled. His mind was reeling. The Shadow Watcher was Michael Slade, Mariah's cruel ex-boyfriend. Why the hell would The Order send a Watcher who in the past had tried to kill the woman he was now assigned to watch? What the hell kind of sense did that make?

Slade glanced at Stephan, some retort clearly on the tip of his tongue. The Watcher, instead, returned his attention to Mariah, shaking his head, jaw slightly open before he spoke. "I left you for dead? What? I could never do anything of the sort. *I* nearly died when I was told you'd been murdered."

If it wasn't for the look of sheer astonishment on his face, Stephan might've started in on Slade where Mariah left off. She placed a trembling hand on Stephan's arm, and said, "No. No, I don't believe you. I heard you planning a murder, and hours later I barely clung to life. Explain that to me."

The sound of switchblades whizzing and clicking open filled the air as Ryan stepped forward. "I think you better leave."

Slade looked from one man to the other as he tightened his bloody hand into a fist. His eyes softened when he looked at Mariah.

Stephan could not block the bolt of pain that shot through his heart. Whatever had happened between Mariah and Slade, there was no way that man could have wanted her dead. He clearly still loved her. If Slade's words were as true as his reactions, Stephan couldn't help but wonder if the man would try to get back into her life as more than just a Watcher.

Slade's appearance hardened as his attention shifted from Mariah to Stephan. As if simply putting on a mask, Slade once again became the Watcher that Stephan had so foolishly approved. "I was sent to do a job and now that I know the full extent of it, I accept its danger wholeheartedly. And I stand fast in front of it. You're not gonna find someone more qualified. So, you can put away your weapons. I don't have it in me to hurt the woman I have loved for so long and was forced to go on without. I already promised I'd give my life for hers. I would never go back on my word."

Mariah's voice shook as she spoke. "Stay away from me, Michael. I almost died because of you. I'm not giving you a second chance." She spun around and stormed toward the exit. Stephan followed Mariah, but she stopped and turned toward him. "No…Stephan, I need time to think…alone. Please…" The need for his understanding was clear in her eyes before she fully retreated from the room. It didn't stop his pang of anger that everything he gave a damn about was rapidly careening out of control. His woman…his best friend…everything was in chaos. And it had all started when Craze came back into their lives.

When would something start making sense?

* * * * *

Question after godforsaken question swirled around in Dusty's head as he walked along the pier toward *Rare and Unusual Imports*, intent upon seeking out Stephan. Happy shoppers went from store to store. Children played tag and jumped from bench to bench without a care in the world other than keeping away from the kid who was "it".

And that was how Dusty felt. Like he was "it". Like his world had just rained a whole gaggle of geese nipping and teasing at him, but as he turned to tackle each question or cruel situation, he came up empty-handed and a little more hurt by each one. Not to mention ten times more frustrated than if he could've just broken out into a full tilt run away from everything.

But that wouldn't do him any good, either. Loneliness was already creeping into his heart, taking up some of the hole Skylar had just created. Why in bloody hell did his heart want her so fucking badly? Stupid question. The complete joining of their bodies and souls had answered that last night.

Last night. There was a topic he could think on for the rest of his life without growing weary. It was everything after it that really irked him. Couldn't time have frozen while he was still in Skylar's embrace? What kind of bad luck did he have to fall in love with a woman who was already taken? He wanted to blame Skylar, but she was just as much of a victim as he was. She couldn't have faked the surprise in her eyes when Hawke walked into the cave, or the pain when she'd told Dusty she was sorry.

And there was another sore subject. Hawke's arrival as a Tracker in Talisman Bay clearly proved that The Order was involved. They were still doing the same bullshit, keeping the truth from those who needed it most, ripping up people's lives without a care beyond their cause. Which was all the more reason Dusty needed to talk to Stephan. He would know more about how to handle The Order and their cruel manipulations. They could band together and present a much stronger force to be reckoned with.

Dusty walked through the delivery door into the backroom of *Rare and Unusual Imports* and was greeted by a mess of scattered newspaper across the floor. Not a good sign. Scooping up the wrinkled sheets, he saw what had caused the paper to be discarded so angrily. There were pictures from the Charity Ball, unsavory photos showing Stephan in a terrible light. Rage crept into Dusty's blood. That should not have been front-page news. Craze was making the game public now. One more reason he needed to die.

Suddenly Stephan's intense anger from earlier made more sense. He'd seen the newspaper then gone to the cave and found Dusty in bed with Skylar. The woman, who by Craze's doing, had effectively driven a wedge between Stephan and Dusty. *Shit.* This was more than Stephan protecting his woman. Craze was crumbling the foundation of the Talisman Bay Shadow Walkers and Dusty really had played right into it.

Dusty, you're an idiot. You're just as involved in this as Stephan is. Skylar's just as involved in this as Mariah is. The Order is just as involved as...

"Dammit, dammit, dammit," Dusty muttered as he quelled his inner frustration and pounded down the stairs into the compound, even more determined to straighten things with Stephan.

Entering the living area, Dusty felt as though something big had just transpired. Residual emotion simmered in the air. Whatever the trouble, he hoped it would require a violent and bloody response. Something to clear his head and help him see what to do about the twists his life had suddenly taken.

Like a whirlwind, Mariah came storming out of the training room, one arm held protectively across her stomach. Angrily, she ran through the main living area then down the hall to the room she shared with Stephan.

Shit! What the hell had just happened? Dusty sprinted across the room and into the training room...and into the middle of a standoff.

Instinctively, Dusty's hands fisted as he drew to a halt just inside the room. It looked like he might get in a good ferocious rumble after all. Stephan was glaring at a tall dark-haired man who Dusty assumed must be some kind of enemy. But on further assessment, the man didn't appear in the least bit hostile, even as he warily returned Stephan's glare. Judging by the two knives strewn on the floor—one of them with traces of blood on it—a melee had happened. Even further illustrating the clash was the blood dripping around the fingers of the man's left hand. Dusty expected Ryan to be the cause, but he was poised, blades out and ready, clearly waiting for Stephan's signal.

Stephan clicked-in before Dusty had the chance. *So, are you here to help, or just to piss me off?*

Damn. Take it easy, man. I ain't here to fuck with you, Dusty replied as he came around to flank Stephan. Even though Stephan remained focused on his prey, his shoulders relaxed just a touch. Then, for a split second, he glanced at Dusty and a flash of understanding passed between the two of them. Although Dusty knew this time was far worse than any other mishap, he was glad to see in Stephan's eyes that the outcome would be the same. Tempers had flared this morning, neither was completely sorry, but both understood why it had happened and they'd move past it to help each other. *So, who's this guy? Someone Craze sent to cause us more hell?*

Stephan was the picture of restrained anger as he addressed the man aloud. "You mind tellin' me what really happened between you and Mariah?" Then he set about answering Dusty's question. *He's Slade…Mariah's Watcher—*

So what's the problem?

He's also her ex-boyfriend.

"Well, shit." Like a gunshot, the words cracked in the silence of the room. The Watcher turned sharply, focusing on Dusty. It was obvious Slade knew there was a click-in conversation going on that he wasn't a part of—and he wasn't happy about it. As though to punctuate his anger, he kicked the discarded blades, knocking them against the wall, away from anyone's grasp.

Dusty studied the man, trying to pin him as a friend or foe. He couldn't help but notice the pain in the man's eyes. It was obvious why Stephan might be worried. Clearly the Watcher still loved Mariah.

The similarity between Stephan's circumstance and his own did not go unnoticed. A Watcher and a Tracker showing up, each having history with the woman of a Talisman Bay Shadow Walker. What the hell was The Order planning?

Slade returned his suspicious stare to Stephan. "I'm not your enemy, Stephan. I don't know why she thinks I tried to kill her. I didn't. I would never do anything like that. Least of all to her. And I know you're wondering, but I had no idea The Order was training me to be her Watcher. I was told I'd be going to Talisman Bay to protect the unborn child of a Shadow Walker leader. A much respected leader. Obviously, The Order neglected to tell me that I'd be walking into an ambush when I got here."

Blood boiled in Dusty's veins. First Skylar's fiancé and now this... *The fucking Order again —*

Themonius should be here momentarily. Fiero put the fires of hell underneath his ass. Stephan shook his head angrily as though for Slade's benefit as well as Dusty's. *We'll straighten out The Order. No more of this bullshit. I get enough games from Craze.*

There's more.

Stephan shot Dusty a nasty glare. *What?*

The Order sent a Tracker after Skylar —

Themonius appeared in a misty cloud, keeping Dusty from giving Stephan the rest of the bad news. The Order's spokesman eyed the four men in the room with his aristocratic stare, then raised an eyebrow as he spoke. "Why is it that you always demand my presence when things aren't going quite the way you thought they would?"

Facing Themonius squarely, Stephan crossed his arms over his chest. "Why is it that the so-called Sacred Order, the purveyors of truth and goodness, don't even inform its officers when there's serious trouble to be dealt with?"

Themonius looked down his nose at Stephan. "You want us to warn you of every impending problem? You are Shadow Walkers. Your lives are in a constant state of flux. Serious trouble is to be expected."

Dusty angrily growled out his reply before Stephan could. "Obviously lies and misinformation are to be expected, too. You turned Skylar's fiancé, a goddamn civilian, into a Tracker. Don't even try to tell me that The Order didn't know about Craze taking Skylar. That's something we should have known. You placed too many peoples' lives in danger." Dusty stepped toward Themonius, while reminding himself that slugging the immortal wouldn't do any good.

"There's no such thing as coincidences." Stephan looked from Dusty to Themonius and back again to Dusty. *Looks like you've been holding out on me as well.*

I got interrupted. I swear that's everything I know about Skylar and the Tracker. Honest. Dusty punctuated his reply with a nod then shifted his attention back to Themonius.

Okay, so click-in etiquette wasn't exactly being enforced today. Themonius looked almost as annoyed as Slade did that there was click-in conversation going on without him being invited. "Now, now, Dusty. Aren't we straight to brass tacks? I was under the impression that Stephan would spout his fury alone." Themonius's gaze shifted to Slade and then to Stephan and Dusty. "I see you two have met the Watcher. We hold him in very high regard. I can't imagine any of you would be displeased."

"I would think that'd be obvious if you really did know as much as you claim," Stephan stated angrily.

Themonius settled his all-knowing gaze on Stephan. "I am not in the business of doling out solutions that are larger than your problems. Motives are not always immediately evident. Your maneuvers, your gleanings play much deeper than you could ever envisage. For instance, Michael Slade." Themonius turned to the Watcher and addressed him directly, but his words were clearly meant for everyone in the room. "When you met Mariah, you knew in your heart that you should be with her, that you should share her every move. You were destined to be with her and she with you. What you didn't realize is that you were not meant to be her lover. You never were. You were meant to watch over her and to ensure that she was delivered to her veridical destiny." During his final phrase, Themonius's attention returned to Stephan.

Ouch. The room grew quiet as the implication behind Themonius's words hit everyone personally. Dusty couldn't tear his gaze from Slade. A grievous darkness had settled across his features, and it echoed in Dusty's soul. Was that his fate as well? To love Skylar from a distance? To keep her safe but watch her love someone else?

"That still doesn't solve the fact that Mariah doesn't want him watching her. I won't let her be in a situation where she feels threatened. That helps none of us. The Order didn't choose him very wisely." Stephan's dissatisfaction practically shook the walls.

"You forget. Slade is not Mariah's Watcher. He is the child's Watcher."

"That's bullshit. Where my child goes, Mariah goes. He can't protect one without the other."

,

"Come now, Stephan, who better to protect her than someone who truly loves her and would give his life for her? What greater sacrifice is there? You are already quite cognizant that The Order would not invest in someone who is not worthy." Themonius shifted his gaze to Dusty. "Adrian Hawke is of high caliber. He was already on the hunt for Skylar Quinn when we approached him. The Order merely offered him the means to find his missing fiancé. Our enhancements are never awarded to the meek. We are all slaves to destiny and fate and their rather acrimonious predilection of truth and all that is inexorable."

Themonius's knowing smile angered Dusty even further. "You're not clarifying how Skylar fits into all this. So far, she's just been another victim of this farce."

"Although not a Shadow Walker by birth, as Mariah's cousin, Skylar is of much importance."

Unable to stop himself, Dusty stormed forward and got in Themonius's face. "Mariah's cousin? Why the hell didn't you tell us about her earlier? She was held prisoner by Craze for two months. We could have done something sooner."

Themonius sneered. "Dusty, do not let your temerarious attitude impede your betterment. I suggest you seek to understand your fate before it is viciously withdrawn from your grasp. Second chances are not given to fools."

Fear rocketed through Dusty. Was that a warning? Shit. Why the hell had he left Skylar in the cave with Hawke? Walking away from her, he'd given the impression that he was giving up on her...on them. What the hell had he been thinking? He was a fighter, not a quitter. Dammit! Skylar was his. In his heart, he knew they belonged together. Even through the crazy circumstances this morning, she had still looked at him with love in her eyes. There was no way they weren't meant to be together. But what if she wanted to rebel against destiny? If he were to show up and try to win her back somehow, would she still want him?

As though privy to the thoughts whirling through Dusty's mind, Themonius's smile widened as he spoke. "You already know all the answers to your heart's questions. Give them merit or you will find yourself a very sullen man."

Ryan spoke from the corner, his voice a quiet strength. "So our futures are already laid out? Why bother living if we can't affect what's going to happen?"

"Every action and reaction has the potential to alter the set course. All of you are important in the roles you play, in the choices you make." Themonius's eyes sought out everyone in the room. "Family goes beyond the bonds of blood. You would do best to let it flourish rather than hinder its progress. The battle cannot be won alone."

"It can't be won by manipulating people either."

Mariah stepped through the doorway into the training room, as the men turned as one to face her. She crossed the room and took her place at Stephan's side. They didn't touch, but just being close to him made her feel stronger, capable of reliving the nightmare she'd forced to the deepest recesses of her mind.

After only spending a minute in her room—long enough to change her clothes and realize running from Michael and her memories wasn't going to solve anything—she'd returned to the scene of her most recent life surprise to confront her past. Instead she'd witnessed a horrible truth unveiled. Michael was as much of a victim as she was. For years she had believed he'd betrayed her in the worst way possible, but her feelings of hatred toward him were based on a circumstance she still didn't understand.

But they weren't the only victims. She had a cousin, Skylar, another innocent being pulled into fate's games. Someone else suffering because of her…

Mariah turned an angry gaze on Themonius. "Tell me about my cousin. Why have I never heard of her before now?"

"Until recently, we were unaware that your fates were linked. Skylar is your father's brother's daughter, but your father never knew of her. When he became a Shadow Walker, he distanced himself from his family until he almost never spoke with his brother. When your father died, the familial connection died with him…or so we thought." Themonius shook his head, his expression growing thoughtful. "Perhaps if we had taken a closer look at her, we would have realized the severity of your connection. Such similarities are far from normal…"

"Similarities? What the hell does that mean?"

Dusty blurted out a reply, surprising Mariah into facing him. "You could be sisters. Essentially, people who don't know you or her could easily mistake her for you. She looks like you, but she doesn't act quite like you do. She…well…she's just similar, but not you at all. Her hair's got red accents, rather than gold like you, and her lips are…"

His voice trailed off and he swallowed hard as though just now realizing he had an audience for his praises. Mariah couldn't hide her grin. It looked like Dusty had it bad for her cousin. Good. At least she'd be well-protected.

Dusty turned his attention toward the door and started walking. "Y'know, I'm actually gonna go find her. I need to…yeah…I gotta go get her."

"Dusty, wait." He stopped and looked over his shoulder, one foot already out the door, his impatience obvious. "Take care of her for me, okay? I don't want what happened to me to happen to her."

Dusty nodded and his pace quickened as he disappeared through the doorway. Heavy footsteps pounded up the stairs as he broke into a run. Stephan glanced at Ryan then nodded toward the door. Ryan nodded his reply and headed out as well.

Mariah spun back around to Themonius. "Got any other surprises from my past you need to tell me?"

"Why do you choose to focus on the past when it is the future that matters?"

Mariah forced the breath into her lungs as she turned and looked at her past—at Michael. "Because the past can affect the future."

Arms crossed over his chest, Michael watched her, his dark, piercing gaze seeming to sear right through her. Just like the first time they'd met. Just like so many times in the past.

Although difficult, Mariah forced herself to meet his eyes. He deserved to hear the truth directly from her. "For five years I thought that you tried to have me killed. Do you know how hard it is to erase that from my memory? Seeing you again…" She clenched her jaw. "Dammit. This is harder than I thought it'd be…"

"Mariah…" Michael's words trailed off. She knew he wasn't begging her to continue. It was as though he wanted too many things from her that he knew he could no longer have.

Stephan placed a warm hand on the back of her neck, caressing and rubbing the special spot he'd jokingly nicknamed her comfort nerve. No matter how horrible she felt, when he touched her there she felt comfortable and relaxed, capable of facing anything. He'd known exactly what she needed.

With new strength, Mariah continued. "There's more, something I haven't let myself think about since it happened. I've never even told anyone. Not even you, Stephan, and I'm sorry for that. I didn't want to think about it. When I almost died all those years ago..." She took another deep breath. "Michael, do you remember that day?"

"Everything changed." He slowly nodded for her to continue, but Mariah wasn't sure he really wanted to hear what she had to say.

"I went to the doctor, because I'd been sick. But I wasn't sick...I...I..."

"Oh God." Michael let out a very ragged breath. "You *were* pregnant." His hoarse whisper sent a chill through the entire room. He stepped toward her, then froze mid-step, his gaze shifting from her to Stephan, as though realizing it was not his place to offer comfort anymore.

Mariah wrapped her arms around herself, suppressing a shiver. "Yeah. I was."

Michael's stone composure cracked. Looking down, his shoulders shuddered. The only sound in the room was rough, uneven breathing.

Stephan moved closer, keeping one hand on her neck as he took her tightly within his embrace. "Mariah, baby—"

A torturous growl interrupted Stephan, and Mariah looked up to see Michael ferociously stalking toward Themonius. "You could have been more specific about who I was being trained to defend. Would that have been too much to ask of you during my twenty-hour training sessions over the past three months?" His voice grew more disgusted with every word. "What? Did it slip your mind? You knew my background. You knew everyth—"

Themonius raised his hands. "We were afraid you wouldn't accept."

"Just as Stephan was disappointed in your choice of me, I am disappointed that you didn't have the *decency* to give me the option...on anything for that matter. You just threw me to the wolves, respect be damned. Did you honestly think that I would not want to be here? To see her again? You are out of your fucking mind!" Slade got in Themonius's face, towering above him.

Themonius recoiled silently.

"I think you've done enough emotional damage for one day, Themonius," Mariah stated emphatically as she and Stephan advanced toward him.

Stephan's voice cut in. "Unless you can actually tell us something that would help us, get the fuck out of here. We have no time for you anymore."

Themonius looked over the threesome closing in on him. "In your dismay, the enemy lies in wait to exploit your every weakness. Do not wait to strike, for you could find greater danger in your diffidence. Darkness follows us all. Even The Order and its organizations may fall prey. Survival lies within your methods of treating the wounded. Attempts will be made to counter hindrances, but you must accomplish your greatest justice of your own accord." Themonius shimmered then disappeared.

The room grew unbearably silent, as though with Themonius's exit, their one common element of shared anger and betrayal had left with him. They watched each other, wondering, waiting...

Stephan reached a hand toward Slade, who shook it, then turned to Mariah as though for approval. She looked at both men and what this moment represented, and the words caught in her throat. All she could do was nod. Somehow they would all make this work.

* * * * *

The cave was empty.

Misery and grief hit Dusty with lightning force as he scoured the cave. Desperately he ran to the hot springs, hoping against all odds that Skylar would be waiting for him there.

The hot springs were untouched. She was gone. She was really gone. What the hell was he supposed to do next? And why the hell had he walked away from her? She'd probably thought he didn't want her anymore. He should have stayed by her side and not given her a chance to disappear from his life.

He returned to the main room of the cave, staring at the bed that just last night had been a paradise. Lying next to it on the floor was Skylar's nightgown, the only evidence that last night had happened. Well, the only physical evidence. The emotional effects would haunt him forever.

Skylar had chosen Hawke, the man she loved, the man who was new to the Shadow Organization and who probably couldn't protect her if Craze came after her again.

Shit.

As long as Craze was nowhere near Skylar, she'd be safe with Hawke. Dusty would make sure Craze never hurt her again even if he had to watch the bastard's every move for the rest of his life. Which would come to an abrupt bloody end as soon as Dusty got his hands on him.

With new purpose, Dusty rushed out of the cave. He clicked-in to Marlin. *Hey, man, is your car still at the beach?*

Yeah, I haven't picked it up yet. Why?

I just need a lift. I'll be good to your car.

Don't fuck it up or I'm not gonna let you borrow it again.

I won't, I won't. Dusty forced a chuckle. *Thanks, man.* He clicked-out and headed straight for Marlin's Jaguar.

Craze was going to go down hard this time. No wussy magic or demons. Hand to hand. Mano y mano.

Using the hidden spare key, Dusty got in and started the car. He took off with a whirl of rage, testing the limits of the Jaguar's handling. The drive took no time at all.

He charged up to Craze's door, slamming his fist on the wood instead of using the snooty brass doorknocker. When that bastard came to the door, his blood would be spilled. Hell, Dusty would even drag the miscreant out onto the lawn in front of the whole damn neighborhood. Craze had hurt his last innocent.

Dusty pounded on the door again. Craze must be scared. Was he looking through the peephole? Did he know that the Grim Reaper was at his door?

Angrily, Dusty tested the handle. It clicked open easily.

Storming through room after godforsaken room, Dusty's furor increased. His hands itched to throttle the bastard. To pummel him. To shred the man that had become his undoing.

Bolting up the central staircase, he surged toward the room where he'd found Skylar before...just last night. Maybe she'd be there once more. *Please let her be there.* Even if her memory had been wiped, he'd make things right, love her all over again.

But he wouldn't get the chance. There was no one there.

In a blind rage, Dusty returned to the main room then spotted a door he'd missed before. He opened it. The stairwell reminded him of the entrance to the compound in *Rare and Unusual Imports.* Was this where Craze hid himself? Dusty blasted down the steps and through another door expecting the magic and mystery of Craze to be revealed. Instead, the room was full of wine, champagne, whiskey, vodka… The many bottles looked so inviting. Like he could just lose himself in drunken oblivion and not have to face ruination ever again.

He forced himself to back out of the room. To not give in to such decadent temptation.

And then he remembered why he was there hunting through that house for the man who'd caused his greatest woes. He clambered through the last two rooms, but the house was empty. Dusty was empty.

Empty. Empty of anything except the urge to run. To just run away. Run away until the fury subsided. If he knew where Skylar was, he'd run to her.

To hell with it. Dusty took off down the street. The ache in his calf heightening with each step he took. It would not stop him. Nothing would stop him. The muscles tightened, threatening his balance, threatening his progress, but he'd be damned if he ever stopped running.

Chapter Nine

Skylar walked down the beach next to Adrian, a million thoughts swirling rapidly around in her head. Every time she tried to focus on one problem or tried to rationalize any decisions she had to make, all the consequences attached to those actions attacked her psyche until she just wanted to scream.

And she'd thought things were complicated when she didn't have a memory.

With the return of her memory, she'd become a complete person again, with attachments, desires, plans and a future. A future that until two months ago had been perfectly laid out. A future that until last night had only included Adrian Hawke.

If Skylar had been near a wall, she would have banged her head against it. It couldn't hurt any more than her heart currently did. No matter what she decided, she was going to hurt one of the men she loved. And she did love them both, just…in different ways. That was where things became even more complicated.

Skylar looked out over the turquoise blue of the Pacific Ocean, the late afternoon sun shooting bright bursts of flame into the water, blinding in its reflection. She didn't even know how long she'd been wandering down the beach, how much time had passed since Dusty had walked out of the cave. The gnawing emptiness inside her grew bigger with every passing step. She couldn't imagine a life without Dusty in it. But she couldn't imagine a life without Adrian, either. They were both an inexplicable part of who she was, and who she wanted to be.

She shot a glance at Adrian beneath lowered eyelids. In the two months since she'd last seen him he had changed. The eyes that had perpetually sparkled with life seemed harder—more lived in. His brown hair, which had always been perfectly styled, was longer, curling around his neck. He'd invariably had a trim physique, but now his body was tighter, his face thinner. And his clothing. Dark jeans, heavy work boots, and a gray waffle knit top. He'd never dressed that casually before, always preferring conservative, button-down shirts and dress pants. Even when they went out just to grab a burger or watch a movie, he dressed business casual. She'd teased him a lot about that. Told him he needed to get more life in his wardrobe. More variety. But he'd stayed the same. Until now.

Now everything was different.

Desperate for the familiar, Skylar placed her hand in his. Sweet comfort settled in her stomach when he laced his fingers with hers. A million times they'd walked this way, in silence, just happy to be together.

He stopped, looking down at where their hands were connected, then raised his gaze to her face. "Skye, if you hadn't gone missing that night, do you think we would've lived happily ever after?"

The familiar comfort became an ache of regret. "I'd like to think so." Except now she knew better. Yes, she would have been happy with Adrian. He was a constant in her life. He would have loved her, treated her with respect and kindness. Their life together would have been simple and sweet with minimal hardships and worries.

But meeting Dusty had changed her. What she felt for him went beyond anything rational. Before Dusty, love had been the light tug of Adrian's hand and tender kisses good night. Dusty was a craving—a life-long burn inflamed in her after only one night. She loved him, ached for him, needed him like she needed air to breathe. It was basic, yet so complex, defying any explanation. Her body and mind equally desired him, as a partner, as a lover, as the one who completed her on every level. She loved Adrian as her best friend, the first man she'd ever loved. But Dusty…Dusty was forever.

Adrian's jaw tightened almost imperceptibly. "Me too, Skye. Me too." He nodded, unable to hide the pain in his eyes before he looked away and began walking again. He still held her hand, but it no longer comfortably bridged the distance between them. Now it felt like their linked hands were the only things keeping them together. It was the most apart from him she'd felt since they'd first met.

When she was ten years old, her parents had moved to a new house and curiosity about her new neighbors had gotten the better of her. She'd climbed a large oak tree that bordered their properties. When she saw a boy doing laps in the Olympic size swimming pool, she'd scooted along an overhanging branch to get a closer look. The branch broke, dropping her into their yard and into Adrian's life. He'd come to her rescue then, jumping out of the pool, hurrying over to make sure she was okay. He'd tended to her scrapes then boosted her back over the wall so her parents wouldn't know the trouble she'd gotten into.

From that moment on, he'd been there for her. It never mattered that he was four years older than her. He was her self-appointed protector. Her confidant. Her best friend.

Their parents had become best friends as well, the six of them—Adrian and Skylar were both only children—became an extended family. They took vacations together, celebrated holidays together. And when she was sixteen and her parents had died in a car accident, Adrian's parents welcomed her into their home, truly making her a part of their family.

Two years later she'd gone off to college, alone. And hated it. She missed Adrian, his daily companionship and the comfort of his presence. She missed teasing him about the fact he never dated, or when he did date, he never went out with a girl more than once. She missed the way he smiled when he saw her. She missed seeing him whenever she wanted to. College life bored her. Not the studying, but the constant partying, the fact that the men she dated either regressed to first grade mentality after a date or two, or they only took her out to get into her pants.

She'd gotten disillusioned with the opposite sex, and with sex in general. Why would she want to get naked with someone who had no interest in anything beyond the two-second orgasm or in how many coeds they could jump each weekend? Thanks, but no thanks. So what if she was the last virgin in her dorm? Sex was a mind game she wasn't interested in playing.

When Skylar had first started fantasizing about love and marriage and the goal of a happily ever after, she'd believed that she would instantly recognize her soulmate the first moment they met. Like lightning would strike or birds would sing a little louder, or there would be that instantaneous zap of startling awareness. But dreams of her Prince Charming showing up and whisking her away to their paradise had dimmed the longer she'd waited, and she had finally dismissed those fantasies as follies born of reading too many romance novels. There was no such thing as all-encompassing love that burned so deep nothing could ever dim the flame. But a tiny part of her kept hoping.

So she'd spent all her free time studying, or on the phone with Adrian. She called him to complain about dates gone wrong, or just to find out what he'd eaten for dinner. And it was over the phone that they began to dream of a future together.

After one of her frequent bad dates, she'd called Adrian.

"Addy, he was all hands. Even his toes were fingerlike, creeping up my leg trying to get down my pants. Every time I tried to talk to him, he'd give me a blank stare like talking was beneath his capabilities." She sighed as she plopped down onto her bed. "Why do I bother?"

He chuckled, but she knew what was going to come next. He'd gotten used to her midnight rants. "Because you keep hoping someone will surprise you."

She snorted. "I keep hoping I'll feel something other than an express desire to get away from the creep. I think I must be dead inside. I just don't give a damn about what every other college student cares about. I'm not going to have sex just to brag that I've had sex."

"And that's absolutely the way it should be. The right guy will love you for more than your body and you shouldn't waste yourself on anyone less. The guy should be willing to give everything for you. To wait until you're ready and not try to play you into something you shouldn't be doing if your heart isn't in it."

Skylar smiled and held the phone closer as she curled up in her bed. "Sounds like you, Adrian."

"I guess it does."

Her heart had started a rapid flutter. Did he really mean it? "So maybe we should date each other…"

She could hear the smile in his words. "Maybe we should."

And they had. From that moment forward, she'd stopped the insane college dating game. Whenever she could, she got away from school and visited Adrian. He did the same. They began to date, and slowly began planning out their future together. She'd been happy…

"You hungry?" Adrian asked, pulling her out of her memories. His free hand gestured toward a smattering of buildings near the pier.

"Yeah." She gave him a tentative smile, her stomach growling at the mention of food. "I can't remember the last time I ate. I guess it's been a while."

He frowned. "You've lost weight."

Skylar looked down at herself. She had lost weight. Her curves weren't quite as curvy as they used to be. "Damn. I didn't even notice earlier." She stepped closer to him and traced her hand along the tightness of his jaw. His chin was sandpaper rough, another new look for him. "You've lost weight, too."

A contemplative depth shone in Adrian's eyes as he intensely, almost angrily, pulled her against him. "Shit, Skye. I hate this. It's pure hell. This…this stilted awkwardness between us is killing me." His tortured gaze seared hers as he continued in a ragged voice. "I can't get the memory of you, naked, in another man's arms out of my mind. It— It's one of the worst memories of my entire life. And out of every fucked up thing that has happened to me since that night… Goddammit…" His lower lip quivered and tears filled his eyes. Roughly, he ran a hand over his hair trying to regain his composure. "I most hate the fact that it took me two months to find you. Because now, I look at you and…and I know I've lost you and there's not a damn thing I can do about it. I just…I just don't know what to do."

Skylar stared up into the pained depths of his eyes, her heart beating so hard against the walls of her chest she thought her ribs would crack. She wanted to somehow wipe the slate clean between them, be the Skylar from two months ago who'd told him she would marry him. But that wasn't who she was any longer. David had changed her. Dusty had changed her. Things weren't that simple anymore.

She struggled to keep the tears at bay, to keep her heart from crumbling into a thousand pieces because of the look in his eyes and the pain in his words. He turned away from her. His voice was rough when he spoke. "I—I'm sorry. C'mon, let's go get something to eat."

A surreal silence surrounded Skylar and Adrian as they walked the remaining distance to Xena's Café. She felt him slipping away from her with each step they took. It hurt like hell, taking away any appetite she'd thought she had.

They slid into opposing sides of a booth, their entwined hands resting on the table between them, a tenuous thread holding them together. They ordered their meals, then sat in silence for several minutes. He stroked his thumb over the back of her hand almost reassuringly before he spoke. "Do you remember what happened the night you disappeared?"

Painful, frightened memories she'd pushed to the back of her consciousness struggled to break free. Since the return of her memory, she'd kept those moments at bay, not wanting to dwell on her captivity, or on the crazy bastard who'd ripped her from her life, altering her perceptions and changing the path of her future. Skylar licked her dry lips and took a drink of the ice water the server had left when she'd taken their order. "I remember...I remember you asking me to marry you."

She squeezed his hand tightly, the memories of that night as clear as if they played on a high definition television in front of her.

"Skylar, will you marry me?" Adrian asked, kneeling in front of her. Candlelight flickered, making the simple band sparkle and shine with a life of its own, shining almost as much as the love in his eyes while he waited for her answer. They'd just finished the dinner he'd cooked for her — broiled lobster, wild rice and asparagus. A dozen peach roses sat in a vase next to a bottle of fine champagne on the decadently laid dinner table. He had made tonight perfect.

So why did she feel like things weren't right? Where were these doubts coming from?

She pushed those thoughts away and smiled at the man she loved. "Yes. Yes, Adrian. Yes."

He kissed her, a long, slow, tender kiss as he slid the ring on her finger. She slipped to the floor, kneeling next to him, wrapping her arms around his body as she deepened the kiss. Tonight, she wanted more...more of him. To finally consummate their relationship. She wanted to feel that burn she'd read about, to understand desire and lust. And who better than with the man she was going to marry?

His breath came out in rough pants as his lips caressed her neck. They had touched and explored each other before, but they'd never made love. Not until tonight.

Skylar struggled to unbutton his shirt. Sweat dampened the palms of her hands. She was nervous...and afraid. She loved Adrian, wanted to spend her life with him, but what if she never felt that incredible all-encompassing spark for him? Would they grow to resent each other for what they didn't have?

And why did she wonder if there should be more between them when Adrian was everything else in her world?

She mentally cursed herself. Rockets and fireworks were short-lived explosions that burned hot, burned fast, then died. It was time to forget those stupid teenage fantasies of "the one". She was damn lucky to have the deep love of her best friend.

Adrian lightly nibbled and teased along her jaw, then lifted his gaze to hers. "Are you sure you want to do this?"

Slowly she nodded. "Yes."

"Let's go to bed." He held his hand out and helped her to her feet. Time seemed to stop as they stared at each other, not moving, the only places they touched were their hands. Frantically, Skylar threw herself at him, kissing him, touching him, loving him, waiting to lose control. Waiting for the insanity of lust to take over. Waiting for something beyond the familiar comfort Adrian's friendship had always given her. Waiting to know she hadn't made a mistake when she'd said yes.

"Whoa, Skylar. What's wrong, baby?"

"Nothing. Nothing. I just need...I just need you."

He set her back on her feet and gave her a crooked grin. "You do have me. And you always will."

Skylar swiped at a runaway tear. "Stupid condoms."

The server interrupted them with the arrival of their salads. Glad for the diversion, Skylar took a few minutes to calm herself before continuing her stroll down memory lane. "The condoms weren't in my purse. Maybe they'd fallen out, maybe I'd forgotten them. I don't know. They just weren't there. You promised you'd be back in twenty minutes, kissed me and ran out the door..."

He spoke through gritted teeth. "I was back in eighteen. You were already gone."

Skylar couldn't look at him, knew if she did she'd see the past in his eyes. "When you left, I couldn't sit still. Nerves, I guess. I decided to take a walk to calm down. I remember looking up at the moon, thinking it was beautiful. Then my world went dark. Everything after that is a blur up until yesterday." That last part wasn't exactly the truth, but she didn't want to tell him that she remembered being chained to a bed, and the pain she'd felt as the pieces of who she was had been stripped away. She didn't want to tell him that she'd clung to his memory long after she'd forgotten his name, when he'd only been a ghost imprint in her mind's eye. Eventually, even that had been taken away from her.

She finally got the nerve to look in his eyes. The sweet friendly spark that had always greeted her with a wondrous enthusiasm for life had faded, as though trying to shine through a dense mist of anguish. That scared her more than anything else did.

A lock of hair fell into his eyes and impatiently he brushed it back. His voice shook as he spoke. "I have another question. Why weren't you wearing the ring when you went out that night?"

"I don't know." His gaze shot up abruptly but before he could ask the questions flashing through his eyes she continued. "As I was walking out the door, I had this overwhelming feeling that I should take it off. My hands were sweaty and the ring was sliding back and forth. I convinced myself that if I wore it outside it would fall off my finger and I'd never see it again." She shrugged her shoulders. "It didn't make sense, but I did it anyway to appease myself."

His free hand skimmed over the table, his long fingers stroking the stained fiberglass. "That's why the police wouldn't believe you'd been kidnapped. They said it looked like an engagement gone wrong. Like you'd just run out on me. Then after you'd been missing for a couple weeks, a friend in the police department told me I was a suspect in your disappearance. I left that night. It was pretty clear that I was the only person who cared enough to even look for you. Everyone else assumed you were already dead. I never stopped believing.

"I came here to bring you home. That was my only goal. Find you and take you home. But now..." He tightened his hand into a fist. "I saw you with Dusty, saw the way you held each other, the looks you two shared." Without any warning he slammed his fist on the table. Skylar jumped, taken aback at the completely un-Adrian-like behavior. She started to pull her hand away from his grasp, but he wouldn't let go. "Dammit Skye, I saw the blood on the sheets. I know what happened. You slept with him. You fell in love with him. I was too late..."

Like magic, the server appeared, eyeing them both contemptuously before tossing their burgers in front of them and quickly departing. Skylar wanted to find humor in the waitress's attitude. She and Adrian would have shared a laugh about it before. But now the laughter wouldn't come.

She struggled for something to say. "I don't want to live without you in my life."

"You can't have us both," he bit out roughly. "I need to know, can I take you home, or are you staying here?"

"Dammit, Adrian, are you telling me if I choose Dusty, I'll never see you again? Is that what this has come down to?" Skylar squeezed his hand painfully tight. She needed to be with Dusty, but the idea of never seeing her best friend again...

"If, Skylar? You've already chosen Dusty. There's no if about it." He laughed cynically. "Look...I—I can't stay here. My life is no longer under my control."

"What the hell does that mean?" Skylar shot back angrily.

His golden brown eyes pierced her soul. "I gave up my life for you."

"Well, damn, Mariah. You always find the gorgeous ones."

Cursing the interruption, Skylar shot her gaze to the woman standing next to their table. She looked familiar but Skylar couldn't quite place her. Although the dark tousled hair, black mini-skirt and red spiked heels triggered imagery.

The woman's eyes grew wide. "You're *not* Mariah, but damn, Marlin was right, you could be her twin." She shook her head in wonder. "Doesn't help you're wearing the sweater I bought her."

Flashes from Mariah's memory filled Skylar's mind and the name spilled from her lips before she could even make the connection. "Twyla?"

"Yeah." Twyla stared down at Skylar's and Adrian's locked hands, then swiftly shifted her concerned gaze to Skylar's face. "Where's Dusty? And why aren't you with him?"

"She's with me," Adrian growled.

Twyla shifted her attention to him. She stared at him for several long moments, looking deep into his eyes, then her face softened with a sad smile. "And you'd give anything for her, wouldn't you? It just royally bites to be the one left behind, huh?" Adrian tensed in Skylar's grasp as Twyla turned back to Skylar and continued speaking. "Look, Craze isn't done with you yet. You need to get to Dusty, stay with the Shadow Walkers. You gotta get somewhere safe, okay?" Her gaze shifted to Adrian once again and she repeated imploringly, "Get her somewhere safe or…well…just get her to Dusty."

She spun as the waitress approached, handing her a to-go bag and two drinks. Twyla glanced over her shoulder as she walked away, her dark eyes piercing. "Just please be careful."

The urgency in her tone and the intense look in her eyes stayed with Skylar long after Twyla had exited the café. "We should go," Skylar whispered.

With sharp, abrupt movements, Adrian stood up and threw fistfuls of money on the table. Skylar kept her hand tucked in his, following him as he strode out of the café. The sun was going down, illuminating the sky in shades of mauve, violet and peach. Nature still had its beauty even when life was spinning out of control.

When she realized they weren't headed toward the pier, Skylar asked, "Where are we going?"

"I'm taking you to Dusty."

"But *Rare and Unusual Imports* is on the pier."

"He's not there," Adrian spit out.

"But...but...how do you know that?"

Adrian stopped so fast Skylar almost stumbled. "I'm a Tracker now. That's what I do."

"Is that how you found me?"

Abruptly, he began walking again, nearly dragging her along with him. "Yeah. Well at first, you were off my radar, so to speak. Focusing on your engagement ring like a talisman that would bring me to you, I just kept heading west. I don't know how I knew. Then The Order gave me a keener tracking ability, but even that didn't do me any good initially." He blew out a frustrated breath and glanced over at her. "You following?"

Although she wasn't, at least not completely, she wanted to hear his side of the story, hoped it would answer her questions about the startling changes visible in him. Nodding, she said, "Enough."

"Okay, well, I still couldn't figure out where exactly I should be looking. I was beginning to think my new sense was some kind of cruel joke. But then like a beacon in a storm, my nerves came alive. You were in Talisman Bay. I drove all night to get here. And then just as I was coming into town, I sensed that you'd moved again. I can't track inter-dimensionally yet, but the last place I felt you was on the rocks just outside the cave. When a man stormed out of the rock face, I knew there had to be a way in somewhere—a way in to you. I'd anticipated having to fight some kind of wicked kidnapper to get you back." The tone of his voice changed, like that of a condemned man. "I didn't think I'd be too late and that you wouldn't want to be rescued."

"That's not fair. I spent two months in hell before Dusty found me. I didn't ask for any of this to happen." She wanted to scream and yell and curse him up and down for making her feel guiltier than she already did. She wasn't going to apologize for getting kidnapped and ripped away from her life. Or for falling in love with Dusty.

Before she could resist he pulled her tight against him, their clasped hands pinned between their bodies. "Of course you didn't ask for any of this. Neither did I. But nothing's fair right now, Skylar. At least not in my world. So don't wor—" he stopped himself with a sigh and brushed a kiss across her forehead. "It'll be okay...I—I'm just gonna play the hand I was given and try not to look back."

Her anger faded, replaced with the muted pain from before and she accepted the small comfort Adrian offered. Things would never be the same between them again, but for this moment she could pretend.

They walked for a couple miles as the sun slipped away and streetlights flickered on around them. Adrian never faltered, his inner radar an invisible hand guiding him toward his goal. Skylar watched him with mixed feelings of awe and fear. He was so much different than she'd initially realized. Harder, darker, and with a new purpose she didn't understand. She combed through Mariah's memories and through what he'd told her, looking for answers. Names of things beyond her comprehension filtered through her mind. Shadow Walkers, Trackers, Watchers. The Sacred Order. Dread Lords. Things that were bigger than her, bigger than life.

But they were her life now. Her life with Dusty. He was a Shadow Walker, his life was always in danger.

And now, so was Adrian's.

Suddenly it was all too much, and Skylar wanted to run. She wanted to hide from the painful reminders of who they'd both become. For one minute she just wanted to pretend that she was Skylar Quinn, resident of Providence, Rhode Island, majoring in Psychology and engaged to Adrian Hawke.

But then they turned a corner and she saw Dusty and she remembered where she wanted to be.

He was facing away from her, raw anger visible in the tension of his body. Even from twenty feet away she could feel his pain, see the darkness in his soul. Skylar's heart rate increased, pumping molten fire through her veins. The inexplicable, burning need to go to him, bury her head against his chest and offer him forever was undeniable.

And then all hell broke loose.

A swarm of beings dark and vile came at Dusty from all sides. Skylar shuddered as a ghastly creature jumped on Dusty. With a vicious grace, he grappled with it until finally, he ripped it apart, throwing its severed limbs at other members of its swarm. Body parts exploded into flame, piles of dust and guts licked the night with fire. The heat shimmer created a wavy illusion as Dusty slugged and kicked with a vengeance. Every appearance suggested that he was outnumbered. That the creatures could overtake him. That he could die at their hands, but the man just dispensed with each one as though he'd done it a million times before. As though the danger wasn't even registering anywhere in the corners of his mind. Gore splattered over Dusty as he punched his fist through a chest and the beast's hands reached out to choke him.

Before she could go to him, Adrian pressed her flat against the wall. She struggled uselessly but he shook his head. "No, there's nothing you can do for him. Just watch him fight. Tell me that you're ready for this kind of life. I want to be sure before I leave you here."

Skylar watched in growing horror as another evil being jumped on Dusty's back. He flung himself to the ground and bashed the beast's skull with his own while his knuckles turned white with the strain of overpowering the choking monster's grasp. Dusty kicked and writhed until the thing's blood finally drained out of the gaping hole he'd left in its chest.

Suddenly the meaning behind Adrian's words hit her and the world came crashing down around her. "Wait. Adrian, you're leaving? When? Not now. Tell me it's not now."

He bent his head to hers, temporarily blocking out the horror happening just feet from her. "Skylar, I became a Tracker to find you. But to become a Tracker, I had to make sacrifices. Once I found you and made sure you were all right, I had to turn myself over to The Order for my training. That was the agreement. When you make your decision, I have to go. I don't have a choice."

"No..." It came out as a mere whisper, the only thing she was capable of saying. Sounds from the battle snared her attention. She was torn, her gaze flickering between Adrian and Dusty. Then she couldn't see Dusty anymore as the swarm increased in number and seemed to swallow him whole. Fear for him rocketed through her and she tried to scream, to run to him but Adrian's hand clamped over her mouth and held her still. "This is what Dusty does. He fights demons every night. It never ends. You need to make your choice with the full knowledge of everything being with a Shadow Walker implies."

Bodies flew from the fray as Dusty reappeared. The demons still moving began a rapid retreat. He met each one with a savage blast, his fists and feet pummeling, tearing each fiend to bits. Each vile creature fell to the earth and began to combust. Even with the stench of burning demon flesh, Dusty's barbarous stance did not falter.

Skylar looked into Adrian's eyes, feeling weak and exhausted, both from watching the fight and from the words she had to say. "Adrian, I'll always love you. Always. But I have to go to Dusty, I have to be with him. I know I can't make you understand, but I love Dusty. He's my soul. I can't walk away from him."

Tears filled her eyes as Adrian pressed his forehead to hers. "I love you, Skye." His lips brushed hers, soft and sweet. "I have to go." He lifted the hand he'd been holding since their time on the beach and kissed it before letting it fall. Then he stepped away.

She grabbed his shirt, not ready to let him go. "Tell me I'll see you again. Tell me this isn't goodbye forever."

He untangled her hands from his shirt and gave her a tired smile. But he didn't respond. That alone told her all she needed to know. She threw her arms around him, holding him close one last time. All the words she wanted to say froze in her throat. He stroked her hair and for that moment she was ten again, being comforted after she'd fallen from a tree and into his life. Just as quickly, the moment was over and he backed away. "Now, go to Dusty. He needs you."

She wiped her tears and tried to smile. "Thank you for finding me."

"I'll always find you." And then Adrian was gone, disappearing into the shadows.

Before the grief could overwhelm her, Skylar turned toward her future, toward the man she couldn't live without. Dusty, coated with green and purple demon gore, slumped at the base of the wall about twenty feet away, his head lowered. God, was he hurt?

Fear for him had her sprinting the distance. His head shot up at her approach and for that brief moment she saw the need to kill in his eyes. Then his eyes flickered awareness and surprise. Disbelief.

And pure, unadulterated, need and love.

Chapter Ten

Carcass fires crackled and popped in the street around Dusty, lighting up the night enough for him to see the beautiful vision in front of him. Was that really Skylar running toward him? It had been awhile since he'd fought Zakamediuls and he couldn't remember if their cruor had hallucinatory effects. It sure stank to high heaven, though. The skin and bones incinerated on their own, but the blood and guts weren't flammable, they just made a gloppy and disgusting mess.

Hell, if the Skylar rapidly approaching him was a hallucination, it was one he never wanted to come out of. With every last ounce of energy, Dusty pushed to his feet, willing his calf to stop its miserable throbbing long enough for him to stand up and take Skylar into his arms. Even if she was only a figment of his imagination, he wanted to hold her again, feel her flesh against his body, her warm mouth opening under his. And a hallucination wouldn't mind the Zakamediul gore that was covering him from head to toe, would it?

Then she was in his arms, her face pressed against his neck, and Dusty knew she was real. There was no imagining the way she smelled like apples and honey or how holding her made him feel complete again. But where had she come from? Was she hurt? Had she see him fighting? *Shit!* Would she hate him for it? Were there more Zakamediuls around the corner just waiting to attack? Where the hell was Hawke? Why wasn't he protecting her?

Dusty scanned the darkness, looking for answers. Hawke stood in the shadows, watching them. Their eyes met, and a moment of understanding passed between the two men. Hawke nodded once, then stepped backward, nebulously disappearing through a brick wall.

A knot tightened in Dusty's chest. Skylar was once again his woman. Now and forever.

All of his fears and worries disappeared as he held her in his arms. As long as she was his, nothing else mattered.

"Mine," he growled as his hands roamed over her body, hungry to feel her naked flesh beneath his palms. "Mine."

"Yours," Skylar whispered as he lowered his mouth over hers.

Like a shockwave, her kiss lit his every sense. Not caring where they were, or who might stumble upon them, Dusty wanted her now. Frantically, he lifted her in his arms…

Until his damaged leg reminded him that he couldn't even put his own weight on it, let alone someone else's. Trying to regain his balance, Dusty stepped back with his good leg, placing his foot directly into a pile of slimy demon guts. There was nothing he could do to stop it. In a tangle of limbs, they both fell to the ground. He cushioned her fall, keeping her on top of him.

Skylar must have thought something else was attacking, because she immediately sat up, her legs straddling his abdomen, eyes wide as she searched the darkness. Demon blood, transferred from his shirt, stained the front of her sweater. The saturated cotton clung to her flesh, silhouetting those incredible breasts of hers. Covered in gore, ready to fight an invisible army on his behalf, she'd never been more beautiful.

Dusty looked up at her in awe, forgetting his pain, wanting to take her with all of the fervor that his recent battle had incited. But she deserved better than a frantic tumble on the dirty streets of Talisman Bay. He stroked his hand down her face, tucking a stray hair back behind her ear. "It's okay, Skylar. The damn demon glop is slippery."

The fear in her eyes switched to concern as she frantically ran her hands over his body. "How badly are you hurt?" Her cunt rocked against him as she moved, distracting him from the pain.

"Keep movin' like that and I'll be feeling great," he said hungrily as he pulled her mouth back down to his.

She sighed against his lips, her tongue tangling with his. She tasted sweet and fresh, a stark contrast to the rest of their surroundings.

A drip, drip, drip sound had them both turning their heads to see the liquid remains of the Zakamediuls draining into the sewer.

Skylar wrinkled her nose. "Oh, yuck. Does that sewer drain into the ocean?"

Dusty kissed away her grimace and said mock-seriously, "Well, let's just say there's a reason I don't swim in Talisman Bay."

Skylar's grimace turned to a giggle as he wrapped his arms around her and held her extra tight.

"We need to get you cleaned up. Where can we go?" She wiped blood from his face. "Is any of this yours?" She looked at her soiled hand.

"I dunno. It might be. Sometimes it's hard to tell." Dusty kissed her forehead, then with a chuckle, wiped away the green lip mark he left. "I've got an apartment around the corner from here. I haven't been there in a few days and should stop in."

The second floor pad wasn't a safe haven like the cave or compound. It was just part of the façade the Shadow Walkers had to keep so the whole of Talisman Bay wouldn't wonder why a bunch of well-off guys lived in the back room of an import store.

She helped him to his feet then stayed at his side, one arm around him as they began a slow walk in the direction of his apartment. Just having her with him brought out deep strength, but his fatigue was still visible, his leg threatening to collapse with every step.

"Just around the corner, huh? It better be that close or you're not gonna make it."

"I'll make it. I promise." He smiled as he looked into her concerned gaze. A flash of movement reflected in her eye and he turned to look in the direction they were walking.

A Mardinlek phantasm wafted swiftly toward them. It levitated three feet above the ground and met them near face-level. Dusty grabbed Skylar to put himself between her and the phantasm and, at the same time, Skylar grabbed Dusty to try to put herself between him and the phantasm. It rattled and clanked its scales, ready to do battle.

"Don't fuck with me today!" Dusty roared as he wound up to punch the phantasm, but it vaporized into a light pink mist, dissipating as two throwing stars clinked to the ground. He lowered his arm and looked around.

"Okay, guys, I won't." Jake laughed as he scaled further along the wall of the building, then down, putting him within safe jumping distance. "I've been trying to kill that damn Mardinlek all night. If it hadn't gotten preoccupied with you guys, I'd still be crawlin' around chasing it." His eyes alight, he landed with usual grace on both feet and picked up his throwing stars. "Zakamediuls are out tonight?" After stowing the stars in his jacket, he motioned to the purple and green mess of their clothing.

"Not any more." Dusty grinned. "Thanks for takin' that thing out, man."

"Hey, don't mention it. Just taking the opportunity to show off in front of the pretty lady. 'Sides, I know your leg still ain't back to normal and bustin' Zakamediuls like you just did is never easy."

"I'm okay. Really." Jake lifted Dusty's free arm and, with Skylar flanking his other side, they helped him limp along. *Dammit!* He cursed the short little demon all over again for wrecking his calf. Months had passed and his leg was still not to be trusted. But he didn't want Jake or Skylar to know just how bad it was. "It's no big deal."

"Yeah, right," Skylar said as she rolled her eyes. Jake snorted. There was an instant camaraderie between the two of them.

"See, even she knows what's up. Oh, hey, pardon my rudeness…and Dusty's as well. You must be Skylar. I'm Jake."

"I know who you are," Skylar replied with a grin. Jake lifted an eyebrow questioningly. "Side effect of my kidnapping and memory swipe. I still have some of Mariah's memories."

"Okay. That's good. Then you know I'm pretty cool to have around, huh? You throw anything at me and I'll take it out. Unless it's a human female, then there'll be a whole 'nother kind of takin' out goin' on. I'm pleased to meet ya." Jake grinned.

Dusty felt like such a third wheel. As they shook wrong hands across Dusty's chest, he blurted out, "She's my fiancée." No need for Jake to think that she was at all available.

"Oh, even better." Jake laughed, then winked at Dusty. "Not bad at all. You gonna start combing your hair for her now?"

Skylar grinned. "I like his hair. It feels really good against my…when he…" She paused, her face turning a bright pink color. "It's perfect just like the rest of him."

Dusty was stunned speechless. Perfect? He'd never imagined she'd ever think him to be perfect. His whole life he'd lived with and accepted that he was a screw-up. Then again, a life with Skylar in it was full of completely new experiences. He could be perfect for her because she'd given him that chance. He lifted his hand from where it rested on her shoulder and trailed his fingers caressingly down her face. She tilted her head and graced him with a heart-stopping smile.

"Hot damn." Jake's mouth dropped open in playful shock. "Dusty, you better hold onto her. Real tight. I mean, she didn't even run away from the Mardinlek. Most chicks run away in fright after just seeing your hair." He chuckled and shook his head.

"Yeah, bite me, Jake. And I ain't letting Skylar go. Ever." He dropped a kiss on top of her head before he teasingly continued, "Unless of course she wants to go to one of those panty parties or Tupperware parties or whatever. Them things scare me. Get a bunch of women together like that and…hell, they're scarier than a pack of Zakamediuls any day." Dusty playfully shuddered as Skylar poked him in the ribcage. "Hey, ouch!" he laughed.

"Just for that I'm throwing a party and Jake can be my date. You up for it, Jake?"

"Oh hell, yeah. You know I'm game. A bunch of hot women all there to check out panties and stuff." Jake was so excited, he nearly lost grip on Dusty's shoulder. "Hey, wait, do they model it? Like, would I get to watch a bunch of women parading around in sexy lingerie? That would kick ass. I'd so be there. You just gimme a time and a place. Hell, I'll even help set up the party. Do you gotta blow up balloons and hang streamers for that kind of thing? Shit yeah. I'll even order pizzas or bake some cookies. Dusty, you can help, too. That'd really be cool."

Dusty watched Skylar as she laughed so hard she nearly gasped for breath. He always wanted her to be this happy. "Naw, man. I mean, it'd be a waste for me. The only woman there I'd even notice would be Skylar. No one else compares."

Through her laughter Skylar beamed him a smile.

Jake let out a mirthful chuckle. "Damn, you got it bad, buddy. But that's good. I'm super happy for ya. 'Sides, I wouldn't really need any help with a whole party full of women. Hell, if I was the only guy there, I would *be* the party. Woohoo!" Jake triumphantly raised his fist in the air. "Aw yeah. You know it. I'm the man."

Dusty laughed. "Yeah, Jake. You are the man. Just don't let the ladies know your technique is as bad as your jokes and you'll be stylin'."

"Hey now, no chick has ever complained about my quick ride."

Tears of laughter streaked Skylar's cheeks. "Wait a second here. Dusty, should I be worried that you're familiar with Jake's technique?"

"Oh hell, no! I was just fuckin' with him." Dusty laughed and almost tripped.

"Shit. That's cold. Why you gotta be like that?" Jake's smile had yet to fade as he shook his head and looked over to Skylar. "You have an open invite to come talk with me about Mr. Smooth here. I'll tell you about all his fifth grade love affairs and the ass he made of himself in first grade with that girl…what was her name…cute redhead…Tracey! Yeah. Your man here was such a stud. He didn't share his ice cream with her during recess. No wonder she ditched you to play hopscotch with that kid, Phillip. Hell, they're probably married by now."

"Jake, I look forward to the day a woman manages to knock you for a loop," Skylar said, still trying to catch her breath.

"Boy, that day would kick ass. Even more than a panty party or something. 'Cause that girl would have to be slick enough not to be wiled by my charms. Shut me down before I even get started. Kinda like you, 'cause you got a great sense of humor. You know how fun it is to get Dusty going. I mean, there's just so much material. I'll bet you and I could go for hours—"

"Home sweet home," Dusty interrupted before Jake got too far out of hand. They'd arrived at the building and Dusty wanted to finally be alone with Skylar…in private, behind closed doors, in close quarters, where he could pretend to be more hurt than he was and see just how well she'd take care of him before he'd surprise her and start taking care of her. "But let's go in through the back. Don't want the neighbors to see me this way."

"Is there any other way in?" Jake joked as he led them around back.

"Fuck," Dusty muttered.

"You okay?" Skylar asked, squeezing him a little tighter.

"The goddamn key. It's at the compound."

"I'll take care of it," Jake said as he leaned Dusty up against the back wall of the apartment building. "You got him?" he asked Skylar. She nodded and stayed at Dusty's side.

"I can stand, you know," Dusty stated emphatically. Was Jake purposely trying to make him look like an invalid in front of Skylar?

Jake raised an eyebrow. "Sure, superman, whatever. If you want to fall on your ass in front of your woman, that's fine by me."

"He already did," Skylar said casually. She and Jake looked at each other then burst out laughing all over again.

"So glad I can be the scapegoat for your comedy routine." Dusty couldn't help but chuckle though. Yeah, he'd deserved that.

Still laughing, Jake set to work on the lock. No one could surpass his breaking and entering skills. Jake had survived foster home after foster home by learning how to break out of the rooms he was locked into. No family could contain him. Funny how Dusty would've just pounded his fist through the glass, cuts be damned, but Jake would sooner work his magic with the lock or run up the side of the building before leaving any trace that something was amiss.

When the door clicked open, Jake and Skylar hoisted Dusty back up and took him upstairs. "I have the key for this one, though." Jake pulled a ring of keys from his pocket and tried several of them.

"Shit, it'd be faster for you to pick it, too." Dusty chuckled.

"Bite me. I'm trying to figure out which one it is so I can give it to you. I gotta get back out patrolling. Ryan just clicked-in. He says he needs help on a cleanup." Jake got the door open and handed the key to Skylar.

"Thanks, Jake." She stuffed it in her pocket, then they both helped Dusty into the apartment.

"Hey, don't mention it. You got him okay, don't you?" Jake asked as they walked Dusty into the bathroom and settled him on the closed toilet seat.

"I'm sure we'll be fine, Jake. Thanks."

"Okay, then. I'm outta here." Jake smiled then clicked-in. *Just call me if anything else goes wrong. I'll be close by. Me and Ryan will cover for you. I'm thinkin' you need some good rest right about now. And with a lady like that who still likes you even with Zakamediul guts all over the place and your hair standin' on end, you better take the time to enjoy her. Let someone take care of you for a change.*

I'm keepin' her as long as she'll have me. Let everyone know where we are and especially tell Mariah that Skylar's with me. She was really worried. Thanks, man. Dusty clicked-out as Jake headed out of the apartment, closing the door behind him.

"So, do you have a first-aid kit?" Skylar rummaged through the cupboards below the sink.

"It's too big to fit under the sink. It's in the other room." Hell, it *was* the other room. "Just grab some bandages. I'm not that messed up."

"Okay, wait here. I want to peel off your clothes myself. I'm going to slowly and carefully inspect every inch of you to make sure you aren't seriously injured." The sparkle in her eyes as she grinned at him before leaving the room made him wait patiently. Well, not too patiently considering that he was fantasizing about her hands all over his skin. Hell, he'd have to inspect her, too, to make sure she wasn't injured, of course.

He was brought out of his reverie by Skylar's laugh. "Dusty, you weren't kidding! Ummm…wheelchairs, crutches, a gurney. A curio full of medicines… You've got enough stuff here to patch up an entire army. Have you ever even used half this stuff?"

"Some of it. I play wheelchair basketball with a couple kids down at the Y whenever I can. They kick my ass, too." He chuckled. "Damn, those kids got game."

Skylar walked back into the bathroom with both arms full of tape, gauze, rubbing alcohol and towels. Her eyes were full of passion as she stepped toward him.

He raised an eyebrow. "You plannin' on tying me up with all that stuff?"

She lowered the supplies to the countertop then straddled him, her hands tangling in his hair as she smashed her lips to his.

The kiss shot fire to his loins, and he grabbed her ass and pulled her tighter against his aching cock. He didn't know what he'd done to deserve this…or her.

She pulled her lips away as quickly as they'd arrived and leaned her forehead against his. "Every time I learn something new about you, I love you even more, Dusty. This is crazy. When I was younger I fantasized about a love like this, but I thought that was all it was, a fantasy. I hoped and prayed for it, but I never really expected I'd fall in love like this, so deeply I can barely breathe because my chest hurts when I look at you. Hell, there are still moments that I can't believe you're real and that you love me back. It's scary and fantastic and awe-inspiring and I don't ever want to not feel like this."

"So you'll still marry me?"

"I don't think I'm willing to give you a choice."

"I don't need a choice, Skylar. I just need you." He spoke with such love and honesty that his own heart felt a twinge, reminding him that they'd both be in for a crazy life together. One that he wished would be easy and lacking in demon, gore at every turn, but he knew that would never be the case. But as he gazed into her blue eyes, he was reassured by the love he saw there, that she'd be with him through it all. No matter how much glop she had to wade through to get to him. Dusty swore he was the absolute luckiest man on the planet.

Their clothing made a sound like Velcro separating as Skylar peeled herself off his lap. "Come on, love. Let's take a shower before my skin becomes permanently discolored by this gunk."

Turning the water on, she squealed as Dusty lifted her from behind and moved them both fully clothed under the hot spray. Immediately, green and purple colored water began streaming off their ruined clothes and swirling down the drain.

"Ooohhhh…it feels so good to get this crap off of me." Skylar sighed as she pulled her sweater over her head.

Dusty lowered himself to the tiled shelf he'd had installed after his injury, letting the heated water work magic on his aches, while his woman worked her own type of magic on his libido. He undid the buttons of his jeans, giving his cock room to breathe.

As he watched, she unclasped her bra, then peeled her jeans and panties down her legs. She bent over, untangling the wet denim from around her ankles. Dusty swallowed his groan, afraid in any way to disturb the moment. She was so damn magnificent enjoying the water, her skin turning pink from the heat.

Eyes closed, she tilted her head back, letting the water run over her exposed breasts, down her belly and through the soft brown curls between her thighs. He wanted to bury himself between her legs, feast on her cream, and listen to her cries for more.

Her hands, which had been resting on her shoulders, lightly skimmed down her body, coming to rest on her upper thighs. Desire flushed her skin, tightening her nipples. Did she have any idea how intoxicating it was to watch her? Dusty leaned against the tiled wall, savoring its coolness contrasting his entire being.

With soap in one hand and shampoo in the other, Skylar approached him. "You know, I've always fantasized about bathing a man." Her voice was husky, yearning as she placed the soap and shampoo on the tile shelf next to him. "Peeling off his clothes, running my soapy hands over every inch of hard muscle, stroking warm, wet skin…"

Her touch was gentle as she straddled his thighs, spreading her pussy wide for him to see. She grasped the hem of his shirt and proceeded to bring it upward, over his head. He lifted his arms as she pressed her breasts against his chest in an effort to tug the shirt completely off. When the fabric barrier was gone, he teased one of her pebbled nipples with his tongue, then suckled it into his mouth with a low groan. More than anything he just wanted to bury himself to the hilt within her and never leave.

He brought one hand over her other breast and she arched her back in response. Her movements were so honest, instinctual. His need echoed inside him with carnal urgency. *Take her. Mate with her. Make her mine.*

"Dusty, I'm not done bathing you yet." Her words were a breathy whisper as she slowly backed away and began inspecting each of the cuts and scrapes along his shoulders and ribs.

Filling the palm of her hand with shampoo, she leaned over him. "Close your eyes."

He followed her instructions as her hands began to massage his scalp. He wondered if she realized she made a soft purring noise low in her throat as she washed him. The quiet noise nearly drove him mad. He wanted to hear her make that noise as she took his cock in her sweet, wet mouth. Dusty shifted on the tile, his balls aching in the confines of his wet jeans.

Skylar traced over his ears, then trailed her fingers down his face and along his jaw. The mouth he'd been fantasizing about brushed across his, a quick flirting of her tongue along the seam of his lips before she stepped away. He groaned in frustration. "Tease," he mumbled.

She laughed, a fascinating mix of seductress and innocent. "Keep your eyes closed." Shifting the water so it sprayed over him, she began rinsing the soap from his hair.

Even above the scents of soap and shampoo, he could smell her musky sweet arousal. Placing his hands over her thighs, he caressed upward toward her heavenly slit, his thumbs massaging the softness leading inward. She gasped as he dipped one thumb into her wet heat. Her breathing hastened, then she gasped again when he moved his other thumb over her clit. Her hands tightened in his hair as his fingers slid through her folds. Hot cream soaked his fingers as she languidly rocked her hips to match his movements.

He opened his eyes to watch her body respond to his touch. Her eyes were closed, lips slightly parted, her breath coming in soft pants. Those perfect breasts of hers were still begging for his attention, the nipples tight and wanting, a deep rose in color. He took one in his mouth, teasing the hardening flesh between his teeth. More moisture seeped over his fingers and he growled his approval around her breast.

Listening to her moans and feeling her body react to his touch was better rehabilitation than any batch of gauze and rubbing alcohol. As long as he held her, bringing her sexuality to life, he felt absolutely zero pain. He'd found his new drug. And she'd agreed to be his wife. He could have and hold her forever.

As her pussy began to spasm around his thumb, he knew she was close. He maintained his rhythm and like music to his ears, she purred her release. Easing his motions, Dusty brought his arms around her as she lowered her mouth to his, drinking hungrily. He returned her kiss with equal fervor, reveling in her satisfaction.

"Was that acceptable?" Dusty teased as he brushed back a few stray locks of hair that the water had stuck to her cheek.

"More than acceptable," she replied as she turned into his touch, drawing one of his fingers deep into the warm recesses of her mouth. Her blue eyes grew wide when she realized she could taste her juices on his finger. His cock pulsed hard against his stomach, pre-come bubbling from the small hole.

Desire replaced the initial shock in her eyes, and her lids drooped as she sucked his finger in deeper. His Skylar had discovered her temptress side. He swallowed hard, wanting that mouth around his cock. Wanting her warm tongue to slide down his shaft, taking him deep against her throat. Wanting her to suck him hard, to taste his come, the way she was tasting her own.

His cock was in total agreement.

Skylar held his hand and with complete attention to detail, cleansed her fluids off every one of his fingers. Dusty broke into a sweat and it took everything within him to keep from throwing her to the floor of the shower and fucking her every which way to Sunday…then Monday, and Tuesday…

She smacked her lips as she trailed the last finger from her mouth. "You know, I'm still not done bathing you…" She lowered to her knees in front of him, her gaze pausing on his cock. He gritted his teeth as her hands reached for the waistband of his jeans and the tips of her fingers brushed against him.

"Lift up just a bit," she said as she struggled to remove the soaking wet denim. She looked up at him with a sly grin. "Remind me next time to strip you naked first so I can have my way with you quicker."

Between the two of them they were able to get the clinging fabric off. Starting at his feet, Skylar lathered the bar of soap over his flesh. Her hands slipped easily across his soap-slickened skin, gliding over various old scars and recently healed scratches with gentle ease. She lightly traced the small scar on his calf, before moving to his knees then up to his thighs. Never once did she cringe at any of the damage his body had sustained. In fact, she touched him so tenderly, he wasn't even sure she noticed his imperfections.

He couldn't get enough of the way she moved, how she was such a mixture of strong and delicate. The whole idea that this woman was truly his, that she wanted him, needed him, desired him, that by her choice she knelt before him, cleansing his body...it completely astounded him.

Searching fingers traced over the whorls of hair on his upper thighs. Dusty held his breath as she studied the part of him that throbbed in want of her. Leaning closer, her warm breath washed over his shaft just moments before she took his cock's thick head into her mouth.

Sweet, heavenly bliss, even better than he'd imagined. Nothing could compare to her wet heat, the tender suckling of her eager mouth. She took her time, learning him with both mouth and fingers.

He repositioned himself on the shelf, spreading his legs a bit wider as one of her slender hands reached down to cup his sac. "Incredible...Skylar." He moaned deeply. "You're..." Words were lost in wondrous sexual oblivion.

She chuckled around his shaft and he nearly came undone. Her tongue exploring every inch, she worked his balls in her hand. Her whole virgin thing had to be a front. There was no way she was inexperienced. Or maybe her expertise was simply based on the fact that they were meant to be together. She instinctually knew exactly what to do to drive him to the edge of sensual madness.

He looked down at her as she stroked him with her tongue and lips. What an amazing sight. He wanted to tell her just how wonderfully she was working him. How hot she made him. How close he was to coming. But all words had disappeared from his vocabulary. All he knew how to do was reach out and caress her as she worked, his breath ragged and fierce, his hips lightly rocking along with her ministrations.

But he felt he should at least warn her. "Skylar, I'm gonna—"

She purred as she pulled his length completely inside, nearly swallowing him. He lost it. He'd meant to give her the option to withdraw, but darn it all to hell, she was too good at pleasuring him.

Thick spurts of come blasted into her mouth, as she continued to work him, drawing out his orgasm until he thought there could be nothing left inside him.

Nothing but love for her.

Chapter Eleven

Mariah approached the house she used to share with Twyla. It was dark, no lights flickering from deep within. It almost appeared void of life. Of memories. But that was probably just her conscience talking.

Unless Twyla was sleeping—highly unlikely since it was still early and she rarely went to sleep before midnight—then she was out somewhere, with someone, doing something. Mariah sighed. She used to know these things. She used to know everything that was going on in Twyla's life, and vice-versa. But now…

Mariah looked at the keys in her hand. She could go inside to wait. When she had moved into the compound with Stephan, Twyla had made it clear that Mariah was welcome back at anytime. But this place, this house that had been her home for five years, didn't feel like home anymore. She felt like she would be violating Twyla's privacy if she barged in now without an invitation.

Instead, she pocketed the keys, sat down on the front porch swing and began a gentle back and forth rocking. It was almost relaxing. Almost, if she wasn't so concerned about Twyla and the state of their friendship. Mariah missed her best friend, the sassy, freaky, weird, amazing woman who had always stood by her side no matter what. It was time to get their friendship back on track, and Mariah wasn't going anywhere until she made things right.

She glanced out into the yard and almost jumped when she saw Michael standing there, watching her.

Of course. He was her Watcher now. Michael was going to be around her all the time. It was just going to take some getting used to.

As he started to step away, Mariah called out to him, "C'mon. You might as well sit up here with me. I might be waiting awhile."

He nodded and climbed the few steps to the porch, but rather than sitting next to her, he leaned against the house and crossed his arms over his chest, his face lost in shadow.

Other than the steady creaking of the swing and the distant sound of the ocean's roar, the night was quiet. It would have been peaceful, but the past day's events were too heavy on her heart.

"So, how do you like Talisman Bay?" Mariah blurted out, immediately realizing just how ridiculous she sounded. "Ugh...sorry about that. It was...it was just too quiet and I wanted to break the silence and that was possibly the stupidest thing I could have said."

"The streets are clean and the air smells fresh," he replied, and although he sounded completely serious, she had a feeling...

"Was that a joke? You're teasing me aren't you?"

His teeth flashed white in the darkness, the first smile she'd seen from him in over five years. "Well, the streets *are* clean...or what I've seen of them from following you here. And yes, I'm teasing you. Is that not allowed?"

Although his tone was light, humorous, the question seemed to have a deeper meaning behind it. He wasn't just asking about teasing. They both had to figure out their boundaries, how they were going to make their new relationship work.

"Yes it's allowed." She smiled. "It just wasn't expected. As for Talisman Bay, it's nice. Something about it grows on you. Even now, after learning about all the creepy crawlies that lurk around here, I still love it. There's no place else that compares."

He didn't reply and the night grew quiet again. Determined to not sit in silence all night, she said, "Okay, next topic. Should we talk about the weather now? Isn't that how most awkward conversations get started?"

"You want to have a conversation?"

"It's better than sitting here in insipid silence, staring at each other uncomfortably while waiting for Twyla to get home."

He shifted against the wall, crossing one leg over the other. "Is this where you used to live? Before Stephan?"

"Yeah. Twyla and I moved here after...after I almost died. It was a fresh start for both of us." She paused, wondering if she should talk to him about Stephan. Michael had to know that Stephan was her life now, that nothing would change her feelings for him, but how could she say that to Michael without rubbing salt into his wounds? Was there ever a right time to talk to an ex-boyfriend who still loved you and was now metaphysically attached to you but could never have you? Mariah blew out a frustrated breath. Dammit! Why couldn't there be a life rulebook for this type of situation?

Before she could say anything difficult and potentially painful, his deep voice broke the silence. "Hey, Mariah? Why did you think I was behind the attempt on your life? I've gone over that day so many times in my head, and I just can't figure that out. Nothing's making sense."

Mariah stopped rocking in the swing. "You want to sit down? This could take awhile."

He shook his head. "I'm fine here. I need to watch the bigger picture. The porch leaves too much unseen."

"Suit yourself." She shrugged her shoulders. It would probably be easier to tell him what she remembered from that day if she wasn't looking him in the eye. "You know, I hate thinking about that day, and kinda forced myself not to think about it much in the last few years."

"You're not the only one, Angel."

"Angel...wow, I haven't been called that..." *since the last time we were together.*

"Well, that's what you were to me." His voice held a glimmer of the tender sweetness they'd once shared. "The only angel in my crazy world of devils."

"Michael..." She squeezed her hands into fists, wishing this could be easier. "You need to know that I love Stephan. There's no chance of you and I getting back to—"

"I know that, Mariah. It obviously wasn't meant to be anyway. That was made painfully clear, don't you think?" His whole body remained tense, but somehow his words came casually, like he wasn't trying to hurt her, but wanted to end discussion of their past love for each other.

She couldn't help but feel a twinge of remorse for the difference in their destinies and how Themonius had viciously exposed their relationship as merely a stolen season. The feelings they'd once shared had been real, no matter what fate had decreed. "Everything The Order did to you, to all of us, really sucks. If you ever want to go, you can. I won't hold you here. You don't deserve to have your life tied to mine. Not like this."

"Mariah, there's a lot that neither of us deserved. But I don't run away from things when they get crazy, I run straight into the middle and try to fix things or at least make them into something I can manage.

This...what we have now, your new life and mine. I can work with this." His voice sounded sure, but Mariah knew it wasn't as simple as he made it out to be. Although what he said was true, the words still pained him. "What we have right now is not my ideal. It's my reality and rather than fight it, I'm handling it and it's not bad. Both of us got to keep our lives. But you still haven't answered my question. Why did you think I wanted you dead? What the hell happened, Mariah?"

"You already know I went to the doctor that day." He nodded. "Well, when I found out I was pregnant, I decided to make a trip to your office, see if we could go to lunch so I could break the news to you. It's funny, I remember now that I never really knew what you did, other than you worked in personal security. It seems rather apropos now." She gave him a half-smile, but he didn't say anything. "Anyway, when I got there, I was getting ready to knock on that ratty door—that whole building was in disrepair, remember?—and it opened a crack, enough for me to realize that you had company. So I started to back away, to come back later, when I overheard the three of you planning a murder. I was shocked, and thinking I must have heard wrong, I eavesdropped. The last thing I heard you say was 'I want her dead, today, the sooner the better. Get this bitch off my case.'"

Mariah stopped in her story telling and looked up toward Michael. Because his face was shadowed, she couldn't see his expression, but his entire body was taut, angry. She continued. "So I'd just found out I was pregnant and discovered the man I loved was a killer. It was a bit overwhelming. I wanted to get away for a while, to think things through so I could figure out what I was going to say to you, what I was going to do about us. But when the same two guys you'd been talking with found me an hour later and tried to kill me, I assumed I was the bitch you'd been talking about." The bitter memories brought a foul taste to her mouth and she crossed her arms over her stomach protectively. "I hated you for a long time," she whispered.

"I'm sorry you hated me and that the secrets I kept put you in such grave danger, but you weren't the female I sent them after. Far from it, actually. I sent them after a Losfun demon who wanted me to work with her...well, it. They're androgynous, but outwardly they look female...well, like an ugly female but they have large breasts."

"I'm familiar with Losfuns." She shuddered, remembering just how unfortunately close she'd come to being a victim. "That's how I met Stephan. He saved me from being impregnated by one of them."

"Then you know that Losfuns are rather tenacious when they see something they want. And this one—its name was Guibar—for some reason decided I would be an appropriate addition to its gang. Yeah, like I would stoop so low. I considered it my job to fight that kind of scum, not work for it. My security company was almost like the Shadow Organization except that we were regular humans...without added or amplified attributes like The Order *installed* in me and the rest of their charges." Resentment laced his words.

"I always knew you were in danger at work. I just had no idea how much."

"Me neither. See, I thought my team was just that. Mine. But they were double agents, had been even through all the years they'd worked for me. Those assholes were just waiting for the perfect moment." He sighed. "Guibar wouldn't get off my case and decided the time had come. She figured that if you were dead, I'd have nothing left to live for and I'd give in and join her. Well, she was right on one count...without you, I had nothing left to live for. But I'd be damned before I'd ever consider going to her."

A car came to a slow stop in front of the house and Michael stopped talking, moving toward the edge of the porch, his attention focused on the vehicle. Giggling teenage girls tumbled out, laughing and waving at the driver as the car took off. The girls crossed the street and entered a house.

Michael lifted his face, gazing at the night sky. He looked so incredibly alone and without thinking twice about it she stood up and joined him there at the railing.

With a ragged voice, he continued. "That night, they came to me. Those same guys. Bragging about how they killed you. Hell-bent on killing me, too, when I refused to join Guibar. They almost had me, but The Order stepped in, taking me while I was unconscious. I didn't have a choice."

Mariah waited for him to resume his story, but he remained quiet. Moonlight washed over his face revealing the grief he'd tried so carefully to hide from her. She slid her hand over his, offering the only thing she could, the comfort of a human touch.

There was surprise in his eyes when he turned to face her. Surprise and uncertainty and...

His face went emotionless, but he didn't pull away. She lifted his hand, turning it over so she could inspect the slash across his palm.

"I'm sorry," she whispered as she lightly traced her finger across the cut she'd given him. "For—"

Before she could finish, he was gone, jumping over the railing, putting himself between her and approaching footsteps.

"What the fuck?" Twyla snarled. "Mariah isn't here, you bastard. Fuck you. Get away from my house." Twyla looked like a captive tiger backed into a corner...her hair tousled, the spark in her eyes threatening to burn out if her last strike wasn't strong enough.

Michael stepped back. "Damn. Sorry. I thought you were someone else."

"Like what? A woman in love? Hell, then you'd just send your cronies to kick my ass instead of getting your hands dirty, huh?"

Hoping to console Twyla, Mariah stepped off the porch. Twyla's furious stare shot to Mariah. "What the fuck did he do to you? Why is he here? Hell, why are you here? What's going on? Are you all right?" Her breathing was fierce, but as she looked from Mariah to Michael, then back again, her guard lowered, apparently realizing she wasn't about to be attacked.

"Twyla, it's okay. I swear. I'll explain—"

"Where's Stephan? Why aren't you with him?" Twyla questioned angrily, back on the defensive.

"Okay, I know what you're thinking. Yes, it's really me. No, I'm not under some magic spell. Yes, that's really Michael, and no, he's not going to kill you or me. A lot...a lot has happened..." Mariah paused, trying to put the events of the day into perspective. "I had another one of those life-changing days today and I really just want to eat some chocolate double-chunk ice cream and girl talk with my best friend. So can you calm down enough to do that?"

"Maybe. But he's not coming in. I don't care what the fuck happened. He is not welcome in my house." She shot him a fierce glance before rummaging through her purse for her keys and heading for the door. "Y'know, Mariah, you really shouldn't be wandering out too far from Stephan. Strange shit's happening again. I mean, for starters I think I might be out of chocolate double-chunk ice cream."

Even though Twyla's words were humorous, her voice was tight with anger. She savagely ran her free hand back and forth through her hair, further tousling the tangled strands, before exhaling roughly and throwing the door open. She didn't look back at Mariah before disappearing inside.

Michael walked up the steps and leaned against the house, resuming the same stance as before. Without saying a word, Mariah knew that Michael would wait for her, that no matter what happened, he'd be there. Yes, it was his job now, but it felt more like he was with her because he was her friend. She nodded at him as she stepped into the house and closed the door behind her.

Twyla was already in the kitchen clattering about, presumably getting out the ice cream. Plastic bowls hit the floor and she let out a string of jumbled curses. Drawers opened and closed as she called out, "Come in here and get out the syrup while I scoop."

Mariah entered the kitchen and found a disaster area. There were no dirty dishes, but nothing was put away anywhere. There were beads, shoes, even various tools littering the countertops and Twyla was completely oblivious as she shoved a pile to the side, plunked down the ice cream and began to carve out two servings.

"Well, phew. You had me worried for a few minutes there."

Twyla raised an eyebrow but didn't say anything as she continued digging into the frozen dessert.

"I mean, we can't girl talk without chocolate double-chunk ice cream. It just wouldn't be right." Mariah opened the refrigerator and stared gape-eyed at the mess inside. "Ummm...Twyla? Do I wanna know why you have a bra in the refrigerator?" She pulled out the chocolate syrup and closed the door, deciding it would be life-threatening to search for the butterscotch. She didn't want to know what else she'd find in there.

Twyla looked up, an expression of frustration morphing into a half-grin. "Aside from my usual, 'I just haven't had time to clean up' excuse, I'd have to say, you probably don't wanna know the exact reason that's in there. Hell, I'm not sure I even remember." She used her finger to swish the last scoop into a bowl before licking her finger and closing the ice cream container. "Why was it you're here again? I know it isn't ice cream. I'm sure you get plenty of that at home." Her half-grin turned to a smirk.

Mariah laughed. "I'm in need of some girl talk. Stephan hasn't quite mastered the art. I don't think he understands the skill involved. He tends to go cross-eyed after the first ten minutes of listening to me rant and rave about bra-sizes. Can you believe it? Then he comes up with some lame excuse that he has to go help one of the guys kill a demon. Men..." Mariah rolled her eyes, while she silently begged for

Stephan's forgiveness for the stories she was spinning about him. But it was for a good cause. Anything to get Twyla and her talking the way they used to.

"Well, I don't suppose most men are really good for anything but fucking and fighting anyway, huh?" Twyla drizzled chocolate syrup over her bowl. "So, what is it you wanna talk about? I mean, obviously, whatever bra I've got in the fridge isn't a good one, so you can take that brand off your list of must-haves."

"Duly noted." Mariah grabbed the chocolate syrup, removed the drizzle cap and poured half the container on the ice cream.

"Still craving chocolate?"

"Nope," Mariah lied as she left the kitchen and settled on the couch in the living room. Twyla followed after her, sitting on the overstuffed recliner. They sat in silence for a few minutes, both munching away on their ice cream.

Twyla leaned forward and placed her empty bowl on the coffee table. Curling her legs underneath her, she relaxed back into the chair. "So, you gonna tell me why the bastard who tried to kill you five years ago is standing on my porch?"

"He didn't try to kill me…it wasn't him." Mariah sighed, put the melting ice cream down, pulled a pillow against her chest and spilled the entire story.

Ten minutes later, Mariah finished. "So that's it. Michael was just as much of a victim of circumstance as I was."

"Okay, but he still freaks me out. Something about the way he looks at me. I dunno. Anyway, I'm still finding it odd that you're not with Stephan. That he let you go out on your own. I mean, weird shit's going down right now. Think about it. Skylar looks just like you and she's running around town, too. I saw her with some other guy a couple hours ago. Clearly someone she's close to."

"Wait a sec…how do you know about Skylar? You've seen her? What?" Mariah spluttered. "Damn, has everyone but me met my cousin already?"

"Cousin?" Twyla frowned. "I guess that would explain the startling resemblance. I was almost figuring more than just cousin. Hell, I thought she was you. I walked into the café to get some dinner and she was sitting with some cute guy with his hand over hers. I started talking to her before I got a good look at her and she knew my name. Very weird. Everything's very weird right now." Twyla sighed, and primped her hair. "And too many coincidences, too close to you, Mariah. You know that's gotta be bad news. You're really making me nervous being here." She fluffed her hair again.

"Nervous? Why? Twyla, what's up? This isn't like you. You've been messing with your hair the whole time we've been talking, you're not meeting my eyes..." Mariah laid her head back on the edge of the couch and stared at the ceiling. "You're keeping things from me and you've never done that before. That's why I came over tonight. I want to know what I did to make you not trust me anymore." Reluctant, angry tears burned in her throat and she choked on them as she spoke. "I just want my best friend back."

"With all due respect, Mariah, and don't take this the wrong way, but I'm not the one who left. I'm happy for you and everything, but I'm still here. And now I'm even more alone than I used to be." Twyla's words came to an abrupt halt.

Stunned, Mariah looked at her friend. Twyla sat, arms crossed, eyebrows furrowed, staring straight ahead. She was still hiding something, and it was starting to piss Mariah off. "Wait, we can only be friends if I live with you? What the hell is that about?" Angry, Mariah got to her feet. "You know, I didn't realize that being in love and keeping our friendship were contradictory experiences. I'm gonna get more ice cream. I don't know what the hell is wrong with you, but I need more chocolate to deal with it."

"I knew you wouldn't understand. You're too happy to understand, Mariah," Twyla said calmly as she entered the kitchen behind Mariah. "As my best friend, you were always around even when I didn't want you to be, but now you're never around and I'm in absolute hell with no one to talk to about it because I can't just barge in on you and Stephan. Hell, every time I've come to the compound to talk to you, you're fucking him. That's great and all. It's about time you had a healthy sex life, so who the hell am I to get in your way?" She washed out her bowl in the sink and set it down near where Mariah was carving out a second serving.

Mariah let out a tired sigh. "I've been waiting three months for you to tell me what happened when Craze took you. Three months. After the first month of reminding you that you could talk to me, I kinda figured you just weren't ready, or didn't want to tell me. Now you're saying it's my fault?" Fed up with trying to scoop out ice cream, Mariah poured in the chocolate syrup and began eating directly from the container.

"No. That's not what I'm saying at all. I'm saying I just don't wanna rain on your parade." Twyla leaned against the counter and studied the floor. "What would you say if I told you that without Freeze, I feel like my life is over?" She pulled an amethyst crystal from her pocket and studied its facets as she slowly rotated it. "What would you say if I told you that even though I was only around the guy for what, five hours total, I knew that I could give up ever fucking another man as long as I lived? What would you say if I told you that he is the only person who has ever breathed more life into me than I have ever breathed into anyone else?" Twyla's voice shook. "What would you say if I told you he was dead?" She palmed the amethyst and darted into the living room, tears falling unhindered down her cheeks.

It was the first time Mariah had ever seen her cry.

Dropping the ice cream on the counter, Mariah hurried after Twyla. She found her sitting on the floor, head down, leaning against the arm of the couch, one knee up as she clasped the amethyst to her chest, her other hand tangled in her hair as her shoulders wracked with each sob.

Mariah sat down next to her best friend. "I don't know what to say," she whispered, as though the fragility of the situation would be shattered if she spoke in a normal voice. She'd never felt so useless, so completely unable to offer any type of comfort. "Why didn't you tell me earlier? Why..." Mariah ran a hand soothingly down Twyla's back. "I love you, Twyla. Just because I'm getting married doesn't mean I can't hurt for you, with you, and curse the fates on your behalf...that will never change. Never."

"I thought I was doing fine. I thought I was getting over it, getting over him. I thought it would go away, but it's not. No matter what I try, he still haunts me. I dream of him every night. Sometimes we're fucking like everything in the world is beautiful and sometimes it's as simple as he's shadowing me, looking out for me as I go off and be my wild and wacky self. Mariah, in the short time I knew him, he taught me things that have changed my life forever. He showed me that I have power. That I can make things happen." She paused and wiped tears from her cheeks, but more tears swiftly took their place. "So now, here I am, somewhere in limbo without anything to hold on to, because why would anyone wanna listen to me whine and cry about some guy I truly can never have? Some guy I killed."

"What?" Mariah asked incredulously.

"That night on the pier, during the battle, I sent Freeze to his death."

Mariah's mind flashed back to that night three months ago when David had tried to steal her to another dimension. A blond man had stepped in, confronting David. Words and fists had flown, and then some type of magic. Twyla had screamed out a name…Freeze. But what had happened and why did she blame herself? "Twyla, I don't understand."

"I saw that Craze was throwing a fireball at you as he fell into the portal and I did what I could to try and stop it. I ended up throwing a spark. Yes, I have that kind of power now. The spark knocked the fireball away from you, but it ricocheted and knocked Freeze to his death." She swallowed hard. "Yeah, I know Craze came back from that hell, but he told me that he watched Freeze die. And even if the bastard was full of shit, Freeze is not here, but Craze is." Twyla lifted her head, her tear-filled eyes begging her to understand. "I know he would be here, Mariah. Freeze would be here with me. I know that. I'm·not making this shit up. I know what I felt—what we felt—was real. He wasn't faking, Mariah. I know it."

Mariah wrapped both arms around her best friend, the tears starting to fall from her eyes as well. "I know, Twyla. I know. But you didn't do anything wrong. It wasn't your fault. Don't blame yourself. Don't go down that path."

"I just don't want the flame to burn out. But I can't get it back. I feel so cold. I was trying to help, but I got hurt…very badly. And I can't undo it. I can't change it. I can't erase it." Twyla wrapped her arms around Mariah and shook with each uncontrollable gut-wrenching sob.

"Do you remember what you told me after Michael? I know it's not the same thing, but hear me out. I still loved him for a while, even though I thought he'd tried to kill me. I couldn't let go of what we'd had, that feeling of being with someone who was such a part of me. But you made me let go. You forced me to see that I could go on. And you can. It'll hurt. It'll always hurt when you think of it…of him. But you can't stop living…you've got too much to live for."

Twyla pulled back, out of Mariah's embrace. "What the hell are you talking about? What have I got left to live for? You're gonna have to enlighten me because I'm just not seeing it. Not at all. I'm still searching for a reason. Still searching for something truly good to come of all of this. Something I can hold onto instead of sacrificing for someone else's sake."

A whooshing, whirring sound filled the air around them and Mariah looked up, startled to see what looked to be a full deck of tarot cards spinning in a furious cyclone around the two of them. Somehow she knew the cause was Twyla, that her rampant emotions were manifesting themselves in the twisting wind.

Needing to break through to her, to calm her down before anything else started flying, she looked Twyla directly in her eyes and spoke matter-of-factly. Hopefully the no bullshit routine would sink in faster than soothing, reassuring words. "Of course, you can't see it now. You're too caught up in the 'what ifs'. I'm not saying you should go out and start fucking every man you see, hoping one of them catches your fancy, but you need to do things for you, start living for you. Screw what you think you *should* do. Do what makes you happy. And I know you're going to tell me nothing makes you happy, but you've got to move past that. Because I know Twyla is in there somewhere." Mariah took a deep breath. "I'm not trying to make light of what happened. I'm not. But I can't keep watching you wither away. I *won't* let you." Her last words came out fiercer than intended, but if that made them sink into Twyla's skull, that was all that mattered.

A glimmer of comprehension flickered in Twyla's eyes just as Michael came blasting through the front door. "What the h—"

With a twist of Twyla's hand, the tarot cards stopped spinning, floating casually onto the coffee table in a perfectly arranged stack, as though she'd done it a million times before. Twyla faced Mariah, a tired smile lifting the corner of her lips. She nodded toward Michael. "You better go."

Mariah glanced at him, then at Twyla. "I can stay as long as you need me."

Twyla shook her head. "No, you go. I'll be fine. I swear it. This," she gestured at Mariah, the cards, and toward the kitchen, "tonight…thank you. I'll call you if things get crazier than they are now." Twyla got to her feet and held out a hand to Mariah. "C'mon pregnant lady, let me help you up."

Mariah smiled and let Twyla help her, then pulled her into a tight hug. "If you need anything…anything…"

"I know." Twyla squeezed her extra tight then pushed her away. "Get home. Be safe."

Mariah gave Twyla a final once over. Twyla just shook her head. "I'm fine. Really." Mariah continued staring at her and Twyla laughed. "Geez, Mom, stop worrying. Okay?"

With the return of Twyla's spunk, Mariah felt like she could finally leave. Things weren't perfect, but they were getting better. As long as they were talking, they were going to be okay. "See you soon?" she asked casually as she walked toward Michael and the door.

"Not if I see you first."

Chapter Twelve

Skylar woke to soft, warm lips pressing kisses down her spine, mixed with the sandpaper rough feel of Dusty's unshaven jaw. Strong, masculine hands skimmed over her curves, stimulating her flesh with a warm buzz of euphoria. If only she could wake to this every morning. Then she smiled. Maybe she would.

Letting out a soft mewl of approval, she blinked her eyes open. Muted light filtered in through the closed vertical blinds. Not the light of dawn, but security lights flanking the apartment's exterior. A digital clock in the room switched from 2:11 to 2:12. Still the middle of the night.

After their shower—after they'd driven each other near senseless—they had stumbled to Dusty's bedroom, curled up together, and fallen immediately asleep. Skylar had never known such serenity as she found with her head resting on Dusty's chest, his muscular arms wrapped around her body, the strong beat of his heart a comforting rhythm.

Warm breath blew along the curve of her back and Skylar whimpered, fisting her hands into the soft sheets beneath her. Lying on her stomach, unable to see Dusty moving above her, caused a curious lustful anticipation. Her body, though still weak from sleep, called out in hot, wet need for him. Moisture pooled between her legs and she drew up on her knees and elbows, angling her hips, instinctively opening for Dusty, wanting him to take her again and again and again.

Fingers pressed deep into her hips, not hurting her, just holding her in place as he continued his slow perusal. His tongue flickered out, teasing the hollow at the base of her spine. Hoarsely she called out his name. Desperate. Wanting.

It was like a dream, his touches coming in slow motion. In her languid state, she ached for him to merge with her, complete her. Yet at the same time, she wanted the simple touches to last forever.

"It will, baby, I promise," Dusty's rough voice murmured from behind her. "I'm never gonna let you go."

Had she spoken her thoughts out loud? She blushed, able to feel her cheeks pinking in the darkness. Then she moaned as Dusty's large hands palmed her other cheeks, lifting and separating them, exposing the area wet with desire for him.

"So fucking beautiful, Skylar," he said reverently as he lowered his mouth to her pussy, tasting her with long, slow licks of his tongue.

If Dusty's hands hadn't held her in place, Skylar knew she would have collapsed after the first swipe of his tongue. He drew out each motion, taking his time, exploring every fold. She rocked against him, her entire body, from her toes to her fingertips, aroused.

Shimmering need thrummed through her like the deep primal pounding of a drum. Her body was no longer hers to control. Wanting to be wrapped in male heat, to feel the hard strokes of her man filling, taking, mating.

One hand trailed from her hip and joined his mouth in play. When two fingers breached her outer folds and slipped inside, Skylar gasped. The fingers of his other hand began circling her clitoris while his tongue continued drinking up all the cream her body offered. His fingers seemed to touch her everywhere at once with incredible dexterity, taking her places she'd never been before.

It was so good, too much sensation. Fingers, tongue, mouth, Dusty. She tossed her head, her tangled hair whipping around her. Sensation of a thousand bolts of lightning surged through her flesh as she cried out her orgasm.

Before the sensations had time to dull, Skylar felt Dusty's erect shaft poised and ready at her entrance. The thick head pushed through her swollen folds, the blood still pulsing hot against the walls of her vagina. Inch by thick inch he penetrated her, her cunt slick and ready for him to slide in to the hilt. But again he took his time, prolonging every moment, every luscious feeling, keeping her on the edge of climax.

After entering her completely, he paused and she tightened her sheath around him, rhythmically milking his cock. He let out a tight, low growl—a warning or perhaps a request?—before beginning a slow retreat.

This went on for what felt like hours, the slow glide in and out, touching every part of her. She relished every moment, the feel of coarse pubic hair against her ass when he was buried deep inside her, the smell of hot, clean sweaty male. He was hers. All hers.

Desperate to claim him, to continue this primal journey with her mate, she thrust back, taking his cock deep and deeper still against her womb. A groan ripped from his throat, urging her on. This time he met her movement with his own until as one they rocked and undulated together. Fast and sure he surged into her again and again and again, his balls slapping rhythmically against her clit.

She felt his orgasm coming, like a mental connection had been built between them allowing her access to all his sexual needs and wants. The room seemed to close in around them until nothing existed but him and her together as one.

The moment she felt his release—the swift pulsing of his cock inside her—and heard his ragged moans, she came harder than she ever had before. The room dimmed around her as her arms trembled and finally gave out and she collapsed onto the bed. Dusty moved with her, keeping them joined, the deep connection still echoing between them.

He draped himself over her back and she snuggled against him. "That was…it…" She paused, unable to put her feelings into words.

"I know." He kissed her neck, her hair.

"I didn't know it could be like that."

"Me either."

He withdrew his cock from her, removing the condom she didn't even remember him putting on. Then he returned, taking her back in his arms, pulling her onto his chest then laying the blankets over them both. One hand stroked her hair, his fingers playing with the tangled strands.

They hadn't used a condom last night. How many times had they made love? She wasn't an idiot, knew it only took one time to get pregnant. Was she ready for that? Was he? "Do you want to have kids?" she blurted out.

Dusty paused, uncertain how he could answer that question. With her, yes he wanted to have kids, if just to see her ripe with pregnancy, to watch her mother his children. But fatherhood scared him, the potential for the cycle of abuse to continue was a constant fear.

Before he could come up with an answer, she lifted her head and looked into his eyes. "Dusty, you will be a fantastic father. I know this. You are the warmest, sweetest, strongest man I have ever met. You are a protector and a provider and so full of love to offer. I can't imagine a better father for my children. So when you're ready, so am I, and I'll wait as long as you need me to."

It still amazed him the things she saw in him that he'd never seen in himself. "Wow. Thank you for having so much faith in me, but really, I'm not all that. My childhood…it wasn't perfect. And parts of it still haunt me to this day." Dusty looked into her eyes, imploring her to understand there was one demon from his past that he was still dealing with. "I am an alcoholic, but I have been sober for over two years. Two years, seven months, nineteen…no, twenty days."

"I know," she said, not an ounce of censure in her voice.

He was prepared for shock or dismay, but not this simple knowledge and acceptance. "You know?" he repeated.

"I still have Mariah's memories, remember?" She smiled. "Dusty, there isn't much you could say that would scare me away. Maybe it's crazy of me to feel that way since we only just met, but a year or a decade isn't going to change what I already know. Even without the knowledge I've gleaned from Mariah's memories, I've seen your soul, your heart. And they're beautiful. So don't think I'm going to run away because you have secrets in your past. We all do. That's what makes us human."

"God, I love you, Skylar." He wrapped his arms tighter around her, ready to sink himself fully inside her again. "But it goes a lot deeper than that. Mariah doesn't know my darkest secrets. The stuff that makes me worry about being a father. She doesn't know the whole picture. She probably thinks I started drinking with my friends. But it was my own mother. I drank with her so I could feel accepted. So that she'd love me instead of throwing things at me and my brother after my dad took off. But it didn't work—I never compared to the pleasure she got from her bottle. I've always tried to live beyond all that and be a better loving person, but I still worry about being a dad because I don't want to repeat even the smallest bit of the cycle."

"You told Mariah once that you were afraid of being a father. Dusty love, you aren't your parents. You've broken the cycle. You stopped drinking. That right there shows your strength." She lifted up on one elbow, one hand resting on his chest. "But I'll wait as long as you need. And I'll just tell you everyday how damn special you are until you believe me." Her eyes sparkled with love and devilish mischief.

"Dammit. There you go again, being the world's most wonderful woman, making me the world's luckiest man. You really are amazing. I—I…I don't even know what to say. I love you, Skylar. I will *always* love you. And I'll do my damnedest to be the man you see inside me."

He held her so tight he thought he would squeeze the air out of her lungs.

She squeezed him back. "Hey, I know what I want when I see it. I knew last night when I first woke up that I could trust you, even when I couldn't trust myself. Although part of it was Mariah's memories of you," she paused, a blush lighting up her face, "it was still more than that. I just *knew*."

"Wait, wait, wait a second. What's with all your skin turning bright red like we just stepped out of the shower? What the hell do you know that I don't and you're blushing about, huh?" He tapped her nose with one finger.

"Well," she squirmed. "I have Mariah's memories. A lot of them. And..."

"And you like them enough that you blush when you think of them? What the hell kind of memories have you got in that pretty little head of yours? Did Mariah watch a lot of porn or something? I mean, I know she was a stripper, but what's making you blush like that?"

"Ummm..." If possible, her blush grew an even brighter shade of red, but something else happened as well. Her nipples swelled and heat radiated from where her sweet pussy was pressed against his leg.

"What, you remember sex? Mariah and Stephan goin' at it all the time?" He ran a hand through her hair, then let it tease down her body.

She nodded, the blush of embarrassment fading into a flush of sexual excitement.

"And the memories enflame you, don't they?" He didn't need to ask. Her desire was obvious, the heat melting him and hardening him simultaneously. "Tell me what you remember," he whispered into her ear as he took the soft flesh of her lobe and tugged on it with his teeth.

She shivered and gasped, arching her body against his. He flipped them over so she lay on her back beneath him, her skin almost opalescent in the slivers of light filtering through the room. Her eyes were hooded, her breath coming out in soft pants. When her tongue peeked out between her lips, teasing at her bottom teeth, Dusty thought his dick was going to grow another six inches.

"I remember..." She mewled as he took a nipple into his mouth, rolling the taut bud on his tongue.

"What? What do you remember?" he asked before turning to her other breast. Curiosity overran his senses. Her sexual memories from

Mariah explained her enchanting mix of innocent and temptress. But what was it in particular that her mind remembered, but her body hadn't experienced until she was with him?

She tangled her fingers in his hair, holding her to him. "Dusty…you're making me forget…what I remember…"

He chuckled around her nipple. "Do you want me to stop?"

"No!"

"Then keep talking. I want to know what turns you on so hot your body's ready to come and we've barely gotten started."

"You do," she whispered. "The memories are just…just a…"

"Stimulant… It's okay, baby. There's nothing wrong with what turns you on."

She was quiet for a moment, and then her eyes fluttered shut. Her lips curled up in a soft smile. "My favorite memory of Mariah's is when you walked in on her and Stephan. The knowledge that someone was watching, someone else was excited because of what I—they—were doing…"

Her fingers pulled tighter on his hair as he tasted her stomach and hips. She arched restlessly beneath him, but continued talking, her voice husky. "It's strange, because I know how Mariah felt. I know how much she loves Stephan, but I also know how much it turned her on to see you watching them…"

"It turns you on, too." He slid a hand over her mound, enjoying the evidence of just how much it aroused her. She was so hot and wet that it almost killed him not to enter her. But he forced himself to wait, knowing the anticipation would heighten their pleasure.

She nodded. "But they're not just memories, Dusty. I can practically feel what she felt. I know what it's like to be Mariah with Stephan."

"Does he lick her like this?" Dusty traced her lips with his tongue. She sighed and opened her mouth, so warm and inviting beneath him. He continued kissing her, loving her.

"Does he touch her like this?" Skin brushed against skin as he lowered his body against hers. Her flesh was soft and warm. His cock slid easily through the moisture welling from her channel. Back and forth, back and forth until he was covered in her juices, trying to show her how much he needed her. "Is this what you remember?"

Blue eyes opened, focusing on his. "Dusty…no one touches me like you do. I have Mariah's memories, and although I know it's Stephan who is with her, in my mind, it's different…I can feel his cock slamming inside of me…can feel the harsh tugs of his fingers on my nipples…and even though I can see you watching, it's still you inside me…not him…all I want is you…I love you…"

She cried out as Dusty easily thrust himself inside her, mimicking her words. One hand fondled her breasts as he increased the speed of his movements. He'd nearly come just listening to her softly spoken words, so when her body trembled beneath his, he shattered, spending himself inside her.

Their bodies still trembled as they held each other, sleep creeping over them like the thick fog of a San Francisco morning. Dusty's last thought before dreaming was that he'd forgotten to tell Skylar that Mariah was her cousin.

Something to talk about tomorrow…

Still lost in dreams, Dusty barely noticed when Skylar slipped out of bed. From a distance, he heard the bathroom door close, water running. Time passed, not long before he heard her walk back into the room.

His eyes flashed open at the sharp, stinging pain. "Skylar?!"

Then the world went black.

* * * * *

"Are you cold?"

There was no response.

Suppressing a curse, Marlin watched Ana out of the corner of his eye as they patrolled in the older, industrial part of town. They'd been working together for half the night, and she hadn't said more than a dozen words to him.

"I said, are you cold?" He waited, hoping she'd give him a dissertation on just how cold she was. All he wanted was for her to talk to him, it didn't even matter what they talked about.

"I'm fine," she replied, then belied that notion by shivering and snuggling deeper into her leather jacket. Shit. What the hell happened to the trust they'd shared? Neither sweet talk nor harassing got anything more than three words out of her. Stephan was going to kick his ass if he didn't fix whatever was broken between them.

When Stephan gave the orders that Ana would team with Marlin during tonight's patrol rounds, there was a very clear motive behind it. Everyone had noticed the thick tension between Marlin and Ana, and it had to stop. The Shadow Walkers could not have any more problems within their organization. They needed to be strong and completely united.

"Should we cut through this alley or the one on the next block?"

"I don't care. It doesn't really matter." Shrugging her shoulders, she kept walking.

Looking almost unfortunately damn sexy in her black denim and leather, her long wavy red hair loosely tied back with a leather strip, and all Marlin wanted was to get her to talk like they used to. Well, maybe that wasn't all he wanted to do. If he'd felt it would be okay, he'd pin her to the wall and kiss her until she remembered how they used to make out on the rocks near the cave and share their deepest darkest secrets while the waves crashed onto the sand and spray blew in their faces.

There was a whole world of stuff he wanted to share with her. But this quiet Ana was not the girl he used to know. The woman next to him looked over her shoulder every ten minutes and stared into the shadows as though willing them alive.

"Okay, then, let's just turn here and take Twenty-eighth Street instead." He turned to her and bit his tongue to avoid going off on her for being so damn terse all night. In his pause, he took a breath and searched for something else to say. "Do you think we should stick to the industrial end tonight or go through some residential, too?"

"Doesn't matter."

What was up with her? They'd never held back before. Twelve years was a long time, but Marlin certainly hadn't forgotten about her and his feelings for her hadn't dulled. What they'd had wasn't earth-shattering love, but it was just as powerful.

When he abruptly turned down an alley, she looked all around, apparently to see if he was going to attack something. Truthfully, he did wish that there was some kind of creepy-crawly to obliterate just so he could let go of some frustration. He wanted his Ana back, the girl who was always on the same wavelength with him, who could match his movements without a word passing between them.

After years of friendship and counseling each other when wickedness overshadowed goodness, it had hurt deeply to lose Ana the day after they had bared both souls and bodies, making love for the first time. That night, they'd escaped death together and desperately needed someone to cling to. The natural choice was each other. When her mom had whisked her out of Talisman Bay, Marlin felt she'd taken a piece of him with her.

He had always assumed Ana would come back, that The Order would make her fulfill her destiny along with the rest of the Talisman Bay Shadow Walkers. He just hadn't anticipated twelve years would pass before her return.

Now that the time had come, he'd expected to see more of her. He'd thought they would resume the close friendship they'd had before she left. Not necessarily the sex, although he wouldn't have minded.

"I thought we were going to cut across on Twenty-eighth," Ana said, interrupting his musings. It was the longest sentence she'd spoken all night.

"I changed my mind. I thought maybe there'd be something down here. I killed a Crayken here a couple weeks ago." He glanced at her. She still only looked at him out of the corner of her eye. Dammit.

What he missed was the girl he could just kiss and talk to for hours without any expectations. The one who always loved to hear his stories about the girls he dated, who offered advice about what a woman wanted both in and out of bed. The girl who kissed his forehead and smiled at him like she gave a damn, and who was honest with him when no one else would be. Hell, he hadn't even told her about Judy. If anyone in the world were capable of understanding the kind of joy and pain he'd felt, it would be Ana. But since she came back, she avoided anything that had to do with him. Apparently it wasn't on her list of priorities to ask him how he'd been. Openly talking with Twyla last night had made him realize what he'd missed about his friendship with Ana.

Maybe Twyla's ultra-forward, get-in-Ana's-face-and-ask-her-what-the-hell-is-going-on tactic would work. Nothing else seemed to.

Marlin abruptly stopped patrolling, stopped walking, hell, he was prepared to stop breathing if it meant that Ana would actually tell him what was really going on between them.

She turned and faced him, an eyebrow raised. "What? Why are you stopping?" She looked around as though she was about to be jumped by a demon. "Where is it?" She even looked up. "Okay, I'm not seeing it, Marlin. And this isn't the first time you've stopped for no reason. What the hell's your problem?"

"No, what the hell is your problem? Me, I'm just pissed that it takes patrol orders to get you to even come close to me and now that you are, you won't hardly talk to me." He stood there, asking with his eyes that she confide in him.

Restlessly, she placed her hands in her pockets...going for the comfort of her weapons perhaps? She threw a quick glance over her shoulder before facing him, but didn't meet his gaze. Her eyes gave her away, though. She wasn't going to give in. She was going to keep fighting whatever *it* was between them rather than just telling him what was on her mind.

Being this close to her and seeing just how profoundly this...thing...was bothering her made him wonder if maybe he'd hurt her in some horrible way. She wasn't afraid to be around him, but she was definitely afraid to talk to him. Was she afraid of saying the wrong thing? The right thing? *Dammit all to hell.* Marlin swore he'd never fall into any kind of caring situation with a woman ever again. There'd be less pain for both parties involved.

Frustrated, Marlin jerked a hand through his hair. "And why the hell do you keep looking behind you like that? Not a single ghoul, wraith or hellion has attacked from behind all night. I'm worried about you, Ana. I really am. I miss the honesty we had. This is rippin' me up."

Ana sighed and looked over her shoulder again. "I've always felt like I'm being watched. It's nothing new. Like someone or something's gonna jump out of the shadows and claim me for good or evil." She stepped closer. "You really don't need to worry about me, Marlin. I've just had a lot on my mind since I got back."

"You can share with me. I'll trade some of what's on my mind if you trade what's on yours."

The corners of Ana's mouth tilted upward in a small smile. "Like the good ol' days... Wasn't that how we ended up in bed the night we became Shadow Walkers?"

So, she hadn't completely blocked their past from her mind. He resisted the urge to kiss her and hold her and tell her that whatever was wrong in her world, he'd make right. But he knew that if he did anything of the sort, she'd likely push him even further away. "Yeah, but now that I know if I sleep with you, you'll disappear the next day, I don't think I wanna take that risk again. I mean, where the hell did you go for twelve years? Why didn't you come back to me?"

He knew he'd said too much before the words were even completely out of his mouth. It was subtle, a change in the air between them. Dammit! He should've waited until he knew she was ready to talk to him. Now, she was going to pull away from him again.

The small smile tilting up Ana's full lips disappeared as she turned back around and started walking. He followed sharply, not wanting her to think she'd won just yet. There was no way he'd let her push him out that easily.

She surprised him when she spoke. "I guess the real question is where haven't I been? I kept moving, looking for...something...someone maybe? I don't know. Maybe just trying to figure out where I belong. I never found it, though." She crossed her arms over her breasts and continued staring straight ahead.

Marlin nodded. They were still so much alike. He matched her stride and lowered his voice, wanting—needing—to share with her, too. "Sometimes I wonder if I even belong here doing what I'm doing. If it wasn't for all the demon mayhem that we knock out every night, I'd swear that The Order was a crock of shit and that I along with the rest of us actually did die in the fire instead of being changed. Like we're just undead and doomed to walk in the shadows for all eternity. Hell, maybe you were better off wandering around in your endless search. At least you got out of here and kept looking."

This time, Ana stopped walking and faced him. "But Marlin, there's a difference. In Talisman Bay, you hunt demons. You know what they are, that they're gonna try to kill you and the rest of the human race or...or...whatever other mischief they're gonna do. I was hunting something that I couldn't even fathom. And it doesn't help that the whole time I was running, I was actually trying to erase all the guilt I felt." She let out a sharp exhale, her hands clenching and unclenching as though she was trying to regain control of her emotions. Then she turned and started walking again.

Marlin didn't move, the shock holding him at a standstill. "What the hell do you have to feel guilty for?"

Ana froze, but didn't turn around. She took a deep breath and looked up into the night sky. Her voice seemed distant, as though she was reliving the words as she spoke them. "For twelve years I thought I was the reason why we became Shadow Walkers. David and I..." She shook her head, a shiver wracking her body. "I was an idiot and fell for his seductive lies. I slept with him a week before…a week before everything happened. And he scared the shit out of me. Marlin, I *knew* he was evil but I was too scared to tell anyone. I mean…God, I didn't know *how* to tell anyone. David was supposed to be our friend! He seemed to think he owned me after that one fuck, and when I told him to get lost, I could tell I'd pissed him off. So when he tried to kill us…when he killed Fiero…I thought it was because of me. I don't know. Maybe I was the reason."

He closed the distance between them, aching to comfort her. "Sweetheart, no. Don't do that to yourself. It was not your fault at all. Ana…you should've come back. I wish you hadn't left. I missed you so much." He stood behind her, his chest an inch away from her back, and laid his hand on her shoulder. He wanted to spin her around into his embrace, but out of fear, held back. She looked at his hand and he almost pulled it away. He just didn't want to scare her.

His heart was set a bit at ease when she stepped backward, resting against him. He slid his hand down her arm and she let out a quiet sigh. "I wanted to come back, Marlin, but…" She turned to face him. With eyes wide, she hollered, "Watch out!"

Ana slammed Marlin aside against the back of the building. He'd already gone for his .45 but hadn't squeezed the trigger. Catching a glimpse of the scaly beast, he swapped his .45 into his left hand and grabbed his Mancation special, a gun built by The Order specifically to take out Roidican and other armor plated demons.

Roidicans preferred human males for sparring into eventual mutilation. After two shots from his .45, Marlin had to hold off from using his Mancation because he couldn't get a clear shot. Ana had wrestled the beast to the ground. It was writhing and fighting so quickly that Marlin could only use the Mancation on its extremities without fear of hurting Ana in the crossfire. He took off one of its three hands as it grabbed for Ana in its frenzy.

She clicked-in. *Marlin, will you just kill this pissant before it kills me with its extreme bad breath?*

You're covering too much. Roll left, we'll combine.

She did as recommended, but the Roidican launched itself at Marlin, knocking him to the ground before he could get out any more than three apparently ineffective shots from each gun. Marlin felt as though he was being pelted with rocks as the thing bashed against him.

I see what you mean about the breath. Get this fucker off me. I don't wanna be a flattened punching bag.

The Roidican burst into flames, incinerating as Marlin rolled away, landing next to the building. He'd never seen a demon ignite like that. He looked up at Ana. "Holy shit. How'd you do that? Light its tail like a fuse or something?"

As he spoke, he noticed fire burning along the palm of her right hand before she slowly curled her fingers, extinguishing the flames. *Hot damn!* Ana was a firestarter? Just how many secrets was she hiding?

She knelt next to Marlin, her fiery hair in reckless disarray, breasts heaving and tempting to fall out of the rips in her skintight tank top. "Something like that." Ana's jeans were frayed from the waistband to one side of her crotch, exposing delicious skin and a few thick red curls that his hand ached to explore.

"You okay?" he asked as his gaze roamed her body, looking for any injuries.

Marlin started as she touched him through a tear in his T-shirt, her fingers unnaturally warm. She lifted her face, the need in her eyes capturing and pulling him in. Marlin had to hold her, connect with her.

There in the deserted alley, Marlin slid his hand under Ana's torn tank top. He cupped her breasts, toying with her erect nipples. A ragged moan provided encouragement and in one swift maneuver, he took a firm hold of the rip in her tank top and tore downward, revealing her deliciously tight stomach and the breasts which he had to take within his mouth's possession. Marlin laved her nipple, bringing forth another deep, lingering moan from Ana's throat.

Before he could taste her further, Ana pulled away and shrugged out of her jacket, letting it crumple to the ground. Naked from the waist up, she was even more breathtaking than he remembered, her red hair falling in frantic waves over creamy shoulders, perfect rosebud nipples tightening and darkening, matching the same color of her hair. But there were differences in her appearance as well. Even in the shadowed darkness, Marlin could see a tattoo curling around her upper arm. Extremely detailed, it appeared to be of ancient design. He reached out to trace it with his fingers. "What does it mean?"

"I don't know." Her eyes pleaded. "Marlin, please...I...I need you..." She leaned into him, pulling the tattered remains of his T-shirt away and lowering her breasts to his naked flesh. The sensuality of her taut nipples rubbing against his chest elicited an overwhelming need to have all of her skin pressed hard against his.

His hands worked their way downward, clearing what little was left of the waist of her jeans and massaging her skin until his fingers intermingled with the already damp curls between her legs. She arched and moved her hips in time with his touch, her need so desperate he could feel it thick and heavy in the air around them. Had she been just as desirous of their connection as he was?

He trailed his tongue along her collarbone and up her neck, tasting the salty-sweetness of her skin. It had been too long since he'd held Ana this way. When he reached her lips, he paused and took his time, tugging on each one, tasting the corners of her mouth. But Ana didn't want it slow. She tangled her tongue with his, kissing him with flaring intensity as she freed his throbbing cock from the confinement of his jeans.

His fingers, now damp from her slick arousal, rubbed back over her clit. He listened to her soft moans of need while she rocked against him, using her reactions to guide his movements. More wetness slid down her thighs, an invitation he couldn't deny. He breached her opening with one finger, then two, slowly gliding them in and out of her pretty pussy. She'd opened a precious part of herself to him and he'd sooner die than not give her body what it needed.

Her body trembled, her pussy clamping around him. Near frantic, she pulled away from his questing fingers and pushed him back toward the wall, straddling him. "I'm on the pill." She answered his question before he could even ask it, then shoving torn denim aside, impaled herself on his cock, both of them moaning at their incredibly desperate connection.

He rocked his hips against her rhythm. He hoped she would understand that his body was hers for the taking. To connect with her, giving her a few minutes of release from what troubled her. He held her need high above any other.

As she worked his cock with her amazingly tight sheath, he massaged her ass through the tattered denim. Their tongues danced within each other's mouths as wildly as their bodies undulated. Her full breasts spilled against his chest, sensitizing him to the heat of her body, urging him to give more of himself than he was in control of.

Yet somehow he knew she was holding back. She responded to every touch, moaned into his mouth, but her body was tight, almost rigid and unforgiving. Her fingers were curled into his shoulders, not a lover's caress, but as though she was afraid if she let go, he'd disappear.

Separating their mouths, he watched her moving above him. Tears dampened the corners of her closed eyes. Stroking a hand down her face, he whispered, "It's okay, Ana. Let go," then leaned in and kissed her softly.

She let out a quiet cry and he felt the blissful beginnings of her orgasm spasming through her sheath. Knowing she was right there on the edge, he let himself lose his last ounce of control to bring both of their bodies to release.

Waves of ecstasy washed over him as his come spurted within her, mingling among her wet heat.

The only thing he wished was that she could use words to speak to him as easily as her body did. Even though she was worth the wait, he didn't want another twelve years to drag by before they connected again.

Chapter Thirteen

"Okay sweetheart, for breakfast we've got cocoa puffs, a chocolate bagel with chocolate cream cheese, and a tall glass of chocolate milk." Stephan set the cocoa-laden breakfast of pregnant champions on the kitchen table in front of Mariah. Her mouth nearly foamed in delight. "Is there anything else I can get for you? Maybe an insulin shot when your body goes into a sugar coma?"

She sighed in pure chocolate contentment as she took her first bite. Then her second. Her mouth was too full to bother replying to Stephan's poor choice of humor at her expense. She just raised her eyebrow and gave him "the look" while she took several more bites.

A very wide grin covered his face. He leaned down and kissed the top of her head. "I love you," he said, then turned as Fiero began to materialize next to the refrigerator.

Before he had even fully shimmered into corporeal form, Fiero was striding across the kitchen toward both of them. Her laughter faded as a tingle of foreboding shot down her spine.

Stephan stood up. "What's up? This doesn't look like a social call."

"I learned some stuff about Skylar. Is she here?"

Stephan shook his head. "No. She's with Dusty at his apartment."

Fiero nodded. "Okay. I tried clicking-in to him. Guess he's sleeping."

"What did you learn about Skylar?" Mariah interjected. The foreboding turned into a gnawing ache in her stomach. Maybe it was all the chocolate, but she didn't think so.

Fiero leaned down, splaying his fingertips on the tabletop. His gaze shot between Mariah and Stephan. "Skylar's not your cousin."

"What?" Mariah and Stephan said simultaneously and Fiero held up one hand in a "hold-off" gesture.

"Biologically, Skylar is your cousin. Your father's brother's wife gave birth to her. But genetically, she's your twin."

"How the—" Stephan started.

"I don't know exactly. Look, Themonius didn't even know. What he told you yesterday he believed to be the truth. Someone more powerful than The Order, Fate or…someone…something…they put a back-up plan in place. Gave Mariah a twin, a sister, but planted her in another woman's womb. If Mariah were to be killed, the prophecy could still live on in Skylar."

"Then she's a Shadow Walker like Mariah," Stephan concluded.

"And she's in just as much danger as I am," Mariah stated, the implications hitting her faster than the realization that she had a sister. "If David discovers this information…"

Mariah turned toward Stephan, to ask him to click-in to Dusty, to warn him of the further danger Skylar faced. Stephan had that far off look he often had when he was clicked-in. Good, maybe he was already talking to Dusty.

"Dusty's still not responding." Stephan paused again, and the minute he was quiet felt like hours to Mariah. The foreboding was growing, expanding, until Mariah felt like she was going to crawl out of her skin if she couldn't do something to make it stop. This was one of those times she wished she could click-in. As a Shadow Walker, the ability was inside her, but like everything else it required training. A training she hadn't bothered worrying about yet.

She blew out a frustrated breath and waited for Stephan or Fiero to update her. "Jake's headed over to Dusty's," Stephan informed her. "Just as a precaution. He'll be there in a few minutes. I'm sure everything's fine."

But Mariah could tell he was worried too. Deep furrows lined his forehead and his body was tight and anxious. He glanced at Fiero. "Any other news?"

Fiero shook his head. "Isn't this enough?"

The three of them turned as the door from the stairway opened and a laughing Marlin and Ana stepped through. Their laughter came to an abrupt halt as their gazes landed on the worried group.

"Uh-oh. What's up?" Marlin asked.

"More Skylar surprises," Stephan said as he walked around the table toward them. "And Dusty's not responding to a click-in."

"Well it is still early and he sleeps like a log," Marlin replied. "He hasn't slept much the last couple days."

"Still, anything out of the ordinary happen last night?" Stephan inquired.

"Normal patrol rounds, Marlin nearly got his ass kicked by a Roidican, nothing special." Ana tossed Marlin a grin. "But we didn't see Dusty, either."

Stephan held up a hand to stop them from talking. "Wait. Jake made it to Dusty's..."

His eyes narrowed and he uttered only one word.

"Shit."

* * * * *

The delicious fragrance of freshly brewed coffee, crisp bacon and sweet maple syrup woke Skylar from a deep, dreamless sleep. Keeping her eyes closed, she stretched languidly under the heavy blankets, deeply inhaling the scents of a homemade, energy-inspiring breakfast. Her man was a keeper. He kept her warm, happy and sated all night long, then cooked her breakfast in the morning. What more could she ask for?

Muffled footsteps crossed the carpet toward her and the bed shifted beneath his weight. With a smile—and hoping she didn't have too hearty of morning breath so she could greet her lover properly—Skylar opened her eyes...

And screamed.

It wasn't Dusty leaning over ready to wake her with a smile and a kiss, but the bastard who had taken her away from her life before.

Not again...not again!

Desperate to get away from him, she rolled backward out of bed, jumping to her feet and facing her worst nightmare.

He looked...different. Dark circles shadowed his bloodshot eyes and his clothes were rumpled, like he'd slept in them last night. What had happened to the perfectly put-together David she was used to seeing? Was this part of his game, too?

"Where the hell is Dusty? What did you do to him?" she growled. If David had hurt Dusty, nothing could stop her from ripping the bastard apart. Her entire body boiled over, shaking in anger.

But as she glared at David, she made a startling revelation. This wasn't Dusty's apartment and that wasn't the bed she'd fallen asleep in last night. This was the place from her memories…Mariah's memories, shit, she didn't even know which memories they were anymore. This was the room where Dusty had first found her. She was back in David's house. But how had this happened? When? How long had she been here?

Jesus, was she losing her mind? For one moment she was afraid…afraid that she'd made up Dusty, that the last couple days were only a figment of an imagination desperate for some type of escape.

Scared and unsure, wondering if anything would ever make sense again, she wrapped her arms around herself, feeling soft cotton beneath her fingertips. A T-shirt. Lifting it to her nose, she inhaled. Dusty's T-shirt.

Memories from last night flitted through her consciousness. Waking up with a desperate need to use the bathroom. Sliding out of Dusty's arms while he still slept, grabbing a rumpled T-shirt off the floor to battle the chill, stepping into the bathroom…

Then nothing but blackness. So reminiscent of the first time she'd been captured.

"What did you do to Dusty?" she repeated through clenched teeth.

A warning buzzed low in her abdomen as David spoke. "What I had to—"

"No!" Hands fisted, she threw herself at David, pummeling him. Tears of rage, of fear, poured down her cheeks. Not Dusty! "You bastard! I'll kill you for this!"

David surrounded her, pinning her arms to her sides. She struggled uselessly against him. "Shhh…Skylar. Shhh…" Still holding her tightly, he lifted and carried her to the bed, sitting down with her on his lap. He stroked a hand down her hair and back, letting out a troubled sigh. "Dusty will be fine. I just needed him out of the way for a while. I'm sorry it had to go this far, but some things are beyond even my control."

"Who are you trying to fool?" she snarled. She couldn't let the sincerity in his voice mislead her. "You've ripped me away from my life twice now, turned me into someone I'm not and you dare tell me you're sorry? Screw you," she spit out.

David flinched. Shock rippled through Skylar's system. He had flinched? What the hell was going on?

"This is bigger than you and me, Skylar. We're both just playing our many roles." He wiped a hand down his face, rubbing his bloodshot eyes.

This situation, this David, none of it made sense. He'd always had such a commanding presence, but at this moment he was acting afraid, vulnerable, even somewhat fragile. His demeanor was hard to place, foreign to everything she knew about him. It was as though his control was teetering on the edge of either a confession or condemnation. She pushed her advantage, hoping to retrieve some information she could use against him later. A name connected to David's past jumped into her memory. "Is it the Dread Lords? Are they behind this?"

He chuckled, but it sounded lifeless. "The Dread Lords are nothing but a small-minded operation. There is so much more to this, don't you see? It is all part of a deeper source of power than mere Truth."

Although she didn't understand his riddles, she knew she needed to keep him talking, hoping he'd say something that would make some sense. "What do they want with me?"

He shuffled her off his lap, placing her next to him on the bed. His shoulders slumped, hands resting on his knees. His voice was quiet, weary, as he began to speak. "It started out as a simple switch. You for Mariah." He cast a glance in her direction, but didn't turn his head, seemingly afraid to look her in the eye. "I made you believe that you—as Mariah—had been abused, to create confusion and buy time. And to make Stephan look bad in Talisman Bay society. But things didn't go quite as planned."

"You mean your plans were ruined when Dusty rescued me."

"Dusty and Twyla." He shook his head, an amused grin lifting the corners of his pinched lips. "Twyla...she continues to amaze me. I won't underestimate her again. But she wasn't the only one I underestimated. If only we'd discovered the truth about you earlier..."

"What truth?" Skylar asked on a mere whisper. Excitement and a twinge of fear made her tremble.

"Mariah's twin sister..." He shook his head. "Not that it matters anymore. Plans have changed. Hell, you've changed."

Skylar bit her lip to keep from shouting at him to tell her more. She was Mariah's sister? How? A part of her wanted to deny it, yet she knew he wasn't lying. Not because she had any reason to trust him but because she just *knew*.

Turning to face him, she caught him watching her. His eyes were a mixture of darkness and light as he studied her intently. Suddenly the deeper realization hit her. "But if I'm Mariah's sister…"

At her utterance, his dark eyes sparked maliciously, all traces of vulnerability disappearing from his demeanor. Skylar shivered and subtly moved an inch away from him. With one lightning quick movement, his hand clamped down on her knee, painfully holding her in place. "The prophecy has changed and I need to verify your place in it. So do you stay or do you go? Is it more prudent for you to return to Providence, to forget your life here? Or do I let you stay and love Dusty?" He smiled, and all light seemed to retreat from the room. "Maybe I'll keep you instead. The possibilities are endless."

"You're not in control of my destiny," Skylar ground out.

"We'll see about that," and before she could struggle, his lips were fastened over hers.

* * * * *

Playing dominoes with Skylar is my favorite pastime.

What do you mean you ran out of Kool-Aid? I thought that's all you have here.

Skylar was supposed to bring some to the park, but she's *gone* tobogganing instead.

Skylar? I love her. She's wonderful.

Trouble. Lots of trouble.

What? Damn, I've got a headache. What did you say?

You are in too *deep*. Are you deaf? *You* should *go*.

Why?

Because *Skylar's* there and she really *needs you* because she's *crazy* in love with you and—

She's here with me and I'll love her forever.

Wake up! There's work to be done. We can't *find Skylar* a pineapple.

Wake up!

"Wake up! Dusty!" Jake's voice permeated the cacophonous din in Dusty's skull as loud banging came from somewhere nearby.

Get your eyes open, Dusty!

Dammit, Dusty. Wake the fuck up! Where the hell is Skylar?

Dusty managed to get his eyes open but nothing was making sense. There were voices in his head. They sounded urgent. Hell, they also sounded like Stephan. And Jake sounded like he was close by, but was he clicked-in?

Clicked-in. Is Stephan clicked-in to me? Jake's clicked-in? What?

Glass shattered all over the room as Jake came crashing through the window. Dusty jumped out of bed, incredulous, and promptly lost his balance, falling against the wall. He tried to scramble back to his feet, unsure whether he was being attacked by friend or foe, but certain there was a huge problem because Jake never broke anything when he entered.

"Dusty! Holy shit, man. What the hell happened, buddy? You okay? We've been trying to get to you and you wouldn't wake up. You're scarin' me." Jake hoisted Dusty up.

Dusty blinked. That was all he could do. He knew something was real bad somehow, but he couldn't make heads or tails of it or even find the right muscles to move. There was broken glass everywhere.

You gonna make it? What's going on? Stephan's voice held incredible worry. *I know you're there, Dusty. Come on. You gotta tell me what you need. I can't help you unless you help me. Do you know where Skylar is? We just learned that she's actually Mariah's twin sister. You gotta tell us where she is. Talk to me, man.*

Dusty's alive, but there's somethin' wrong with him. Jake paused. *It's like he's fuckin' drunk. He's awake, but he's not responding to me. And Skylar's not here. I dunno what happened but it doesn't look good.* Jake's voice was in Dusty's head, too. How did that happen? And who was drunk? Nobody drank around him anymore.

"Dusty? What happened to Skylar? What happened after I left you two here last night? I thought you guys were good. Did she leave you? You need to tell us what happened. Dammit! Hello? You there, man? Your eyes are open, but are you seeing me?" Jake waved his hand in front of Dusty's face. He squinted and tried to focus on Jake's three very concerned heads. Why did he keep mentioning Skylar? Where was she? That's right, she went to the bathroom…

Jake's heads disappeared and Dusty rubbed his blurry eyes. Suddenly, a pair of jeans and a T-shirt were thrust in his face and Dusty figured he should probably put them on, but he wasn't entirely sure why.

Stephan's voice once again blared in his head. *Bring him to the compound for Fiero. And keep tryin' to get him talkin' about Skylar.*

While pulling up his jeans, Dusty shook his head, attempting to clear a fog that wasn't easily lifting. Skylar was taking a long time in the restroom. Maybe she wanted him to join her in the shower. Hot water. Hot Skylar.

Jake brought a pair of boots and Dusty sat back down on the chair to put them on. Everything was hazy. If Jake hadn't leaned down to tie Dusty's boots, he would have just given up and stuffed the laces inside. Dusty slid on his T-shirt and shook his head again. The fog was not nearly as dense as it had been.

But what was he forgetting?

Jake helped him up and they took two steps before something crunched beneath his boot. He looked down and saw a crushed syringe.

Images of Skylar limply flung over Craze's shoulder as he stabbed the needle into Dusty's thigh. Trying to reach out to Skylar or punch Craze. Everything going black just before he could click-in to the guys.

Click-in. Find the words. Talk. Find the words.

C'mon man, talk to me. I gotta know what happened to you. Where's Skylar? Stephan had remained clicked-in but Dusty couldn't find a way to reply. All he could think about was Skylar in that evil bastard's clutches. All he could think about was finding her.

Before Dusty was aware of leaving the building, he was in Jake's car, but they weren't heading toward David's house to get Skylar. They were headed toward the compound. "No!" Dusty found his voice to shout as he pointed across Jake's face. "David. Now!"

Jake glanced over at Dusty, then turned the car in the direction that Dusty had pointed out. "You comin' back to us, buddy? Talk to me."

"Craze. The needle. David. Skylar." Dusty managed to formulate a few words as he fought mind-over-matter to gain control of himself.

Jake had told Stephan that Dusty was acting drunk. But he wasn't. Didn't. "I didn't drink. It was Craze. Set me up. Took Skylar." He didn't know what was thicker, the fog or all the red. "I'm gonna bust his fucking skull in."

"You'll get your chance, man. I'm takin' ya there, but you gotta get a hold of yourself. Can you even see straight yet?"

The anger pulsing through him helped dissipate his mind's fog and made his words fly out clear and sharp. "I can see well enough to beat down his door and take back what he stole from me. I don't need to see anything else." Dusty gritted his teeth as more feeling returned to his body. Random parts of him tingled and a few more were sore.

Talk to me, guys. What the fuck is going on!? Stephan persisted.

Jake replied before Dusty could figure out how to get his click-in connection functioning properly again. *Shit, sorry. Dusty's good to go. Craze took Skylar and fucked Dusty up. We're almost to Craze's.* "Well damn, Dusty. Looks like Marlin's already there." Jake nodded toward Marlin's car parked where Dusty had left it the day before.

"No, he isn't. And don't tell him I left his car there yesterday when I was lookin' for Skylar."

Jake snorted. "Well, shit. You were a day early."

Jake was taking too long to park his damn car. Dusty pitched himself out of the still-moving car almost drunkenly. Skylar needed him. He gained his balance as he charged toward Craze's door. Jake's hollering was only heard in some distant corner of Dusty's mind. "Get your fucking ass back here. Wait for backup! You tryin' to get yourself killed?"

Raising his fist, ready to waste the door into oblivion, Dusty watched the brass knocker shake. His punch swished unobstructed through the air as the door was opened by Craze.

"Hello, Dusty. Three times in three days. Maybe I should just give you a key."

Dusty wrested himself upright as the force of his punch took him over the threshold and past Craze. Whipping about, Dusty readied himself for an attack.

But the man just stood there, his hands in his pockets, a snide grin on his face. Craze looked…different. Far from put-together. And it wasn't just the black eye Stephan had given him. Craze's clothes were rumpled, his eyes bloodshot…for once his looks matched his name. Almost like he was slowly losing control.

"Where is she?" Dusty demanded.

"Shhh… She's resting." Craze lifted a finger to his lips, illustrating his words. "I'm sure she'll be down soon." His demeanor was too relaxed, too comfortable, and it pissed Dusty off even more.

"What the hell did you do to her? Why is she here?" Dusty growled as he advanced toward Craze.

"I needed to confirm my suspicions about her. Things are changing, the prophecy is evolving…" He shrugged. "She is of no use to me anymore."

"No *use*? You fucking bastard! You stole an innocent woman's life—"

"And you stole her innocence. Who's the real *fucking* bastard here?"

Dusty landed his fist squarely under Craze's jaw then hooked upward, knocking him backward against the wall. But it wasn't enough. He launched himself at Craze, the rage taking over.

Two strong arms grabbed him from behind, pulling Dusty away from his prey. "Don't, Dusty," Stephan said harshly as he hauled Dusty backward. "I want to kill him, too, but we can't. Not like this. Who do you think would be the first one questioned if he were found dead? Not to mention Jake and Marlin's cars are out front. We'd be setting ourselves up."

Craze stood up, rubbing his jaw, but his smile didn't falter. "Now if only you'd realized that at the ball the other night. The past few days haven't been a complete waste. I may not have gotten Mariah, but I did get something I wanted. My brother is no longer the golden boy of Talisman Bay society."

"But you didn't get what you really wanted, now did you, David," Skylar said calmly as she walked down the stairs wearing nothing but a T-shirt that fell to mid-thigh.

Crossing the room, Dusty pulled her into his arms, inhaling her sweet scent, wanting to caress every inch of her to make sure she was okay. "Skylar, did he hurt you?"

"No, but I'm sure he wanted to when he realized he couldn't use me like he planned." She kissed him. "I love you. Things are going to be better now. I know this…" She pulled out of his embrace and stepped toward Craze.

"You say you have no use for me anymore? Isn't it more that you can't control me? I'm not the pliable weak puppet you thought I was. You can't climb into my mind and make me do things I don't want to do." She stepped closer to Craze while Dusty shadowed her every move. And it wasn't even really about protecting her. Skylar was every bit strong enough to fight this battle. He just didn't want to miss a moment of her getting her punches in.

Stephan watched from the sidelines, a look of intent interest on his face.

"It took you two months to get me to believe I was Mariah. Two months of daily mind torture. And you still couldn't control me. Not really. You made me believe I was someone else, you put outside memories into my head, but you couldn't *make* me act a certain way. You couldn't control my reactions. You couldn't make me betray the Shadow Walkers and you couldn't get to Mariah through me. All that time you spent, all the effort you put into manipulating me, and nothing. Did that bother you? Did it drive you just a little bit crazier to know that my mind was that strong?"

Craze lifted a hand toward her face, and Dusty reacted immediately, pulling Skylar out of his reach. Smirking, Craze said, "You are most definitely Mariah's sister. The similarities go beyond the physical. Her strength lies in her eyes, yours in your mind. I should have recognized it earlier, but Fate hid her plans well. But the ride was fun now, wasn't it? I would have loved exploring your mind a bit more, but Mariah and you are no longer my primary concern. Things are changing in Talisman Bay. Having you here makes things a lot more interesting. I'm looking forward to seeing how this little drama plays out."

Craze stepped past everyone, dismissing them as he placed a hand high on the edge of his opened door. "Now that you've gotten what you came for, it's time to leave. Stephan, shouldn't you be at home tending your woman? I'm going to be an uncle soon—"

"You will have no part in my child's life." Stephan's words were spat like venom.

"Funny, that's what I hoped your mom would've said to my dad." David lounged against the door.

This time it was Dusty who held Stephan back. "Remember what you told me. He's still gonna be an asshole even after you deck him."

"He lost," Skylar said dismissively as she turned her back on David. She tucked her hand in Dusty's. "Let's go home."

The trio walked out the door, leaving David behind them. His quiet words echoed after them. "I always win, one way or another."

David's yard had become a Shadow Walker meeting place. Marlin, one hand in his jacket, probably on his .38, Jake crouched near a window looking ready to hop up on the side of the house, Ryan with hands in pockets, switchblades ready to strike, Ana, hands fisted at her sides, eyes full of angry fire. The entire crew had come out in force, prepared to do whatever necessary to get Skylar back.

Jake jogged by. "You must be cold. Let me get a blanket from my car."

Dusty pulled Skylar to him. "Shit. You got goosebumps. Do you even have anything on under that shirt?" He ran his hands up and down her arms.

"I'm fine." She smiled up at him. "I don't think I'll ever take this shirt off."

Dusty gave her a questioning stare.

"David tried to wipe my memories again, tried to see if he could turn me into Mariah. But he couldn't, because of you."

Jake interrupted with the blanket and Dusty wrapped it around her. "Now what were you saying about what Craze did?"

"David tried to force himself into my mind. Just like he did before. But I fought back. I wouldn't let him take you from me. I could smell you on the T-shirt, and with your scent filling me, I focused on every memory we've shared, everything between us. And I won. We won."

The thought of all he could have lost hit him, and he pulled Skylar into his arms, needing her close to him. He kissed her upturned face. "I love you."

Stephan's Mercedes S65AMG whipped around the corner, pulling up across the street. Mariah bolted out of the passenger side and dashed toward David's house.

Skylar let out a quiet gasp. Dusty looked down at her face as her eyes widened and she whispered, "Mariah?"

The two sisters approached each other slowly, their faces matching expressions of awe and wonder. And then they were in each other's arms, hugging and crying and talking so fast no one could understand a word they were saying.

Stephan faced Slade. "I thought you were going to keep her in the compound?"

Slade met Stephan's intense gaze with a matching one of his own. "You should know by now you can't stop her when she wants to do something."

They both turned, watching the women chatter while they moved toward the cars. "And now there are two of them," Stephan said with a wry chuckle as he began to follow them. "Fate definitely has a sense of humor."

"Hey! What the fuck is my car doing here?" Marlin asked.

Dusty didn't answer. He just wrapped an arm around his woman and smiled.

Epilogue
One month later

"I want to watch you while you come, Mrs. Clements." Dusty slid his hands up her thighs, pushing up her white silk sheath dress and bunching it around her hips. She raised and lowered herself almost lazily on Dusty's cock, enjoying the slow glide of hard flesh moving in and out of her.

"I like…the way that sounds," Skylar gasped as Dusty thrust even deeper. "Mrs. Clements…"

She lowered her hands to his chest, the new diamond ring on her finger shining brilliantly. Yesterday, Stephan and Mariah, Dusty and Skylar had gotten married in a small service at city hall. They'd kept it simple, to avoid the press and the potential problem of David inviting himself to their wedding.

But today was the real ceremony.

Skylar could feel the beginnings of her orgasm rippling across her skin, could feel the tension of Dusty's impending release, and could "feel" Mariah in her mind. It still took some getting used to, considering she pretty much always knew what was going on in her sister's head. Since the very first moment they'd hugged a month ago, a link had flared to life between them. Senses, emotions, and even thoughts and phrases passed unhindered from mind to mind. Sometimes they were able to block, but it seemed the higher the emotion, the stronger the connection.

Skylar had gotten used to tangibly experiencing Mariah and Stephan's sexual interludes. It was an interesting type of voyeurism that the sisters had learned to live with and even enjoy.

But sometimes the voyeurism went a little farther.

Skylar moaned as Dusty sped up his movements. She was so close, she had trouble forming a coherent thought, let alone a complete sentence. "Dusty…more than just you…are going to…watch me come," she panted.

"Oh God, not again," he groaned as Mariah stepped out of his closet.

Skylar just smiled. The mental bond between her and Mariah was so strong, it didn't bother Skylar to have her sister watch her make love to Dusty. They already felt what the other felt, and watching was just a continuation of that shared connection.

But their men still weren't quite used to it.

Dusty stopped thrusting and dropped Skylar's dress so it covered where they were joined. "Dammit. I thought The Order fixed that portal—" He broke on a moan as Skylar shifted her hips "—so it didn't dump you off in my closet anymore," he finished in a mad rush.

Mariah laughed. "Oh, they did. There's another door in the main room…but I had them keep this one available in case I need to get to Skylar fast, or if she needs to get to me…"

"Or if she wants to catch us in the act," Skylar finished between panting breaths.

"Which isn't hard considering it's a frequent pastime." Mariah snorted.

"Oh, it's hard, all right," Skylar teased as she rocked on Dusty. He let out a muffled groan, his jaw locked as he tried to hold back. Skylar fought the desire to come right then. Too close…

She closed her eyes and immediately got lost in the moment, letting herself go completely, forgetting about anything but the need to take Dusty and herself to paradise. Her whole body shuddered, the waves of release shaking her to her core. Dusty moaned and came inside her. His warm spurts of semen bursting against her womb took her over the edge again.

In the corner of the room, Mariah let out a soft gasp.

As the three of them began to recover, Stephan called out from the closet. "Mariah, you in there?"

Skylar's eyes shot open as Stephan stepped out of the closet. "God, not again," he groaned.

"Again," Mariah growled, tackling Stephan and pushing him back through the closet.

"Again?" Skylar asked Dusty.

"Again," he replied, his cock already thickening inside her.

* * * * *

"Can I come in?" Twyla asked as she walked in the door of Skylar and Dusty's room in the compound.

"Nope," Mariah teased.

"Hey Twyla." Skylar threw a casual smile at Mariah's best friend. Twyla returned the smile before looking away, moving toward the mirror, adjusting her dark green velvet dress.

In the past month, Skylar had spent a lot of time with Twyla. Yet even with Mariah's memories and feelings toward Twyla filling Skylar's subconscious, she still didn't feel like she really knew Twyla. Skylar couldn't quite put her finger on it, but it was like Twyla was unapproachable, as though she was wearing a big "do not trespass" sign. Skylar wondered if even Mariah knew Twyla as well as she thought she did.

Skylar swiped on her deodorant, then tossed it to her sister. "You and Stephan were going at it pretty hard so you should probably reapply."

"Subtle hint taken." Mariah rolled her eyes and slid a hand down the front of her silver and lavender dress, putting on the deodorant.

Twyla grinned. "Do the four of you do anything else but fuck like rabid bunnies?"

"I still eat chocolate," Mariah called out as though it was a huge accomplishment.

Twyla snorted. "Yeah, I know. I brought you a little…ur…a big something. Probably not as big as Stephan though." She tossed Mariah a gaily-wrapped package then tossed one to Skylar, too. "Not like either of you need a backup…"

Skylar and Mariah looked at each other, then tore into their packages. Both of them burst into laughter when they opened their boxes.

A beautiful, large and solid chocolate cock was nestled in red satin. It was decadent, luscious and Skylar had to take a bite. She put the sweet package up to her lips at the same moment Mariah did the same with hers.

"Such a Kodak moment," Twyla said wryly. "The two of you all dressed up fancy for this binding ceremony, big chocolate dicks hanging out of your mouths."

Mariah bit the tip off, and grinned. "Thanks, Twyla."

Tucking the luscious dessert back in the box for later, Skylar wiped her hands free of any remaining chocolate before straightening her simple white silk sheath dress, and slipping into a pair of matching sandals. "I'm ready to go."

"Let's do this." Mariah's dress shimmered as she stood up from the bed. The sometimes-lavender, sometimes-silver fabric was gorgeous, and somehow managed to both reveal and conceal. The necklace Twyla had made for her months ago, that had helped bring her and Stephan together, hung proudly around her neck.

"Not yet." Twyla halted them. "C'mere you two. I'm gonna get mushy. I want to offer up a toast…a blessing…whatever you want to call it. Something about you two finding the men of your dreams, you lucky bitches." She put a hand to her chest, then winked. "Oh, did I say that? Naw, seriously, I want to endow you with further…umm…sanctity." She grinned.

Twyla took one of each woman's hands, but hers was cold to the touch and Skylar shivered. Twyla squeezed their hands and her eyes fell shut as the mere whisper of strange sounding words fell from her lips. Every time Skylar tried to focus on what she was saying, the words seemed to become even less clear.

Twyla's eyes blinked open and she smiled just as the door behind them burst open. Michael ran in, weapons drawn, eyes sharp as he scanned the room. "What's going on? You okay?" He stepped closer to Mariah. "What just happened? I felt you in danger."

"Ummm, no, we're fine." Twyla pulled her hands from the two sisters and stepped away.

Mariah narrowed her eyes. "Danger? We're fine. Girl-talkin' and getting ready. Your senses must be off."

Michael shook his head and warily watched Twyla as she walked through the door and into the hallway.

He turned back to Mariah, somehow managing to look even more striking than usual in his dark charcoal gray high-collared suit. "It's time."

"You two ready in there?" Jake shouted from down the hall. "I'm getting gray hairs waitin' for this thing to start."

"You can't rush perfection," Skylar called back. She linked arms with Mariah and together they exited the room, Michael following.

The group waiting for them in the living area was almost unrecognizable. Quite a motley crew, but she wouldn't have it any other way. Jake was done up in a green button-down shirt and dark blue trousers—quite the departure from his patrol clothes. Marlin, dapper but sleek in a gray silk shirt and black pants. Ana stood next to him, dressed in a pale blue strapless dress that made her look like an elegant starlet from the fifties. Ryan in neatly cut all black. Stephan wore a sharp ultra-dark plum tuxedo with tails, and a bowtie the same shimmery material of Mariah's dress. Few men could get away with what he was wearing, but Stephan looked stunning. Skylar could feel Mariah's appreciation, and her desire to remove Stephan's tuxedo as soon as possible.

But the only one Skylar really had eyes for was Dusty. He was dressed to the nines in a royal blue tuxedo similar to Stephan's, but finished off with a pair of white sneakers. Skylar smiled. At least they were new sneakers.

She stepped up to him, straightening his bowtie. "Some things never change," she teased. Sliding her hands around his neck, she pulled him down to her level so she could kiss him.

He grinned against her mouth and lifted her to face level, holding her tight to his chest so he could kiss her more thoroughly.

A flash of blue light interrupted their kiss and Fiero appeared, a pleased smile wide across his face. He was dressed in a silver-grey ceremonial robe with runic lettering embroidered on thick white ribbons streaming down from his neck to the floor.

"Nice robe," Jake snickered.

"Jealous, Jake?" asked Ana. "You wouldn't look that hot in it."

"Hey!" Jake interjected. "You didn't say anything last time you saw me in a robe."

Ana rolled her eyes. "You were wearing a fuzzy, stained and full-of-holes bathrobe and were about as far from sexy as I've ever seen."

As Jake fumbled for a reply, Fiero chimed in. "Just because I'm dead doesn't mean I don't make a pretty corpse." He walked over to Ana, took her in his arms and dipped her deeply before ravishing her with a kiss. "If you were dead, I'd be in heaven."

Ana playfully swatted Fiero as he set her back on her feet. He waved a hand while uttering a low chant and a portal opened up. "Come on through. The party's just beginning. Go on in to the sacellum. That's where the ceremony will take place."

"Are you nervous?" Skylar whispered to Dusty.

"Not about being bound to you. I'm just wondering about the rest of this…"

Together, they stepped into a whole new world. The binding ceremony would take place on a sacred level, a dimension not often opened to anyone outside of the Sacred Order. Skylar stood at Dusty's side, her eyes wide as her gaze drifted from the façade of a huge white castle-like building and over the grounds surrounding it.

Everything seemed a little brighter, a little cleaner, a little more colorful here. Sunlight—was it a sun?—shone down on them with a pleasant warmth. The sky was a crystal blue, completely pure in its color. Brilliant green grass stretched for miles and miles, over rolling hills and valleys.

It was almost too perfect. Skylar was afraid that by breathing she would somehow damage the perfection. But she inhaled anyway, and even her lungs seemed to wallow in the glory of this place.

Dusty leaned over and whispered in her ear. "I'm afraid I'm going to burp and lightning will strike me down."

Skylar slapped a hand over her mouth before she could snort out her laughter. "You are horrible," she mumbled between her gaping fingers.

"I know," he replied mischievously, then pulled her fingers from her mouth and brushed his lips over hers. "You ready to do this?"

"Of course. You trying to back out?"

"Oh, hell no. I want to be bound to you forever. I want to know that through this life and into the next and even the one after that, you'll be at my side. In fact, I won't give you a chance to back out." He picked her up and carefully slung her over his shoulder. "Where's this ceremony taking place?"

Skylar giggled as she bounced along, Dusty lightly smacking her ass in time with his footsteps.

Without warning, he quickly lowered her to the ground. Still somewhat dizzy, she stumbled, and turned around.

Adrian stood a few feet away, watching them. "Hey Skye…"

It had been a month since she'd seen him. A month of wondering if he was okay, if the strange new world they'd both stumbled into would ever allow her to see her best friend again.

Her heart stuttered as she discovered the changes in him. He'd gained muscle and his eyes looked more intense. Like he was becoming a sharpened version of himself. A man who used instinct and cunning to find his prey. But he was still her Adrian. She ran into his arms, the tears blurring her vision. "Adrian? God, I can hardly believe it's you. How?"

"Got the day off for good behavior."

She pulled back to look into his eyes to see if he was telling the truth, if his new life was really that bad. He smiled. "I'm joking, Skye. Well, kinda. But I wouldn't miss this for the world. I wouldn't miss seeing you…" He brushed a stray lock of hair off her face then dropped his hand back to his side.

"But you're okay?"

"Yeah. They're working me hard, but I feel like I'm really getting somewhere. I can almost find a needle in a haystack." At that, he grinned, and a spark of the old Adrian shone through. She smiled.

Skylar…come…something to see…

Mariah's thoughts registered enough to bring Skylar out of the shock of seeing Adrian again. She reached out for Dusty's hand. "I need to go inside now." She gestured to the sacellum behind them. "You're coming, right?" she asked Adrian.

He nodded and the three of them walked into the building.

It was just as beautiful as the rest of everything she'd seen so far since stepping through the portal. Roses and other flowering vines climbed sections of the walls giving off an incredibly delicate fragrance. The ceiling was the brilliant blue sky and birds perched among the crenellations as though in audience of the ceremony. It was almost like a sacred walled garden, but it felt more powerful. Fountains poured scented water into a pool at the heart of the sacellum.

There were people milling around. A lot of people. Skylar wondered who they all were and why they'd turned out to see the binding ceremony. "Do you know who any of these people are?" Skylar asked both Dusty and Adrian.

Dusty shook his head. "A few. But mostly not."

"Higher beings, and some lookie loos. Your joining today is being celebrated all over," Adrian said. Although his voice was casual, there was a bit of pain behind his words. "This doesn't happen often."

Mariah came rushing through the crowd, her eyes alight with love and excitement. "Skylar, come here. There's someone…well, someones, I want you to meet."

Hands clasped, Mariah and Skylar stepped through the crowd. Eyes followed their every move. Mariah didn't seem to notice, but Skylar did. It was strange. Very strange to be considered so important. She wanted to shout out that she was just Skylar, nothing more than that…but she knew it wouldn't do any good. Somewhere along the way someone had decided she was important. She stifled a nervous giggle.

Mariah suddenly drew to a halt in front of a stunning couple. The man was incredibly handsome, his dark brown hair and mustache both sprinkled with gray, his eyes a deep silver blue. The woman standing next to him was obviously his wife or partner—the love pulsing between the two was obvious. Her dark blonde hair fell in long waves over her shoulders and tears filled her light hazel green eyes. Skylar smiled lightly, and looked to Mariah for the answer to why they were here.

"Skylar, this…" Mariah choked up. "I want you to meet our mom and dad."

Amazement. Shock. The world seemed to spin as she stared into the faces of the parents she'd never known. The parents who had died before she'd even known of their existence.

Mariah? How?

Instead of Mariah answering, her father stepped forward, taking her hand. His eyes sparkled, a mix of happiness and tears. "My little one. Death does not always signify the end. Just as in life, there are many levels of existence. Sometimes life and death can meet. This is one of those places."

Skylar stepped into her parents' waiting arms, Mariah at her side. Although the story of her strange birth still seemed unbelievable to her, at this moment, everything became real. These were her parents. Somehow, someway, she'd come from them.

Thirty minutes later, the couples stood side by side, as the ceremony commenced. The crowd from earlier, including Adrian and her parents—had gathered en masse, watching as the binding took place.

A spiritual aura emanated from Fiero, surrounding the couples as he spoke the binding words, only a few of which Skylar understood.

But the meaning was clear. Their souls were linked, their lives, their very existences forever joined through this life and beyond.

Fiero led the couples to a nearby fountain and in turn, dipped their hands in the viscous fluid. It was warm and comforting to the touch, almost like paraffin. Dusty intertwined his fingers with hers beneath the liquid and together they pulled their hands free. Skylar was surprised that they were completely devoid of any residue.

Dusty looked down at her and winked, his sweet smile touching her heart the way it always did. Skylar could feel the excitement of the crowd, could feel Mariah's joy, could feel Dusty's love wrapping around her, through her, completing her.

Skylar sighed contentedly as Dusty lowered his mouth to hers, sealing the ceremony. They'd won. Nothing and no one would ever come between them.

* * * * *

The binding ceremony was lovely, but it was no less than what Twyla had expected. Stephan and Mariah, Dusty and Skylar, they were the lucky ones. They got their happy ending.

And that was wonderful. It was great. Really.

A vase of roses on the nightstand perfumed the air of her bedroom. Candlelight glinted off the amethyst in her hand as she pondered the powerful purple hued crystal point. Her happy ending would never come. Without Freeze, there was no happiness to be found. Months had passed, the memories hadn't faded and she was feeling just as dead as Freeze.

Letting him go would likely pain her forever.

Thankfully, her life was not yet completely over. There were many ways in which Freeze's magic could sustain her, keep her flame from burning out, add his wisdom to hers. Just without his body or soul...without his enchanting touch.

Twyla knelt down and opened the bottom drawer of her dresser, buried the amethyst underneath a stack of men's T-shirts—Freeze's T-shirts—and closed the drawer with a sigh.

It was for the best.

At the sound of her bedroom door opening, she shot back up to standing, but did not face the man. "Hello, lover." The words fell from her lips as anticipatory wetness pooled between her legs…just as it had every time since she'd first fucked him one month earlier.

"Did you do it? Am I joined to them?"

Twyla slid the straps of her dress off her shoulders and let the green fabric fall to the floor. "Yes." She stepped out of the dress. "You are bound to them as they are bound to you. Perfect equality."

She turned and faced her smiling lover, as his midnight black gaze swept her from toe to head.

"Not as perfect as our union, Twyla." Craze's voice echoed in the candlelit bedroom as he hungrily closed the distance between their bodies.

It was for the best…

The End

(When a vampire and a Shadow Walker come together, death is not the only option. Watch for Eternal Talisman, coming soon…)

Chapter One

This was not like the parties she'd been to in high school—which, it was sad for her to admit, was the last time she'd been to a party. All of the people she had seen so far were thin, built and gorgeous…even the damn valets. She was far from a size zero, or negative, or whatever these women were. Sam wore her double-digit clothing with pride. She was a baker for goodness sake; no one would eat her food if she looked anorexic. She had curves and rounded hips and big boobs. Around these women, she was an anomaly. Maybe she should have worn Blaina's too small purple paisley and leather outfit, although she doubted she could stick out any more than she already did.

Blaina put a hand out to stop her before they reached the door. "Wait, before we go in there, you gotta know a few things about these kinds of parties. There will be sex. There will be drugs. There will be alcohol. And a few other surprises, I'm sure. Don't drink anything that you haven't had your eye on all night and never go anywhere with a guy who gives you the creeps, because he definitely is a creep. And by the way, before you even ask, yes, ninety-eight percent of the boobs in there are fake, so don't feel like your big beautiful naturals are tiny, okay? You're gonna have a blast. That's what our adventures are all about." Blaina didn't give Sam a chance to reply before she turned and spoke to the doorman, pointing out her name on the list. The fellow gave them a sideways glance before welcoming them in with a smile. It was obvious to Sam that they didn't look like most of the vapid starlets in attendance.

"Okay, you're on your own because if I don't leave you now, you'll never talk to anyone. I'm gonna see if Eric is here. On the last show we worked on, he claimed to know Jimmy Maxson, but never invited me to one of these parties."

Blaina hiked up her electric blue mini-skirt to ass-flashing level, pushed up her little cleavage so it popped out the top of her multi-shaded green corset, then ruffled her hair as much as a person can primp a red porcupine on acid. She tossed a killer grin over her shoulder as she walked away. "Have fun! Later!"

Sam looked around. The revelers were even more beautiful up close. They moved and talked and walked and even ate as though it were a show. These people were so used to being in the limelight, they never stopped performing. She spent an hour wandering the huge rooms watching crazy, drunken but clearly happy people participate in lots of illicit activities. The only people she managed to strike up a conversation with were the help. She even gave her business card to the head caterer because he was looking to expand his services.

Every time she caught a glimpse of Blaina, she was making out with another hot man. Sam smiled. Blaina was the kind of girl who would enjoy kissing many Mr. Wrongs until she found Mr. Right. Listening to Blaina talk about her sexual escapades was the closest to sex Sam had gotten since she'd conceived Gina. She'd had one lover in her life, her asshole ex-husband. The only orgasms she'd ever had were self-induced. Although she would never admit it, she was a tad jealous of Blaina's sexual freedom. But her daughter and her career came first. Sam let out a wry chuckle. And she didn't come at all.

Hoping to escape some of the music and revelry, she walked down a quiet hallway and opened a door. All she could see were bare breasts, laving tongues, writhing women, and cocks galore. Her eyes bugged and she felt the heat of a blush cover her entire body. With lightning speed, she shut the door. She leaned back against it and closed her eyes. She was way out of her league here.

Sam walked away from the debauchery and took a deep, calming breath. She wasn't into voyeurism, or group sex, or anything like that, but her body had still responded to the stimuli offered. Her thong was rubbing her in a way that was no longer uncomfortable and leaned more toward invigorating. The moans of the room's participants seemed to echo in her mind and throb in her pussy. She desperately wanted to let go of her inhibitions, to have one true night of mindless pleasure.

Sam tried to shake it off. What she really needed was some cool night air to chill the heat rising off her flesh.

With that decision made, she headed for the backyard where she could call her daughter, enjoy the view…and clear her mind of all her wanton thoughts.

About the author:

Sometimes two people meet, become good friends, and share a lot in common. When you're really lucky, you meet someone who understands you, who thinks like you, can finish your sentences and together, the both of you can create whole new worlds.

Ashleigh Raine is the pen name for two best friends, Jennifer and Lisa, who share a passion for strong alpha males that succumb to the women they fall in love with. These two met in junior high where they were band geeks (but they swear they really were cool…they were percussionists after all!) But love of the arts didn't end with band. By high school, the two had a small following of fans for their stories and the characters they created…characters that would become the inspiration for their Talisman Bay series. They want to thank those fans for their continued support and interest. They couldn't have done it without them!

Both Lisa and Jennifer are married to their soul mates, who are the best support and inspiration. As Ashleigh Raine, this duo has many stories to tell, as their collective mind never stops creating fantasies that must be written down. They write larger than life stories, with adventures, hot sex, peril, hot sex, mystery, and more hot sex…but most assuredly they have a happy ending, usually with hot sex. Watch for many titles coming soon from this duo who are glad to have found their niche in writing erotic romances. Visit both halves of Ashleigh Raine on the web at www.asleighraine.com or drop them an email at Ashleigh@asleighraine.com

Ashleigh Raine welcomes mail from readers. You can write to her c/o Ellora's Cave Publishing at 1337 Commerce Drive, Suite 13, Stow OH 44224.

Why an electronic book?

We live in the Information Age—an exciting time in the history of human civilization in which technology rules supreme and continues to progress in leaps and bounds every minute of every hour of every day. For a multitude of reasons, more and more avid literary fans are opting to purchase e-books instead of paperbacks. The question to those not yet initiated to the world of electronic reading is simply: *why?*

1. *Price.* An electronic title at Ellora's Cave Publishing runs anywhere from 40-75% less than the cover price of the <u>exact same title</u> in paperback format. Why? Cold mathematics. It is less expensive to publish an e-book than it is to publish a paperback, so the savings are passed along to the consumer.

2. *Space.* Running out of room to house your paperback books? That is one worry you will never have with electronic novels. For a low one-time cost, you can purchase a handheld computer designed specifically for e-reading purposes. Many e-readers are larger than the average handheld, giving you plenty of screen room. Better yet, hundreds of titles can be stored within your new library—a single microchip. (Please note that Ellora's Cave does not endorse any specific brands. You can check our website at www.ellorascave.com for customer

recommendations we make available to new consumers.)

3. *Mobility.* Because your new library now consists of only a microchip, your entire cache of books can be taken with you wherever you go.

4. *Personal preferences are accounted for.* Are the words you are currently reading too small? Too large? Too…**ANNOYING**? Paperback books cannot be modified according to personal preferences, but e-books can.

5. *Innovation.* The way you read a book is not the only advancement the Information Age has gifted the literary community with. There is also the factor of what you can read. Ellora's Cave Publishing will be introducing a new line of interactive titles that are available in e-book format only.

6. *Instant gratification.* Is it the middle of the night and all the bookstores are closed? Are you tired of waiting days—sometimes weeks—for online and offline bookstores to ship the novels you bought? Ellora's Cave Publishing sells instantaneous downloads 24 hours a day, 7 days a week, 365 days a year. Our e-book delivery system is 100% automated, meaning your order is filled as soon as you pay for it.

Those are a few of the top reasons why electronic novels are displacing paperbacks for many an avid reader. As always, Ellora's Cave Publishing welcomes your questions and comments. We invite you to email us at service@ellorascave.com or write to us directly at: 1337 Commerce Drive, Suite 13, Stow OH 44224.

Discover for yourself why readers can't get enough of the multiple award-winning publisher Ellora's Cave. Whether you prefer e-books or paperbacks, be sure to visit EC on the web at www.ellorascave.com for an erotic reading experience that will leave you breathless.

WWW.ELLORASCAVE.COM

Printed in the United States
27587LVS00005B/70-255